*continued . . .*

"Ms. Sweeney is a talented writer who has peopled this series with some extremely likable characters.... She is adept at weaving the history of the textile industry into *The Cat, the Mill and the Murder*, giving the reader just enough to keep their interest without boring them. This series just gets better and better." —Fresh Fiction

"Leann Sweeney has written another well-plotted page-turner. I loved this book. I enjoy a good mystery that features my furry favorites as well as quirky characters. Jillian is such a loving character that you can't help getting drawn into her life and wish that you could help her solve the problems she encounters. So if you enjoy mysteries that feature adorable cats, then *The Cat, the Mill and the Murder* is a book you should read."
—MyShelf.com

"I cannot recommend this series enough to animal lovers and fans of a darn good mystery. The mystery was multilayered and kept me guessing right to the end, and, as always, I'm anxious for the next Cats in Trouble book!"
—Cozy Mystery Book Reviews

### *The Cat, the Wife and the Weapon*

"A light and easy cozy mystery that strikes a nice balance between the murder mystery and the intricacy of human relationships.... I give this book four paws up!"
—MyShelf.com

"[An] amusing and enthralling regional amateur sleuth tale starring an eccentric cast led by a likable, peacemaking heroine." —Genre Go Round Reviews

### *The Cat, the Lady and the Liar*

"A lighthearted, fun cozy starring an engaging cast of characters. . . . Feline frolic fans will enjoy."
—The Best Reviews

"Tightly plotted, with likable characters, and filled with cat trivia, this entertaining mystery will become a favorite for cozy and cat lovers alike." —The Conscious Cat

### *The Cat, the Professor and the Poison*

"A fun, entertaining story. . . . The mystery will keep the reader guessing." —Fresh Fiction

"The characters and friends Jillian makes along the way, and the care she gives to the cats she encounters, will make her a fast favorite." —The Mystery Reader

### *The Cat, the Quilt and the Corpse*

"The cats are entertaining four-legged assistants . . . [and] kitty lovers will enjoy the feline trivia."
—*Publishers Weekly*

"[Leann Sweeney's] brand-new series about adorable cats that just can't stay out of trouble is bound to be a hit!" —Fantastic Fiction

Other Novels by Leann Sweeney

The Cats in Trouble Mysteries

*The Cat, the Vagabond and the Victim*
*The Cat, the Mill and the Murder*
*The Cat, the Wife and the Weapon*
*The Cat, the Lady and the Liar*
*The Cat, the Professor and the Poison*
*The Cat, the Quilt and the Corpse*

The Yellow Rose Mysteries

*Pushing Up Bluebonnets*
*Shoot from the Lip*
*Dead Giveaway*
*A Wedding to Die For*
*Pick Your Poison*

# THE CAT, THE SNEAK AND THE SECRET

## A CATS IN TROUBLE MYSTERY

## LEANN SWEENEY

AN OBSIDIAN MYSTERY

OBSIDIAN
Published by the Penguin Group
Penguin Group (USA) LLC, 375 Hudson Street,
New York, New York 10014

USA | Canada | UK | Ireland | Australia | New Zealand | India | South Africa | China

A Penguin Random House Company

First published by Obsidian, an imprint of New American Library,
a division of Penguin Group (USA) LLC

ISBN 978-1-62953-585-2

Printed in the United States of America

*This book is dedicated to my precious Marlowe, who awaits me on the Rainbow Bridge—and to all those who gave me so much support as that precious kitty and I followed a difficult path together.*

# Acknowledgments

The Cats in Trouble mystery series would not have this seventh installment without the readers who have embraced my books. I thank you and am so glad I interact with many of you on social media regularly. My dear friends, the Cozy Chicks (Lorraine Bartlett, Jennifer Stanley, Mary Jane Maffini, Mary Kennedy, Kate Collins and Maggie Sefton), have been kind and wonderful supporters. I treasure their friendship and feel privileged to blog once a week with a cast that includes so many best-selling authors. My agent, Carol Mann, and her staff have been with me on this journey, always there to help whenever I ask. Last, these books would never have happened without the kindness, understanding and expertise of my editor, Claire Zion. Thank you from the bottom of my heart.

*"One of the most striking differences between a cat and a lie is that a cat has only nine lives."*

—Mark Twain

# One

The cramped office that served the Mercy Animal Sanctuary smelled like hay and kitty litter and kibble and pine-scented air freshener—or as I liked to call it, *love*. There was nothing I enjoyed more than being here to cuddle with a cat or a dog starved for affection.

But on this particular sunny October morning, I had not come to comfort the shelter's inhabitants. Instead I sat beside my future stepson, Finn, as we waited for the owner, Shawn Cuddahee. He would be bringing a very special girl from the cattery.

Finn was in town on a college break. His stepdad, Tom Stewart, and I were getting married in a week and Finn had handed in research papers and taken a few tests early so he could be part of our celebration. As usual he planned to volunteer at the shelter during his stay in town. But he had something else on his mind today. Since his last time volunteering, Finn hadn't been able to get a certain cat out of his head—a little tortoiseshell kitty, or "tortie" as they were usually called. Since she was still available, Finn wanted to adopt her. But the cat would have to live with Tom and me until he moved from the dorm into his own apartment next semester.

As we sat on folding chairs in the cluttered space, Snug, the African gray parrot who believed he was in charge of the office, entertained us. He promenaded back and forth on the horizontal dowel Shawn had nailed up near the ceiling, saying, "Hello, Jillian Hart. Hello there," and "Finn, clean the dog crates. Clean the dog crates."

When Shawn finally rushed through the door from the kennel and cattery, his face was flushed with agitation. And he wasn't holding the tortie. "Sorry, Finn, but she's gone again. She is the sneakiest little girl we've ever had."

Finn stood. "That's okay. I planned on working today anyway and she always comes back. She'll probably be here by the time Jillian picks me up later." He looked my way. "Anything I need to do to help you guys with the wedding setup when I'm done here?"

I laughed. "Though I'm certain you're dying to wrap vines and rosebuds on Kara's banister, we'll take care of it." Kara was my stepdaughter—my late husband's only child. She was hosting the reception at her gorgeous new house.

"Yeah, I'd probably be more useful here." Finn looked at Shawn. "Where should I start?"

Snug piped in with "Clean the dog crates, Finn. Clean the dog crates."

Shawn still seemed a little annoyed and preoccupied, but not with Snug. He bent and retrieved a shoe box from under the desk and set it down on the battered metal surface. He glanced back and forth between us.

"You sure you want a cat who brings this kind of stuff home all the time? 'Cause I got a couple across the road from here who'll always take the difficult cats. They've got a barnful to protect their chicken feed from rodents. Cats do that quite efficiently."

I leaned forward and examined the contents of the box while Finn merely seemed amused.

Shawn picked out a shoelace and held it up. "This is so old it couldn't hold anything together."

I spied what looked like a ragged sock, several coins, buttons, more shoelaces, a filthy little sachet pillow and a baby's knitted hat. I looked up at Finn and smiled. "Are you adopting a cat or a magpie?"

Snug said, "Magpie" three times and did a wolf whistle to top it off. None of us could keep a straight face after that one.

"That's it." Finn grinned. "I'll call her Magpie. It's perfect, Jillian."

Shawn shook his head. "All I can say is you'll have your hands full. She may become a domestic indoor cat right away, since she's real friendly, but she's an escape artist." Shawn looked at me. "She's always sneaking out to hunt for anything she can drag back here." He waved his hand at the box. "This stuff is just from the last few days. I wanted you to see evidence of what you're getting yourself into if you plan on keeping her through the holidays, Jillian."

Finn glanced my way, a hint of anxiety in his eyes. "You said it would be no problem, right?"

"Absolutely no problem. I'm excited to have her with us." I smiled because it was true. What kitty didn't challenge its human caretaker?

Finn went on as if Shawn and I needed more convincing. "Plus, I'll be living with her and Tom starting the second week in December and through most of January when we have semester break."

I could tell this kitty must indeed be special. Finn *really* wanted to bring her home.

Shawn's phone rang and he answered, "Mercy Animal Sanctuary." After listening for several seconds, he said, "This cat is wearing one of *my* collars? You're sure?" He nodded and glanced at Finn. "What does the kitty look like?" More listening and more pointed looks at Finn. "I'll be right there."

Finn cocked his head and stared at Shawn. "Was that about Magpie?"

"Oh yeah. Did you bring a crate for this girl?" Shawn asked.

I nodded. "It's in my van. Someone found her, I take it?"

"Yup. And you'll never guess who. You can follow me and then *please* take this little troublemaker off my hands." But Shawn smiled. He had a soft spot for the troublemakers.

We left the office with Snug bobbing his head and chanting "Magpie" over and over.

The route Shawn took confused me at first. True, I'd lived in Mercy for seven years, but there were more back roads than people in this town. Then I recognized where we were headed and turned to Finn sitting beside me. "How did Magpie end up at Ed's Swap Shop?"

"You got me. This should be a fun mystery to unravel, Jillian. I love it."

I couldn't help smiling. "A cat who collects other people's trash ends up with a man who does the same thing. Seems fitting."

Finn laughed. "It's perfect she's with Ed."

We considered Ed Duffy a relative. He was the lovable, gentle live-in companion of Tom's mother, Karen. Ed had been collecting junk for years and actually did a steady business either swapping his treasures for different items that caught his fancy, taking things on consignment or selling some things for cash. Finn spent almost as much time with Karen and Ed as he did with Tom. In fact, when we pulled onto the neglected patch of asphalt Ed called a parking lot, the old guy opened the door and Finn's rat terrier, Yoshi, raced straight for him. Ed often kept Yoshi at the shop when Finn or Tom didn't plan on being home. Tom must have dropped the dog off before he went to pick up the new suit he'd bought for our wedding.

Finn opened his arms and the dog leapt into them. After licking his beloved Finn's face and wiggling with joy, Yoshi jumped down and greeted me as he'd been taught— by sitting and waiting for me to pet him. Then it was time to say hello to Shawn, who was already crouched and waiting to scratch Yoshi behind the ears.

Ed called, "Y'all come on and help me with this little feline problem I'm presented with."

Soon we all crowded into the store. Decades ago it had been a family home and the stacks of toys, tools, small appliances, magazines, books, lamps, fishing gear and so much more made what had once been the living area seem tiny. And there before us was this battered old love seat—obviously a recent addition. It filled what little space had been left in the center of the room. Since we couldn't get past it, we all stood staring down at its dingy brown upholstery.

Ed stroked his gray beard. "This here is my dilemma." He looked down at a whining Yoshi. "Help me out, fella. Make some noise."

Yoshi complied by jumping on the love seat and yelping at the space between the love seat cushions.

We all heard a cat meow in reply. I would have expected a hiss if one of my three cats found itself trapped in a sofa, but Magpie had been at the shelter so long she was probably used to barking dogs.

I put my hand to my mouth and muttered, "Oh my. Is she stuck?"

"Darn right," Ed replied. "Only good thing is she can almost get her head through that crack and I saw the tag on the collar, got a flashlight for a better look. Like I said on the phone, she's one of yours, Shawn. But I've been working for an hour to coax her out of there and it ain't happenin'."

"Actually, Gramps, she's now my cat." Finn smiled at Ed. He'd taken to calling him Gramps not long after he came to live with Tom.

Ed's bushy eyebrows rose in surprise. "Well, there's a new development. Guess she needs savin' right quick, then."

Shawn addressed Finn. "Yoshi's done his job. Maybe he needs to go in the back while we work on this problem. The cat's probably spooked a little."

Finn had to squeeze past the sofa, and as soon as Yoshi was closed up in the back room, he returned and stood by Shawn again. I fit my fingers between the back of the love seat and the attached cushions. I used a soft coaxing voice. "Hey, baby. You okay?" I wiggled my fingers. The sofa was old and dirty, and I was thankful the dark brown of the cushions hid a lot more than the stickiness I felt.

It only took a minute for Magpie to pop her head out. Finn laughed and whipped out his phone to snap a picture. "Got to think of a caption for this when I put it up on Instagram."

"Such a pretty girl," I whispered, stroking the side of her face.

Meanwhile, Shawn was looking underneath the love seat in the back to check if she'd gotten in through a rip in the fabric. He stood and shook his head. "She either got in there the way she's trying to come out, or came in through the bottom."

"There's no hole in the bottom, Shawn," Ed said. "I woulda seen it."

"So she can get out, but she's choosing not to." Shawn smiled wryly. "Typical cat."

Sure enough, Magpie began to worm through the space and finally Finn couldn't stand it anymore. He grabbed hold under her front legs and eased her out.

It was then that we saw she had a thin gold chain wrapped around one front leg.

"Ah. So you were Dumpster-diving again." Finn held her up and looked into her eyes so Shawn and I could free the chain. It seemed to have an etched gold locket attached.

Magpie, with her mottled black-and-gold fur and pale green eyes, was indeed a beauty. Shawn held her back legs firmly so I could untangle the jewelry. I felt the same stickiness on her paws. Had someone spilled a soft drink on the sofa? An *entire* soft drink? Because that was what her fur felt like.

When we were finished, Finn held his new friend close. I stared down at the locket and saw something grimy on my hands.

*Wait a minute. What's gotten all over me?*

I slipped the jewelry into my pocket. My palms were rusty red and I held my fingers to my nose. I immediately recognized the smell.

*Blood.*

# Two

"I—I have blood on my hands." I tried my best not to sound as panicked as I felt. "Shawn, please check Magpie. She might be injured."

I stared down at my palms again and realized my hands were shaking. Did the cat sneak into that sofa because she was wounded? Or vomiting blood? Cats usually hide when they're ill or hurt, so that might explain why she was hunkered down in an old piece of furniture.

Finn held her firmly for Shawn's inspection, and after a thorough examination, Shawn smiled at me. "She's fine. Looks as healthy as the last time I saw her before she managed to open her crate and get out the cattery door."

"Then there's blood on that sofa. Or under the cushions." I glanced at Ed. "Could there be a dead animal in there? Because this is *not* just a little bit of blood." I held my hands out to him.

He grimaced. "Guess we have to tear the thing apart and then I'm takin' it to the dump. Sure as heck can't trade this old thing to anyone and I don't want it around. I'll get my big knife and start taking it apart . . . see what we got."

"You find this outside somewhere, Ed?" Shawn asked.

The old guy had already wrangled around the sofa and was behind the store counter. "Yup. By the clothing donation box they got set up on Harkins Road." Ed held up a container of disinfecting wipes. "Catch, Jillian."

He tossed them to me and I started cleaning my hands, grateful to be rid of the mess. Meanwhile, Finn fetched the crate from my car and brought it in. With my help, Finn put his new kitty in. Within seconds she began fiddling with the latch.

All of us now had blood somewhere on us and I passed the wipes around.

Ed said, "That's what you get for sticking your hand in there. I wasn't about to get chewed up by an angry cat."

"She's not angry, Gramps. She's scared."

"Whatever you say, son." Ed sounded unconvinced.

Shawn put his face close to the sofa cushions. "Can't hear anything, can't smell anything but blood. Probably any animal in there was freshly killed by our friend Magpie."

"You think so?" I didn't want to believe it, but cats *are* predators.

Shawn read my mind. "You've been around cats long enough to know that's probably what happened. A bird or squirrel or a rat, no doubt. I'll help Ed take this old thing to the dump after we find out what's inside. A critter that needs burying, if you're up to the job."

Finn said, "Are we dismantling the sofa right now? I hate to leave Yoshi locked up much longer."

I had plenty to do myself and didn't want to end up with the task of burying a poor, dead animal. I did have a wedding in my imminent future, after all. Then something caught my eye—a coppery glint between the cushions. I almost touched it, but Shawn grabbed my hand. He'd seen it, too.

I looked at him, my heart beating a lot faster than seconds ago. "Is that what I think it is?"

"Looks like a bullet to me. Guess we won't be touching this thing until our favorite evidence collector checks it out first. I'm sure you or Ed can call up Deputy Candace Carson, tell her we've just made her day." Shawn glanced at Finn. "I need to get back to the shelter. You coming?"

"Somebody probably shot a squirrel or something, huh?" Finn said, sounding concerned.

Shawn and Ed exchanged skeptical glances. Shawn said, "Looks like .22 ammo to me. Not exactly a hunting gun. But we can't make assumptions. Lord knows Candace has drilled that into me by now."

"I promised to help Shawn with the bales of hay he has to move or I'd stay until you and Candace get this figured out." Finn looked at Ed. "I can come back and we can move this out of here later, okay, Gramps?"

"Son, I got it in here and I can get it out. Been hauling stuff for years, long before you were born."

"Um, hello?" I said. "What's with y'all? You think I can't lift a little piece of furniture? Ed, Candace and I can handle this. Go on, you two."

Finn smiled. "Sorry. We're sounding like a bunch of macho guys, aren't we? I'll let Yoshi out, say good-bye and meet you outside, Shawn."

Soon they were gone, leaving Ed, Yoshi and me alone with a dirty love seat and a determined cat. How long before she got out of that crate?

I focused on the sofa and felt a stirring inside that told me we wouldn't be finding any dead animals today. Maybe because after all the times I'd helped Candace on cases, she'd taught me well, taught me to pay attention to my instincts and even the tiniest of fears.

I tossed the dirty hand wipes into the wastebasket by the shop door and pulled my phone from my jeans pocket. Tom had installed a brand-new cat cam with all sorts of amazing features last month. I could interact with my Chablis, Syrah and Merlot. The cameras in my house moved so I could see them anywhere, and if I wanted to tell them I would be home soon or I missed them, I could turn on the "talk feature." Technology was so fantastic.

I resisted the urge to activate a chat, though. This whole sofa mystery came first.

I hit the speed dial for Mercy PD, and B.J., the dispatcher, answered and put me through to Candace.

"Hey there," she said. "I hope you're calling to meet me for lunch. I'm starving already."

"You realize it's only ten in the morning?"

"I know. Long, boring day. What's up?"

I told her and you'd have thought a bag of gold just landed smack in the middle of her desk. She didn't even bother to say she was on her way, but of course she was.

While we waited, Ed squatted and secured the crate latch with a wire before Magpie worked her way out. Candace would probably treat her as evidence even if we ended up finding a dead squirrel.

It couldn't have been more than five minutes before

my best friend and the finest police officer in Mercy burst through Ed's door.

Her forest green uniform pants and khaki shirt hid her curves, but she was a beautiful young woman. Candace agreed to actually wear a dress when she and my stepdaughter stood up for me at my wedding this coming Saturday. I'd seen the dress and I was sure she'd be gorgeous that day even if she felt less than comfortable.

She tucked a loose strand of blond hair behind her ear. "I take it this nasty-looking thing is the sofa in question?"

She set her evidence kit on the floor, put her hands behind her back and leaned over to give the love seat a thorough visual inspection. "I see the bullet you told me about. I can smell the blood, too. From my experience, I'd say the stain's not that old."

I said, "Since Ed found this thing outside and there was a cat hiding under the cushions, it's probably animal blood, right?"

Candace nodded. "I see plenty of cat hair. Could be another cat in there. Maybe a dead one."

"No way." I couldn't stomach the thought. Any animal we found would be terrible, but a cat? *No, no, no.*

She took her camera from the evidence bag and snapped a lot of pictures—front and back, above and below, and finally focused on the bullet. "Now, let's find out what we've got here." She removed a small jar and a pair of thick tweezers from the satchel. "I'll collect this bullet. Looks like a .22 caliber."

Ed nodded his agreement.

The bullet wasn't embedded in the cushions, just sort of tucked between them. When Candace grasped it and held it up, a speck of blood was barely visible on the small copper object. Candace dropped it in the jar, and it clinked when it hit the glass. Such an innocent, almost pretty sound. I found it grating and . . . *wrong.*

Candace held up the jar and studied the bullet. "Not too damaged. I'll bag and tag this even if I end up throwing it out. Can't be too careful." Out came an evidence bag and she took her time writing the where, when and whatever concerning the bullet using a permanent marker. Then she signed her name.

Her slow and deliberate pace only made my anxiety grow. I was almost wishing for a dead squirrel about now, but immediately felt guilty. There could be a completely innocent explanation for the blood—one I couldn't think of off the top of my head.

Next, Candace snapped on a pair of latex gloves and removed a packaged swab. She smiled. "Science is great. This is a test for blood. Just have to rub it in one little spot." She glanced between me and Ed, who'd retreated behind the counter. I got the feeling he was nervous, too. "By the way, this is just what we call a presumptive test. If we find anything suspicious, then—"

"Can you please get on with it?" I sounded impatient and I'm usually a pretty easygoing person. Maybe my feelings about this sofa and its secrets had merged with my anxiety about getting married, because I was anything but calm about now.

When Candace's eyes widened as she saw the change in color on the swab, I understood what we were dealing with before she said a word.

She spoke the words I didn't want to hear. "It's blood and it's human."

Goose bumps rose on my arms.

Ed piped in then. "Don't have to be ominous, right? Nosebleed? Female troubles? Kid with a busted head from a fall?"

"Yes. Some kind of accident, right?" I added.

Candace nodded. "Sure. All possible. But see, there's this bullet. Not an unused bullet, by the way. One that's been fired and bears a spot of blood."

Ed's eyes filled with sadness. "I should have followed my gut, left that thing where it was dumped. An uneasy feeling come on when I was shoving it up in my pickup. When I got back here and heard the cat inside, I thought that's why I was all troubled inside."

"Ed, you did right." Candace was staring at the love seat, hands on hips. "I'll need your help, though. Tell me again exactly where you found this darn thing."

"I can write it down," he said.

"I'm the one who needs to write it down for my report," she replied. "You, on the other hand, need to come with me to show me the exact spot where you found it."

"What you need me for? I don't know nothin' else, Candace."

"It'll be fine. I simply need to know the position of the sofa when you found it, where you pulled your truck in . . . details like that. I'm a detail girl." She smiled broadly, probably hoping to quell Ed's obvious apprehension.

"But who'll watch my shop? And—"

"I can do that," I offered.

Candace removed the gloves and took out her cell phone. "Nope. Need an officer here to keep this as official as possible. The furniture could be evidence or it could be nothing, but I'm not taking any chances. I'm thinking you

got a cat and dog who could use your attention, Jillian."
She nodded at the crate. Yoshi was lying next to it, looking
far too calm for Yoshi. Maybe he was scared, too.

"Yoshi can stay with Ed. But are you saying Magpie's
not evidence?" I asked.

"Not really. I'll get a cat hair sample for comparison
to what's on the sofa. Other than that, I don't need anything."

After she put a bit of Magpie's fur in an evidence en-
velope, it was time for me to leave. Not wanting to get
near the sofa, I blew Ed a kiss from the entrance rather
than giving him the hug I was sure he could use about
now. "I'll be in touch. And don't worry, Ed."

Soon Magpie and I were on our way, but my nervous-
ness had merged with curiosity. How *did* that blood get on
the sofa? And what would they find when they returned
to the spot where Ed found it this morning? These
thoughts would nag at me until Candace filled me in.

I glanced at the crate on the passenger seat next to
me. Magpie would have much preferred to be out of
there if her continued clawing on the latch was any clue.

"What do you know about blood and bullets, Magpie?" I said softly.

# Three

I pulled into my driveway, feeling an urgent need for sweet tea, a cat on my lap and Animal Planet on the TV. But Magpie came first. I didn't want a kitty smeared with human blood visiting with my three resident fur friends.

Before Merlot, my red Maine coon, Chablis, my Himalayan, and Syrah, my Abyssinian, could blink—they were waiting by the back door—I quickly took our new friend to the basement for a bath. I shut the stairway door before Syrah could stick out a paw and stop me. I didn't need company for this particular job.

Cats and baths don't often go well together. Perhaps they feel as if it's humiliating. Two out of my three cats hated getting in the tub—because they believed they could clean themselves just fine, thank you very much. Chablis was different. Any and all attention was welcome, even if it involved water.

Turned out, Magpie was like Chablis. She purred as I shampooed her. When I rinsed her off, the lather was rusty red and had I not known about the blood, I would have thought she'd been rolling in South Carolina clay. I finished the bath as quickly as I could, not wanting to dwell on what had just gone down the drain.

The downstairs bathroom was always ready for guests—whether the guests were feline or human. Since Finn had already dropped off his bag in the bedroom down here, I used his hair dryer on Magpie. I was worried this part of the process wouldn't go quite as well and kept my thick rubber gloves on to prevent scratches. But this little tortie seemed unflappable. She even rolled onto her back at one point to make sure I thoroughly dried off her tummy.

Merlot and Syrah should have been watching this and maybe learning a lesson on how to behave when it was their turn. They rarely needed baths, but when they did, I often wished I owned a suit of armor.

Worried that the carrier I'd used for this baby would have traces of blood left inside, I stowed it in a corner of the basement for now, knowing it was probably headed for the trash. I had a soft-sided carrier in the storage room and used that to take Magpie upstairs for the meet and greet.

My cats were immensely curious when I set the carrier down on the window seat where the afternoon sun would warm Magpie up. Syrah offered an openmouthed hiss when he saw the new visitor and ran off. Chablis sniffed her and walked away, but Merlot was quite interested and parked himself next to the carrier and stared at Magpie through the mesh. It seemed she would have one friend right away—even though I was certain my other two would come around.

After I had a PBJ sandwich for lunch along with some

freshly made sweet tea, it was time to work on the hem of my wedding dress. When John and I had married, we'd chosen the courthouse in Houston. No dress, no flowers, no fuss, mostly because John's daughter, Kara, in her late teens at the time, had been none too happy about her father remarrying.

Kara and I were close now. I loved her and she felt the same about me. After John's heart attack seven years ago, his recliner was my haven. I'd sit there and feel wrapped in his arms. But now it had been moved to the master bedroom in Kara's house. That chair had comforted me through the dark days following John's sudden death. Now it belonged with her.

For my wedding to Tom, I would be wearing my grandmother's cream satin dress, and it needed alterations. I was almost done with the hem but would need help from Martha at the local quilt shop for the rest. She was an expert seamstress as well as a quilter. Before I got started with my needle and thread, I heard Magpie softly mewing. She was probably hungry. I opened the crate and set a dish of kibble on the window seat while Merlot continued to stare at our new addition to the family.

Before the tortie even smelled the kibble, she bumped noses with Merlot. He blinked—that loving blink all cats use—and sat nearby to watch her eat.

"Does my big red boy suddenly have a girlfriend?" I asked.

Merlot warbled a response but kept his eyes on Magpie. *How sweet,* I thought.

I usually felt comfortable leaving the cats to get to know each other, since I fostered kitties all the time for Shawn, but this baby was a little different. She was used to more outdoor time than indoor. I figured about ninety minutes was the max I could work on the hem.

In the meantime, I hoped Magpie would be entertained by my three amigos. I went to my quilting room and set the timer on my phone. I heard no loud protests once I closed the door, nor did I hear sounds of a catfight as I worked. Paws appeared under the door several times, but the addition of a new visitor was probably more interesting than watching me sew. I was putting the finishing touches on the hem when I heard Candace's familiar knock at my back door—a rather booming version because I no doubt hadn't heard her the first time.

I carefully boxed up the dress to keep it away from prying cats' paws and hurried out to greet her. By the time I reached the kitchen, Candace had already let herself in and was taking the pitcher of sweet tea from the fridge. Syrah and Chablis watched her closely.

"Your back door's not locked—*again*." She set the pitcher on the counter and reached for a glass above the breakfast bar that separated the kitchen from the living area. "Tea?"

"Absolutely. Just finished the hem on my dress and couldn't have so much as a glass of water near it for fear of spilling anything."

"It's finished?"

"Almost," I answered. "A few alterations are still needed."

"Did you hear what I said to you, Jillian? It's not safe to leave your door unlocked." She added ice to our glasses and poured the tea.

"But I had to hurry in here and get Magpie downstairs for a bath without a clowder of cats on my heels."

"I get that." She sounded like a mother scolding a child. "But Tom added that app to your phone where you can remotely lock up the house. Why not use it?" She handed me my glass.

"You're right." I smiled. "But wait until you're my age in twenty or so years and see how well you remember what apps are on your phone."

Candace laughed. "You're only forty-something, so don't think I buy that excuse. I only want you to be careful."

"Let's sit. You look tired and it's not even the end of your shift."

"I can talk for a bit, but first, you have something I need." She pulled a small plastic evidence bag from her pocket.

"What are you talking about?"

"Ed told me about a locket. I sure hope you still have it."

"Oh my gosh. I forgot all about it." I pulled it from my pocket and held it up. "You want me to drop it in the evidence bag?"

I suddenly had Syrah's complete attention. He stood up on his back legs for a second to get a better look. In his world, dangling objects must be focused on—and attacked whenever possible.

"Hang on a sec." She set the evidence bag on the counter and then I noticed she had her camera strapped across her chest. She gave a quick pet to both Syrah and Chablis. Merlot and Magpie remained where I'd last seen them, sniffing each other as they sat about an inch apart on the window seat.

Candace took several pictures of the locket and then backed up her photos by taking shots with her phone.

"Did you open that thing up?" she asked.

"No. I haven't touched it since we unwound it from Magpie's leg—because I forgot all about it. There is a major life event in my near future, if you remember."

Her blue eyes brightened. "An exciting one, for sure." She took latex gloves from her pocket and pulled them on. "Okay, I'll carefully open the locket so I can catch a few pics and then close it up again. Just keep holding on the way you're doing now."

Syrah jumped on the kitchen counter. He definitely wanted a closer look.

"You better hurry up, Candace, or another cat will take off with this tempting piece of jewelry."

But Syrah, to my surprise, didn't paw at the locket as I expected, though it certainly held his attention. Once Candace finished taking photos of the etched gold locket while it was open, she took the chain, carefully grasping it in the same place I had done. She asked me to open the evidence bag so she could place the necklace inside.

"I couldn't see what was in there, Candace—and I sure want to know."

"A picture of a baby. Don't know how old, but an infant for sure. Maybe the crime lab can give us an approximate date of the photo." She showed me the baby's picture on the camera.

"Just this one picture?" I asked.

"Yup. Bald baby, so whether it's a boy or a girl is anyone's guess."

"Maybe there'll be a clue when the crime lab people

take it apart—like writing on the back. By the way, I am so sorry I've been walking around all day with the necklace."

Candace was dating the evidence bag with a Sharpie she'd pulled from her breast pocket. "I have it now, so no problem. I did find more possible evidence of a crime when Ed took me over to that donation box. Unfortunately, when he picked up the sofa, his truck ran over any previous tire impressions in the ground."

"So you *did* find something." I was almost afraid to hear what it was.

"More blood in the dirt where the sofa had been sitting. I'm surprised Ed didn't see it, but then he was dragging that sofa all by himself and probably overlooked it. Man's gonna have a heart attack one day if he keeps trying to do everything by himself."

"You'll never get him to understand that. Karen has tried and failed to convince him many times. So, what's next? Because somebody could be hurt somewhere, right?" I gestured for Candace to take a seat at the small mosaic-topped table in my breakfast nook that overlooked the lake. "Why not get off your feet for a bit and we can enjoy our tea while you tell me what's happening?"

Candace nodded and once seated across from me, she sighed before taking a long drink. "I phoned the hospital, not to mention every doctor in town about a possible GSW victim. Came up with nothing. It's frustrating. We don't have the ability to search such a large grassy area without help. The county sheriff's K-9 unit is backed up with cases, so I'm stuck. If I put crime scene tape up, it will draw attention and folks will march all over the place. Besides, I'm not sure it *is* a crime scene."

"My gut tells me it is. And I'm guessing you think so, too."

"Oh, something happened all right, but it could be a secondary scene." She closed her eyes. "It makes me antsy because more evidence might be destroyed before we can thoroughly investigate the area."

"I'll bet a few people already saw you by that box and are talking about it," I said.

"Oh, no doubt. Nothing gets by people in Mercy. I'm meeting a woman over there later today and she'll open the donation box. Maybe I'll get lucky and find a clue to this mystery in there."

"Who's the woman? Because I know some of the ladies who volunteer at the charity that services that box. Those people can be pretty . . . um, let's call them *talkative*."

"Her name is Rebecca Marner. You know her?"

"Oh, for sure. She's the head of about three volunteer committees. I can see why she'd have the key to that box."

Candace raised her eyebrows. "Busybody or know-it-all?"

"How did you—"

"Your tone, Jillian. You don't want to say anything unkind about anyone, but don't forget how well I understand you. So give me the skinny on this woman."

"I'd put her in the 'know-it-all' category." I whispered "know-it-all" as if Rebecca Marner might overhear me.

Candace's shoulders sagged with disappointment. "Great. I have problems relating to know-it-alls. And Chief Baca has even told me I need to work on my *people skills* as he calls them. Ms. Marner's name sounds familiar, but I'm not sure I've ever met her."

"You'll probably recognize her when you see her. I've run into her quite a few times when I took quilts I've made for soldiers' children over to the community center. Do you know Zoe? She's over there all the time volunteering."

Candace nodded. "Nice woman."

"She is," I replied. "Anyway, she introduced me to Rebecca, who within minutes was telling me everything she does to help out in Mercy—which is nice, of course, but most folks around here don't start conversations that way. Anyhow, her husband owns a construction company. And get this. Zoe is married to Rebecca's first husband, yet she's saying all this sweet stuff about her. That's a rare thing."

Candace's eyes widened in surprise. "Wait a minute. Are you talking about Rhett Marner? Those women have both been married to *him*?"

"Zoe still is. You'd think it would make for a few awkward moments in the charity volunteer circles, but they're quite friendly. So you know Rhett Marner?"

"Oh, yes. He builds mostly commercial stuff. Mercy is growing and he's been pretty busy on various projects— like the new office building. We've had to break up a few fistfights there as well as at other sites he supervises. Some of the workers he hires must have cut their teeth on their daddies' rifle barrels."

"Gosh, we never had any problems like that when John and I built this house. But then, John was very hands-on and such a kind man. The atmosphere set by the people in charge can really make a difference."

"Speaking of your late husband, is the wedding bringing up lots of . . . *memories*?"

"It is. But even though it sounds like a cliché, I know John would want me to be happy. Tom makes me happy." I smiled.

She answered with a grin, "He's a good man. If I didn't think he was great, I wouldn't be putting on a dress to stand by your side in church."

"I can't wait to see you in that dress. It looked so pretty on the hanger."

Candace picked up the evidence bag with the locket, her cheeks pink with embarrassment. "I need to book this as evidence—of what I'm not sure yet." Then she just stared at her shoes for several seconds.

"What's bothering you, Candace?"

She met my gaze. "I know you're crazy busy with your wedding preparations, so—"

"If you need my help, just ask."

"You know this Rebecca person and I tend to suffer from foot-in-mouth disease when it comes to know-it-alls. Would you mind coming with me to meet her—not only to introduce me but to keep me in line? Maybe you can clear your throat or something when I say something I shouldn't?"

I laughed. "Since when has anyone been able to keep you in line? But of course I'll go with you."

# Four

Once Candace booked the locket into the evidence room, we had thirty minutes to spare before meeting Rebecca at the donation box, so we decided to stop at Belle's Beans and pick up coffee. The afternoon was growing chilly, bringing enough wind to knock plenty of leaves off the many trees that lined the street. Candace mumbled about her fear of any impending rain destroying potential evidence near that donation box.

Luckily for us, she found a parking spot in front of Belle's Beans just as someone was pulling out. Main Street seemed pretty crowded for late afternoon. We both ordered coffee to go from the Belle of the Day—whose real name was Tina. Owner and good friend Belle Lowry always had her baristas wear a name tag that said "Belle."

I suggested we also buy a coffee for Rebecca, and Candace agreed it was a good idea. We added that to the order. I'd carry sugar and creamer with me so she could doctor her own drink.

As we waited for our order to come up, I noted that Belle's Beans buzzed with conversation. Each lacquered table was occupied and every barstool along the wall was taken. Either Mercy's population was booming or teenagers were growing into adults way too fast. I had a feeling the cooler October weather might also have something to do with the influx of customers.

Candace's double-shot flavor of the day was up, as well as the plain coffee for Rebecca. We were still waiting on my decaf vanilla latte when Belle walked toward us. She'd been in the back room and carried a tray of pastries to refill the display case on top of the counter. The sight of cupcakes with thick, rich-looking frosting, raspberry bars and brownies made my mouth water. She baked all these goodies herself and I wondered how the woman ever had time to sleep.

"Hey there. My girls are here." Her smile was lopsided because of her misapplied lipstick. She wasn't wearing her new glasses, which explained the makeup malfunction.

After shoving the tray on top of the display case, she came around the counter and hugged us both.

"At my age, you can call me one of your girls all day long," I said.

"You're a bride-to-be and that makes you ageless. Besides, you're twenty years younger than me, so that makes you a girl, at least to my way of thinking." Belle's snow-white hair and laugh lines made her as beautiful as any twenty-year-old to me. "What kind of trouble are you two up to now?" she asked.

"Trouble? Us?" Candace's tone sounded mischievous.

"I do see a problem lurking in those pretty blue eyes, Deputy Candace Carson—even though you're smiling."

Belle glanced at Tina. "Sweet pea, would you replenish the bakery case, please?"

Tina nodded.

Candace said, "You are correct as usual, Belle. I am a little . . . *puzzled*." I saw a spark light her eyes. "Maybe you can help." She unclipped her phone from her utility belt.

While Candace unlocked her phone, I said, "It's so busy in here. Tell me you *will* make it to my wedding and not be tied up working."

"Does a fifty-pound sack of flour make a giant biscuit? Of course I'll be there."

I smiled. "Whew. It wouldn't be the same without you."

Candace swiped her phone screen looking for a picture and then held it out to Belle. "Have you ever seen this piece of jewelry on any of your customers?"

Belle squinted at the screen and I almost asked her where those new glasses were. But I kept my mouth shut, not wanting her to think I was a meddler. She was quite capable of taking care of herself.

"It does look familiar." Belle cocked her head. "Why do you need to know?"

"I don't want to contaminate your memory with any knowledge I have concerning this locket—which is precious little, by the way."

Belle nodded. "Shoulda known I'd get nothing out of you. Can I think on it? Sometimes I need to wade through the maze I call my mind before something comes to me. After sixty-eight years there's a lotta junk in my personal attic."

Candace and I laughed.

"I'm counting on you, Belle, so yes, think on it." Candace put her phone back on her belt. "You know how to reach me." She looked my way. "We gotta get moving, Jillian."

I hugged Belle. "Glad you'll be there next Saturday," I whispered.

"Wouldn't miss it for the world. Now get after Miss Speed Demon or she'll be halfway to wherever before you can blink."

Belle was right. Candace drove as though she wanted to join Danica Patrick on the NASCAR circuit. I grabbed my latte as well as the sugar and cream, then hurried out of the shop. Candace was already climbing into her squad car.

Worried I might trip and spill my coffee, I went as fast as possible without running. Wasting Belle's coffee would be a sin. By the time I set Rebecca's drink down in the cup holder and was hitching up my seat belt, Candace had already lurched into drive and we were on our way.

The charity drop box was about a tenth of a mile from the turnoff to Mercy Animal Sanctuary. The large wooden donation box was painted green and on the side that faced the rural road was a sign that read CHARITY THRIFT STORE. PLEASE DONATE SHOES, CLOTHING, COATS AND SMALL HOUSEHOLD ITEMS. Though in a rather remote spot, it was so close to the busy animal adoption site that many people with good intentions visited. I remembered one of the volunteers at the charity store saying how surprised she was at the amount of nice stuff they received from this particular box. It had to be checked for overflow at least once a week.

Candace and I stood by the sign to wait for Rebecca. The already brisk wind was picking up, making me glad I'd worn a sweatshirt with a front pouch where I could tuck my hands. The brown, shriveled leaves that had been on the ground now danced around us everywhere.

Candace said, "When Ms. Marner shows up, I won't say much about what I'm looking for, so if you could keep her occupied, I'd sure appreciate it."

"I'll try. But you can bet she'll be asking questions. What should I say?"

Candace thought for a second. "Say someone isn't sure if they threw something in here by accident or if the item was stolen from their house. Tell her you don't know much more than that. It might be a white lie—but I'm not really sure what I'm looking for."

"Maybe she'll take the lead and mention something about thefts in Mercy. She does like to talk—though mostly about herself."

"I'll bet you can make that happen without much prompting, Jillian. I don't want her looking over my shoulder, is all. We could find bloody clothes or even a weapon in this box and she'd be sure to spread the word all over town about a find like that."

I glanced toward the road. "Nothing like a little pressure—and I believe that's her pulling over behind your squad car right now in her pretty Lexus SUV. She always dresses as if she has money. Guess she does."

Rebecca Marner did not come dressed to collect anything from a donation box. She wore a fuchsia suit—looked expensive—and shoes that would probably pay someone's mortgage for the month. Certainly not walking-around-in-the-country shoes, that's for sure. The wind couldn't budge even one highlighted blond hair as she approached us. She'd probably put on enough spray and gel to protect against a hurricane.

In the past, I always thought she seemed younger than me—maybe late thirties. But as she approached us today, she seemed older than that, maybe even late forties. Could be the tightness I detected in her jaw. But then she produced a smile that belonged on a campaign poster as she greeted me with double fake kisses on my cheeks—*fake* being the key word. Her smile made all the difference and I decided I had no idea how old she was.

She thanked me for the coffee I offered, but refused, saying she didn't want to ruin her lipstick or spill it on her suit. I took a deep breath as she shook Candace's hand, knowing it would help me remain calm in the face of such a phony. I liked most people, could look past their flaws and find something good. But people who pretended to be more than they were always bothered me the most. This week I felt on edge with so much going on and I only hoped I could find the good in Rebecca Marner to help me through this little meeting while Candace did her job.

Rebecca pulled a key ring from the dark pink-and-black leather tote hung in the crook of her elbow. "Let me see. I empty all the boxes and each one has a unique key. Not that the locks keep vandals away. Our philosophy is, however, if they need clothes and shoes that badly, they are welcome to break into our boxes." She offered a constrained tittering laugh that, to me, meant "I don't believe what I just said for a minute."

She unlocked the box and Candace helped her open the swinging door that protected the contents. The place on top where people dropped in their donations had a grill so that once items were deposited, it was impossible to retrieve them—sort of like the spikes at a parking lot that warned you not to go backward or risk tire damage.

As I expected, Rebecca bent at the waist and peered inside, so I did the same. The box smelled like old socks and perspiration. I stepped back.

"Exactly what are you looking for, Deputy Carson?" Rebecca said.

I piped in with "Do you have to keep repairing the boxes? I mean, after someone breaks in?"

She turned to me. "We've had to make locks and grills line items on the budget, it happens so often. There's no keeping people out if they truly believe they need clothes or shoes that desperately. Can you believe they actually use a saw to cut through the grills?"

"How awful." I'd left my unfinished latte in the squad car and now gripped the full coffee cup intended for Rebecca, not quite knowing what to do with it. "Do they understand they could come to the charity store and you'd make sure anyone who couldn't afford clothes or shoes—especially for their children—would get what they needed?"

"We do need to have money to pay the store rent and utilities, Jillian. Contributions are wonderful, but every charity must have a budget. Not that there haven't been times when we have offered the most destitute shopper a helping hand." She glanced back at Candace, who began to remove a few trash bags stuffed to near bursting.

"Deputy Carson, I only emptied this box a few days ago, so if I can be of any help, then—"

"Does that happen often?" I needed to keep her attention on me and not Candace.

Rebecca turned to me, and her tone was impatient. "Does *what* happen often?"

"People in need have to ask you to give them things?"

My attempt at a diversionary conversation was making me pretty depressed. It struck me that if I walked into the charity store, I wouldn't feel comfortable asking Rebecca Marner for *anything*.

"We do price items reasonably. It's not like they're shopping at Belk."

Belk was a fancy department store in the shopping mall by the freeway that was quite a ways away. Her condescension, her obvious disdain for those she was supposed to be helping, only made me feel more down.

I forced a smile. "Of course they're not shopping at Belk. I guess I need to learn more about the store and how it works. After my wedding, I might even volunteer."

Rebecca returned the smile. "Your wedding? When is that event again?"

"This coming weekend. At the little church in the Mill Town." I was surprised to notice that, this time, thinking about the wedding didn't make me tense. In fact, I had a quick vision of Tom and me walking out of the church as man and wife. The image eased the constriction and sadness this brief talk with Rebecca had created.

She raised her perfectly sculpted eyebrows. "You're getting married in the *Mill Town*? Oh my. That is an interesting choice. But historic, I suppose. There is *that*."

"It's the right choice for us." This time I couldn't keep the testiness out of my voice.

"Because?" She was mining for gossip.

"Because the pastor and his wife are two of the finest people I have ever met."

I could see the probing glint in her eyes fade. I had shut her down. "I'm certain it will be a lovely affair. And by all means, do volunteer. We need all the help we can get."

As long as Rebecca Marner wasn't on duty the same day I volunteered, I might consider it. That way I could find out what people needed and how I could get it to them without this person standing in their way.

Unfortunately my thoughts made me waver from my assigned task for a second. That was all the time Rebecca needed to whirl and focus on Candace, who was kneeling amid about a dozen trash bags now.

Rebecca stood over her, her curiosity obviously not quelled by my attempt at distraction. "Let me help you, Deputy Carson."

"I got this." Candace peered into the bag she'd steadied between her knees. "If you trust me with the key for an hour or so, I can go through all this and return it to the box or bring this stuff to the store. Either way I'll get the key back to you as soon as possible."

"That doesn't work for me. I'll be out of pocket the rest of today with several committee meetings." She tapped her foot as she pondered this. "But I suppose you could drop the key by my home. My daughter will be there after her class in . . . whatever it is she's taking this semester at the community college."

As I listened from several feet away, the two of them made the arrangements. Candace would take the bags to the store and then drop the key off at Rebecca's home. The woman then sped off in her luxury car.

"How can I help?" I knelt next to Candace.

She pulled a pair of latex gloves from her pocket and handed them to me. I traded them for the untouched coffee. She said, "I'll examine the contents of these bags and then you keep what I hand you separate from what, if anything, I might consider as evidence."

Candace gulped down that extra dose of coffee as if it were water in the desert before she continued working.

The job took us more than an hour and in the end, Candace found nothing with blood on it, nothing that screamed "a murderer dumped evidence in here." She sat back on her heels. "There's no way the cat could get inside this donation box and get out with that blood all over her. And certainly not with a locket wrapped around her leg. It's all about the darn sofa." Candace tucked loose strands of hair behind her ear. "I wish that kitty could talk. She's my witness."

I was sitting cross-legged, folding old clothes and returning them to the bags Candace had emptied. "She may have climbed between those cushions to hide if something was happening—and by something I mean a gun going off."

Candace shook her head and didn't bother folding anything as she shoved clothes and toys back into bags. "Bullets and blood concern me and I won't give up on this problem until I have answers."

She didn't need to tell me what I already knew.

We loaded the bags into the trunk of her squad car. Candace drove to the charity store as if she were driving a getaway car with me gripping the sides of the passenger seat tightly. Not only was she driving like a demon, but she had a look in her eye that I knew only too well.

She *would* get to the bottom of this mysterious blood. And because she'd decided I could talk to people she felt uncomfortable with, I'd be smack in the middle again.

I didn't mind. I needed the distraction.

# Five

After we dropped off the contents of the donation box at the Charity Thrift Store, Candace got a call from B.J., who said she was needed back at the station. She took me home and handed me the key to the box, asking if I wouldn't mind dropping it off whenever I got the chance.

I stared at her as we sat in my driveway. "Whenever I get the chance? Shouldn't I take this to her house right now?"

"That would be no. You are busy. I am busy. She can wait."

"But—"

"I don't want you to take it to her house until at least tomorrow. That woman needs to learn that police business trumps her social schedule."

I shoved the key in my jeans pocket. "If you say so—*boss.*"

Her expression softened. "Sorry to sound like a bear, but I don't like her attitude."

"Okay, tomorrow—if I get the chance. How does that sound?" I smiled, afraid I was sounding a little like a bear myself.

"Perfect."

With that, I climbed out of the car and waved a good-bye that went unnoticed. Candace was definitely preoccupied by what had gone on today.

My cats greeted me with sleepy eyes and I was relieved to see Magpie hadn't managed to find an escape route, though perhaps she'd put a plan in place during my absence.

My phone pinged. Finn texted me that Shawn would be dropping him off in about an hour so I didn't need to pick him up. After doling out crunchy treats to all four cats, I considered what to feed the hungry men in my life.

This week was so packed with planning and sewing and now a mystery, food was the last thing on my mind. Tom was across the lake on a PI job, and I didn't want to risk ringing him if he was busy. I texted him and asked if he could bring home sandwiches from the local sub shop.

He responded by calling to ask what Finn and I wanted, since he was halfway back to Mercy. I asked for a hot pulled pork sub and told him to pick up something he knew Finn liked. I would have to learn more of his favorites, since he would be living with us for a spell. So far, I hadn't seen him refuse any hot meal . . . or cold meal . . . or snack. He was twenty years old and still growing, maybe even making up for lost time when he'd lived with his emotionally abusive mother. Kids do pick up the tab for their parents' problems. Finn was an unhappy young man when we first met. Tom, though not his biological father, certainly was the best thing that ever happened to him. His mother and father were out of the picture now and had no say in where he lived. Finn was over eighteen and could make his own decisions.

By the time we sat down to eat at the dining room table situated between the breakfast bar and the living area—we'd designed the house to be very open to give us optimal lake views—Syrah was already sniffing around. He loved pork and was always disappointed when we spoiled it with the mustard-based Carolina barbecue sauce.

Tom told Finn that he'd asked Ed and his mother, Karen, to keep Yoshi for the coming week, since we'd all be so busy with the wedding drawing near. "That dog loves to go fishing with Ed and enjoys being at the shop."

Finn didn't seem too thrilled about this; in fact, when he'd arrived here from college, he asked if Yoshi could come stay here as soon as possible. I thought it was fine, but apparently Tom had other ideas.

Rather than voice his disappointment, Finn changed the subject. "Did you figure out where the blood came from?"

Tom's eyes opened so wide the lids disappeared for a second. "Did you say *blood*?"

"He did," I answered. "I can explain."

"Please. This sounds far more interesting than my day following a guy who's cheating on his wife. Divorce keeps me in business, but I can't say I enjoy documenting a cheater's behavior."

I filled Tom and Finn in on the rest of my day, which to me didn't sound any more exciting than Tom's.

"Sounds like the lady's full of herself." Finn balled up

the wrapping from his Italian sub, wiped his mouth with a napkin and tossed these things in the bag the subs came in.

"She is. But I've been pulling memories of conversations I heard between folks who volunteer in her circles. I recall she had some kind of personal trouble a couple years back. Maybe she's hiding bitterness or depression over whatever it was."

"Or she's full of herself." Finn stood, seemingly anxious to remove himself from the conversation. "Now, where's Magpie? Getting acquainted with every hiding place in your house?"

The cat must understand plenty of words, because as soon as Finn spoke she came sauntering from the hallway. A spool of thread bounced behind her. Thread was wrapped around her paw, but she appeared completely unbothered. In fact, she seemed quite proud of herself.

When I went to help get her untangled, I realized she had something in her mouth. I tried to remove it, but she turned her head away. Cats, no matter how small, are quite strong when they want to be. I wasn't about to fight with her.

"Finn, I need your help," I called.

Both Finn and Tom came to the rescue and only then was I able to extricate my very expensive Roxanne gold thimble from her mouth. She blinked slowly at me as if to say, "You may have caught me this time, but just wait." This girl had been busy and there were plenty more treasures in my sewing room where this thread and thimble came from.

"Bet she thinks she's come to kleptomaniac heaven," I said.

Finn cradled her as Tom removed the last of the thread from her paws.

Tom smiled. "Finn tells me all doors leading to outside are a challenge to this one. She's an escape artist like our last feline friend, Clyde."

"Gosh, I miss that big orange guy." I'd fostered him and he now lived in New York City. "Anyway, cats hate a closed door, and your fur baby Dashiell is no different, as I recall. But this one must really dislike them—or love the opportunity to show how smart she is."

"Syrah will show her all the ways to get around this place," Tom said.

"Oh yes, he will." Syrah knew how to open doors, too, but he didn't find it necessary too often. It was easier for me to leave closet doors ajar and other entrances open. Otherwise he'd work away at them and scratch the wood.

"You guys realize," Finn said as he stroked Magpie, "we'll have five cats here when Tom moves in after the wedding."

"The more the merrier." I stroked the side of Magpie's cheek and she began to purr.

The next morning, the key to the donation box was burning a hole in my pocket as I pulled into Rebecca Marner's driveway around ten. Would she be home? Would I face her wrath for keeping the key longer than she'd wanted us to? I did have a ready-made excuse—my wedding plans—even though Kara was making the whole thing quite easy by taking over on all fronts.

I took a deep breath and walked up the stone-and-slate walkway to the two-story brick home. The house had to be at least four thousand square feet. I noticed it was quite isolated here, with huge white oaks and pines canopying bright green ferns. The leaves had turned to burnished gold and deep red. Their beauty made me forget that the nearest house was maybe a half mile away. And what did that matter, anyway? It wasn't as if I was walking into a trap. Okay, maybe I was a little worried about Rebecca's reaction. That *could* be a bit of a trap.

I pushed the thought aside as I reached the double front doors with beautiful lead glass windows and side-lights. The doorbell was backlit and I pressed it quickly—as if that would help me end this chore swiftly so I could leave. *Not really, Jillian. It doesn't work that way.*

A girl who looked to be about Finn's age—late teens or early twenties—answered the door wide enough to wedge her petite body in the space between me and the interior of the house. Too bad her clear-skinned oval face was marred by disdain as she appraised me. "What do you want?"

"Is Rebecca here?" I asked.

"Nope."

"Are you her daughter?"

"Unfortunately I am. Come back later—and call first, because she's not home very much." She was about to close the door.

"Wait." I held out the key. "She said to leave this with you."

The daughter screwed up her face and stared at the

key as if it were a snake ready to strike. "What am *I* supposed to do with it?"

Best to counter insolence with kindness, I decided. "Just give it to her if you would, please?"

"Funny how she can get people to do stuff for her, like *all the time*. You . . . and now me. Doesn't that *bug* you?"

"It's no problem. What's your name, by the way?" I smiled warmly. I detected melancholy in her brown eyes and knew her attitude was masking pain of some kind. Or maybe hiding loneliness?

Her eyebrows rose. "Oh. Are you supposed to report back exactly who has possession of this precious *key to the kingdom of charity*?"

*Smart girl,* I thought. *Sarcastic comebacks require a quick mind.* "No. I just kind of like you, so I'd like to know your name."

I could see surprise overtake surliness. "Lindsey, okay? Now, if you don't mind, I have an exam to study for."

She took the key and closed the door before I could even say thank you. So I pressed my mouth close to the door and called my thanks—and heard a "You're welcome" in response.

Yup. For some reason, I liked that girl. Maybe the old "the enemy of my enemy is my friend" thing was going on. And this girl did speak of her mother like an enemy. But did I consider Rebecca an enemy? No. It was Lindsey's spunk I liked.

Since Kara and I had an errand to run for the wedding, my next stop was the *Mercy Messenger* offices. She was the owner, editor and photographer of the town paper.

I didn't even have to leave the van. A smiling Kara

was waiting for me on the sidewalk, her dark brown satchel-type bag strapped over a stylish short jean jacket. She climbed into the passenger seat. "How's the bride-to-be? Nervous?"

"Not really. Okay . . . maybe a little. I need to finish the dress. Martha at the Cotton Company will be helping me with the fitting. Besides being an amazing quilter, she's quite the seamstress. I need a few alterations that I sure can't handle myself."

Kara shook her head. "Sorry. I'm of no help in that department. I'm useless when it comes to sewing and I'll bet your beautiful other bridesmaid, Candace, is as well. Leaving these final details in the hands of other people is probably part of your anxiety. I know how independent you are."

"You're probably right, Dr. Kara." I laughed. "Next thing you know you'll be writing an advice column for the *Messenger*."

She laughed. "Maybe I will. Please don't worry too much. Your day will be perfect and joyful and all the things a wedding is supposed to be."

We drove several blocks to a gift shop on Main Street where we'd had favors made for all the guests. Lynn Summer's Specialty Gifts combined the owner's creative talent for making unique gifts with her expertise in ordering items to sell in her store that always fit the season.

Greeted by the scent of pumpkin spice and a smiling Lynn behind the glass counter, I relaxed the minute I walked through the door.

She grinned at us. "They're ready. I hope you like them."

Kara and I walked up to the counter and Kara said, "I can't wait to see them."

Lynn's eyes, magnified by thick lenses in horn-rimmed frames, sparkled with pride as she carefully lifted a box from behind the counter. "Check them out. See what you think."

The flat box was packed with stemless wineglasses, each one engraved in a scrolling white font with my name, Tom's name and our wedding date. Lynn had filled each glass with Hershey's foil-wrapped candy. She'd sealed the glasses with delicate ivory tulle and secured the tulle with a satin ribbon. Attached to the ribbon was a heart-shaped antique-looking tag that said "Hugs and Kisses from Tom and Jillian."

Kara said, "Wow. These will look so beautiful surrounding the giant vases of peonies. You nailed it, Lynn. We'll have one gorgeous table at the reception."

She smiled, looking almost embarrassed. "Where is the reception?"

"At Kara's house," I answered.

"Ah. Good choice." Lynn looked at Kara. "Maybe one day, I can do something special for you and Liam."

Liam, an assistant prosecutor for the county, was Kara's steady boyfriend—if that was the appropriate name for a thirty-something good-looking man.

"Maybe. Right now it's Jillian's time. She's done pretty well for herself in the future-husband department." Kara picked up the box and Lynn lifted another from beneath the counter.

"By your expression, Jillian, you're happy with these?" Lynn said.

I touched the ribbon on one glass, staring at our names linked together. I felt tears sting behind my eyes. "You have no idea. These are so special."

Kara, Lynn and I each took a flat box of the filled glasses and carefully packed them in the back of my minivan. I'd brought along several old quilts to cover each box. The quilts would also keep them from knocking together.

When we were done and Lynn assured me I'd paid the right amount up front when I placed the order, she said, "Would you mind showing me your cats on that phone of yours? You know I have two of my own, but I can't get enough of seeing yours."

I pulled my cell from my jeans pocket. "I could never say no to *that* request."

Soon we were watching Syrah batting at a lounging, sleepy Chablis. He was trying to get her to play and she was having none of it. Then I swiped the phone to pan the camera, and Merlot and Magpie came into view. Merlot had his big paws around her neck and was cleaning her face.

"Aw," Lynn said. "Who's the new addition?"

I explained about Finn and his newfound fur friend.

While we talked, Kara had sat in the passenger seat to check text messages. Suddenly she called out, "Jillian, we have to go. *Now*."

Lynn backed up onto the sidewalk. "Sounds important. You better get to it. Have a wonderful wedding, Jillian."

I wanted to give her a hug, but since something was up, I hurried to the driver's side, climbed in and stabbed the key in the ignition. "What's wrong?"

"My police source texted me and says they've found a body. Let's go."

# Six

Kara directed me to a construction site on the other side of town and before I headed that way, I asked if I should drop her at the newspaper office so she could drive herself there. But it was in the opposite direction and I already knew her answer. She didn't want to waste a second backtracking to the office. Besides, she had everything she needed for a story—the camera she always had with her in her satchel, as well as her notebook computer.

I said, "This is where they're constructing that new high-rise office building. It's rumored to be some big company relocating and bringing in plenty of white-collar jobs."

"Can you go faster? I want to be on the scene and talk to Candace before she leaves or gets too busy with interviews and canvassing and all that police stuff."

"Those wineglasses in the back are fragile and—"

"Lynn packed them well and so did we. Please step on it, Jillian."

"Okay, but if I hear clinking glass, I'm slowing down." I pressed on the gas pedal. The entire police force was probably at the site, so I surely wasn't at risk of getting a speeding ticket. Besides, I was certain this happened to be new construction Rhett Marner managed. I was as curious as Kara about what had happened there.

A vast area that looked like the planned parking lot for the office building was partially cordoned off with crime scene tape. We couldn't get very close to the spot where officers stood looking down at what I assumed was the body Kara mentioned.

A cement truck rattled by my van, apparently leaving without dumping its load. It kicked up the gravel from the temporary roads and parking area where my van now sat. At least I assumed it hadn't poured any concrete, because I couldn't spot any. Someone had placed plywood over the rebar crosshatch that was prepared in the area that would be poured. Before I even killed the engine, a shiver ran up both arms. Something awful had happened here. I could tell by the look on Candace's face as she talked to Morris Ebeling, her partner, and the chief of Mercy PD, Mike Baca.

Then I spied an additional sight that only added to my discomfort. Lydia Monk was standing behind Mike, hands on hips. One high-heeled, booted toe tapped impatiently. How could she walk around this precarious place with those silly boots on? The last thing Candace and Mike needed was a coroner's investigator with an ego the size of that office building, but that was what Lydia was and they were stuck with her. Why couldn't Lydia just do her job—which was basically to take down the facts and report to the elected county coroner—and leave Candace and the rest of the force alone?

After Kara took in the scene as I had done, she slid out of the passenger seat, camera ready. Was this more trouble for Rhett Marner? An industrial accident? Or something more sinister? Or had someone thought they found the perfect spot to hide a body forever?

I stayed put, not wanting to interfere, but Kara carefully maneuvered on the plywood paths in place. She stopped when she reached the crime scene tape. Deputy Lois Jewel, notebook in hand, was making sure no one breached the barrier. She nodded at Kara and smiled briefly, but I could tell she was trying to block Kara's view of what was happening beyond that tape. Trouble was, I couldn't spot much of anything myself. I expected to at least catch sight of a covered body, but didn't. What was everyone standing around for? Usually there was plenty going on when a body was found.

While Kara took photos of the office building, the unfinished parking lot and the area where the police had gathered, a pickup truck arrived and two men, maybe mid-forties, got out and hurried around to the back of the truck. They each hefted a large handheld saw out of the truck bed. The saws had scary-looking circular blades and I worried they might hurt themselves as they ran to where Lois and Kara stood. *Oh, wait,* I thought. *There must be guards on the saws.* The men wouldn't run with giant, jagged blades next to their legs.

Lois wrote in her notebook before she lifted the crime scene tape and pointed to the plywood path leading to where everyone was gathered. She was probably making sure they stayed right on those planks so as not to destroy any potential evidence.

As Kara took pictures of them talking to the chief, my curiosity could no longer be contained. I had to find out what the heck was going on.

Lois greeted me with a warm smile, thank goodness. She was an "all business" kind of cop, but we'd become friends during my frequent visits to Candace at the station. That friendship must have counted for something, because she didn't object to me hanging around where I probably shouldn't be.

Kara seemed not to notice that I now stood beside her. She'd lifted her camera again and was watching as Candace and Morris unfolded what looked like a brand-new tarp. From what I could tell as they knelt, the two of them were carefully fitting the tarp beneath the rebar, folding and unfolding as they painstakingly completed their task.

Kara mumbled, "Protecting the body."

"So there is a body?" I didn't know why I said that. Maybe I was hoping against hope everyone was wrong.

Neither Lois nor Kara replied. They didn't have to.

Once the tarp was in place, the men with saws got to work cutting away the rebar. The noise was jarring in the late-morning quiet. Then I had a puzzling thought. Why wasn't the fire department here to do this job? Surely they had saws and tarps and equipment to handle this? They always showed up at times like this.

I asked Lois and she said, "Because for now, the chief wants this kept quiet and you know how those young firemen love to talk. Puts teenage girls to shame the way they gossip. That's why this didn't go out on the scanner."

Lois eyed me, her stare serious. "That means you and your daughter better keep this quiet until the chief gives the okay."

The police were keeping a secret from the firemen? That was a first. Something about whatever had happened here was different.

Kara, her gaze still on the unfolding drama, addressed Lois in a curt tone. "If there's a serious crime involved, I never print a story that hasn't been approved through police channels. We don't shout out about anything that might jeopardize an investigation."

"I know. I'm just doing my job, Kara," Lois replied.

"Is this a murder?" I glanced between Lois and Kara.

Lois's lips tightened into a line. She looked toward the work being done and remained silent.

"Kara?" I touched her arm.

"Well, you don't get buried under dirt, gravel and re-bar, and perhaps even *concrete*—which I'm guessing was about to happen if not for an observant someone—by *accident.*"

"Oh. The body's *buried.*" I felt silly then. That meant this interment was premeditated, planned to make some-one disappear forever—a thought that made my skin crawl.

# Seven

We watched along with the folks inside the crime scene tape as the men carefully cut away rebar. The debris from their work was caught by the tarp. The noisy job seemed to take forever, but finally the guys with the saws stepped away.

Candace knelt and seemed to be deciding whether they had enough room to lift out the body. But if I thought the waiting was over and we'd know what happened, I was wrong. As the men with saws walked back to their truck, heads down, Candace made a call on her cell. She then crossed her arms. A silent vigil began that seemed to fill the fall air with a bitter chill.

In the meantime, despite no news about this on the scanner, word got out that something was happening at this construction site. Onlookers began to gather, mostly hesitant at first to come close enough to ask questions.

Deputy Morris Ebeling noticed them, hitched his

heavy police belt higher and made his way outside the crime scene tape.

The old grouch, about ready for retirement, nodded at Kara and me as he passed. He might have been grumpy, but he was a good man—and he did have the town's respect. About a dozen people were edging closer by the second. He raised his arms and shouted, "Y'all, this is police business. No one's in danger. Miss Kara is right here, so you know you'll get the straight story from her in the *Messenger*. Now go on about your business." He cleared his throat and added, "Please."

The "please" seemed to do it because they all complied. Some walked away; others got in their cars and left.

Morris ambled back to where we stood. "That's gonna keep happening. Wish that doc would get here. She said she wasn't too far away."

Kara appeared puzzled. "A doctor?"

"You know. That forensic woman—archaeologist or something. The one we had out at the mill that time a while back."

"Dr. Worthy?" I asked.

Morris stabbed a gnarled finger my way. "That's the one."

"You've found a skeleton?" Kara said.

"Nope. Fresh corpse, from what we can tell. We all saw the skin on an ankle. But we gotta *preserve* the evidence, you know." Morris nodded in Candace's direction. "She'd never let me forget it if we just dug the thing up and got it over with. Gotta do it by the book." He grinned at me. "I'm getting too old for this, Miss Jillian."

I caught Lois nod in silent agreement and withheld a smile.

"Morris, you know Candace is right," I said.

"Ain't she always?" He smiled again and patted my arm. "I see more rubberneckers pulling up. I'd rather deal with them than the crazy lady who wears high heels to a crime scene. Don't get that Lydia Monk. Not for one minute."

Morris and I surely agreed on that.

But the latest rubbernecker, as Morris mentioned, wasn't a curious onlooker. I recognized Dr. Worthy the minute she stepped out of her vehicle. She wore a white paper suit over her clothes, as did the three other people who climbed out of the SUV she'd arrived in—two young men and a young woman. They all carried what looked to be large toolboxes.

Once the crew reached us, Dr. Worthy broke into a smile. "Are you a crime scene junkie like me, Jillian?"

"Actually I'm the chauffeur for the reporter here." I introduced her to Kara and asked if she knew Deputy Jewel. They shook hands and Lois wrote something in her notebook.

Dr. Worthy gestured at the three people she'd brought with her and said, "Students of mine." She gave Lois their names, which I didn't catch. The doctor then looked at Kara and me. "Nice seeing you folks and wish it were under better circumstances." Her expression grew serious. "Let's get to work, young people. The police have waited on us long enough."

I thought I understood why she was here. If gravel and dirt covered the corpse—and how I hated the word *corpse*—then everything would have to be painstakingly removed. I'd seen work like that done on the Discovery Channel. It would take a while, for sure.

"Kara, why don't I take the wedding favors home and pick us up some lunch?"

Kara nodded absently, her attention on the new arrivals.

I looked at Lois. "Would you like a sandwich or a burger?"

"No, thanks. Gotta stay focused here." She stared back at those white-suited forensic experts kneeling by the space where the rebar had been cut away.

Kara lifted her camera. "Black bean burger. Not messy, though. Just ketchup and mustard. Large coffee would be nice."

That got Lois's attention. "Guess a coffee would help."

I made a mental note of what she and Kara wanted and left. As soon as I drove away I felt the tension leave my shoulders. A body had nearly been buried in concrete. It dawned on me that I'd seen no construction crews hanging around. Maybe Mike sent them all home? Even so, I would think Rhett Marner might be lurking. This was his project, after all, but so far, I hadn't caught sight of him.

As I pulled out onto the nearby side street, I nearly collided with Rebecca Marner's SUV. Maybe that was Rhett now, but I couldn't be sure, since the windows were tinted and I couldn't see the driver.

I drove home first, still filled with questions. But I had work to do and I pushed all that I'd just witnessed to the back of my mind.

I stored the favors in my office closet and locked the door, much to the chagrin of four kitties. Cats plus ribbon and tulle spelled disaster. I wasn't about to let them ruin all of Lynn's work. None of them seemed too happy with me once I'd thwarted their future mischief. They considered a *locked* door an affront at the very least, and perhaps more of a personal insult. Merlot chattered up at me as if to ask, how could I do this to them?

I looked down at the four of them, sitting in a row by that closed door. I took the time to snap a picture with my phone before I said the magic word hoping to distract them. "Treats?"

But though my three amigos followed me eagerly to the kitchen, Magpie stayed back. Maybe she thought she could get inside the closet if she tried hard enough.

I doled out tuna munchies, making sure Chablis didn't steal from the others—because she was, after all, addicted to these things. Merlot liked to savor his and often lost out to her because of this. I sat cross-legged on the floor and petted each of them. My world had been busy the last few months as I prepared for the wedding, but I never neglected my dear friends.

I was talking and petting and they were purring and bunting—bunting is what cats do when they want to show affection by rubbing their head against you—when I burst into laughter. Merlot jumped at the noise, but I couldn't help myself.

Magpie was dragging a large spool of ribbon that she'd pilfered from my sewing room. If a human had locked away the fun of satin ribbon and tulle, she decided to fix the problem. She held it in her mouth like a prize mouse, and a stream of ribbon flowed between her legs and trailed behind her.

Oh, this girl was trouble all right.

Thirty minutes later I headed back to town after watching four cats destroy the ribbon I didn't even know I had—which for me meant it was more important for them to have a good time than for me to save it. But where had that little sneak found it? And what else did Magpie have up her paw?

Rather than bring sandwiches and coffee for only the three of us at the crime scene, I called up a Mennonite friend who owned a donut truck. He parked in spots all over the area, but he and I became friends after his wife taught a quilting class I attended. They made the best donuts in the world and he often had homemade bread and jam on the truck as well as candy and sometimes cinnamon rolls. And yes, nice fresh coffee. Not as good as Belle's, and he didn't drink it himself, but he had no problem selling it. He told me he'd been about to close up the truck where he was parked—no problem with him having a cell phone either—but he'd call his wife, restock the truck and head out to the site. After all, the area would be populated by police and other workers for hours, if not the rest of the day.

I stopped at a local chicken spot and bought a dozen sandwiches because donuts and coffee might not be enough to satisfy hungry workers. I'd ordered Kara's burger ahead of time from her favorite vegetarian café on Main Street—Sprouts and Soups. When I passed the construction site before making the turn onto the side street to enter the area, the talkative fire crew was now on the scene along with the paramedics. In Mercy, para-medics were often the ones who transported a body to the morgue about twenty miles away. If no autopsy was needed, the local funeral homes did the unpleasant task of carting a body off.

I parked next to Rebecca's SUV and saw a black car was parked on the other side of hers. Up ahead Rebecca Marner and Rhett's second wife, Zoe, stood silently together, shoulders touching. They'd both crossed their arms, as if trying to hold themselves together. I had a sick feeling in the pit of my stomach because Rhett Marner would have been here if he could. My guess was that he already was here — and about to be unearthed from the kind of grave no one deserved.

I hurried to where Kara and Lois stood, being careful not to send three cups of coffee in a cardboard tray flying. When I'd stopped for the sandwiches earlier, I decided to buy these drinks rather than make them wait for the donut truck to arrive.

The bright day indicated we wouldn't be rained on, but the autumn wind was brisk enough to have colored Kara's cheeks. I noted that Lois had put on her leather gloves. They both thanked me for the coffee, but before I could tell them about the food I'd left in my van, I noticed Candace approaching the two Marner women.

She never even gave Rebecca a glance but focused in on Zoe, who was twirling a blond curl at her temple with so much force I thought she might pull her hair out. Candace held a man's wallet and when she was face-to-face with Zoe, she opened it and showed it her.

The woman's hands went to her mouth and then I heard her cry out as if she'd been cut with a knife. She bent over and then fell to her knees.

Rebecca dropped beside her and put an arm around

the sobbing woman. She looked up at Candace, who wore an anguished expression. She glanced our way before kneeling in front of Zoe and Rebecca. She spoke to them both this time. After a brief conversation where Rebecca nodded in apparent understanding and Zoe continued to cry, Candace stood and returned to where Dr. Worthy and her team continued to work. They needed to completely uncover the body and probably sift through dirt and debris for evidence.

Billy Cranor, one of the firemen who'd stood watching the proceedings from the other side of the crime scene tape, made his way toward the women still on the ground. It was apparent Rebecca was having trouble helping Zoe to stand.

Without even a thought, I reached the two women first. I helped Rebecca raise Zoe to her feet just as Billy got to us.

"The paramedics are standing by to . . . to take the . . ." He lowered his voice. "The *you know*. Should I ask them to check out Mrs. Marner?"

Why he asked me this question, I wasn't sure. Maybe because he knew me better than the other two women.

Zoe spoke haltingly, tears streaming down her cheeks. "I'll be okay. I—I—"

She went limp and fell into Billy's arms. She'd fainted.

The question concerning a paramedic was answered without further conversation.

# Eight

Though Zoe came around quickly, Marcy and Jake, the paramedics, decided to err on the side of caution and have her checked out at the hospital. I heard Zoe say, "What will I tell the kids?" as they pushed the stretcher inside the ambulance. They left without the siren blaring. Rebecca followed in her SUV. I was pretty sure Zoe's condition wasn't too serious. She certainly hadn't gone pale or vomited, two things I probably would have done if they'd found my husband buried here.

Lois remained stoic as the drama unfolded, and though Kara watched in sober silence, she refrained from taking any pictures. Other journalists might have exploited family grief, but not Kara.

I saw Candace reach for her phone. They'd need another ambulance to cart away Rhett Marner once he was extricated from the ground. I assumed that was what she was calling about. It *had* to be Rhett Marner judging from Zoe Marner's reaction.

Where the rebar had been cut away, blue-jeaned legs and work boots were now visible from our vantage point. Kara's zoom lens ensured she could see a whole lot more.

"What's happening, Kara?"

"They're working on the area surrounding the body now that they've uncovered his face and legs. They're using those sifter contraptions to check for any evidence left behind in the dirt. Dr. Worthy is taking great care brushing off dirt with what looks like a paintbrush." She glanced over at me. "Rhett Marner, I assume?"

"That's my guess," I said, "though I know Zoe has two sons. They're teenagers."

Lois spoke for the first time. "We're pretty sure it's not one of the sons. Probably Marner. His wife reported him missing last night. Didn't come home for dinner and she called us about midnight. Course we couldn't do much. He's an adult and lots of adults walk away and are never heard from again. He might never have been found if not for—okay, maybe I've said enough."

"I won't print anything without an okay from Chief Baca. Please tell me how he was discovered."

Lois took a sip of her coffee and glanced at Kara. "This isn't for public consumption, but the security guard noticed a shoelace coming out of the ground under that rebar. At first he thought it was a snake. He told us he wanted to save it from being buried alive under concrete. When he bent over and saw it was a shoelace for a work boot, he pulled—and the thing wouldn't budge."

"A shoelace. Wow. Very observant guy." Kara took out her iPad. "What was this guard's name?"

"Seth Marner. Rhett Marner's boy from the first marriage."

Neither Kara nor I spoke for several seconds. Finally I said, "Oh my gosh. How terrible. Can you imagine finding your father like that?"

"All he saw was the boot. He doesn't know yet. But let's suppose he's the one who put him there in the first place, but decided at the last minute he couldn't go through with the whole cement burial thing." Lois took another sip of her coffee, which seemed to be acting like some kind of truth serum for the usually less-than-chatty Lois.

"You believe that's what happened?" I couldn't keep from sounding incredulous.

"Families. Always look at the families first."

Kara had been tapping on her tablet. "You don't believe his shoelace story?"

"Oh, the shoelace was there all right. And he'd dug around it and found the boot it was attached to. He could be innocent and I don't want to be quoted saying he's guilty of anything more than doing a good job. But you know people will be talking. I'm giving you the facts."

"I appreciate that, Lois. Until the chief gives me the okay, I'll only report what I can describe from being here and whatever statement Mike wants to offer."

"You're a good woman." Lois nodded at me. "Both of you are. Hard for me to trust a lot of folks, but the two of you and Deputy Carson? You're the best."

"Thanks," I said with a small smile. "I'm so glad you came to work in Mercy. Candace said you were on a police force up north?"

"Detroit. Tough job."

I nodded. "I can only imagine."

We fell into silence and thank goodness Yoder's donut truck arrived seconds later. Soon a line formed, mostly composed of the onlookers, but I heard Fred Yoder call out for them to back off. They did. Fred left the truck and walked over to where we stood. He wore a clean canvas apron with "Yoder's Donuts" stamped on it in navy blue ink. His bald head was covered by a baker's hat and his dark red beard and thick sideburns looked to have been recently trimmed.

He addressed Lois. "Deputy Jewel, if you could inform the officers and the firemen that the coffee and donuts are waiting at no charge, I would greatly appreciate it." He looked at me. "Mrs. Hart, I thank you for allowing me to do this service for our community. God tells me this place is filled with trouble, and I feel in my bones that comfort is needed here."

He turned abruptly and walked back to his truck.

Lois texted the information to Candace. While Dr. Worthy and her team continued their painstaking work, the firemen, Candace, Mike, Morris and Lydia all made their way to the truck a few at a time. Lydia's bleached hair was pulled into a ponytail and aside from the spike-heeled boots, her outfit was subdued—all brown. She probably didn't have time to pull her typical inappropriate outfit together—something at the far end of the bell curve when it came to attire. Zebra stripes or purple spandex were often the norm.

I went to my van and brought out the box of sandwiches and had Fred set them out. They were gone in seconds—mostly taken by the firemen.

As I handed Kara her black bean burger, Candace joined us, a donut in one hand, a cup of coffee in the other. "Whoever arranged for the donut truck, thank you. I had no idea how slow this process would be. Billy Cranor brought a couple cases of bottled water, but folks were getting hungry, for sure."

I said, "All this standing around isn't what you want to be doing, I know."

"I hate it almost as much as delivering bad news." She finished off the last of her donut and licked glaze off her fingers.

Lydia seemed to appear out of nowhere and stopped behind Candace. "I could have handled that job. I'm used to dealing with grieving families, you know."

Candace closed her eyes and drew a calming breath before pasting on a smile and turning to face Lydia. "But I was here. So you didn't have to."

Lydia looked me up and down. "What are *you* doing here? Don't you have a wedding to get ready for? By the way, he will leave you standing at the altar. Mark my words."

Kara's cheeks reddened. "Why we're here is none of your business."

"Oh, it's my business, *Lois Lane*. I keep track of what goes on at a crime scene, and as far as I'm concerned Jillian Hart has no reason to be hanging around."

Before I could respond, Candace stepped between me and Lydia. "There are plenty of observers besides Jillian. Let's get back to work."

Lydia didn't budge. "Morris informed me some kid found the body. Did you send him home? Because that's not how you're supposed to—"

"He's resting in my squad car, Lydia. He was up all night working his shift. He doesn't even know it's his father we've found—and *I* will be the one to tell him."

"His *father*? Why didn't you tell me this when I got here?"

"Because we didn't *know* it was his father until not long ago."

Lydia pointed a finger at Candace. "You need to interrogate him *now*. And I'll be right beside you. Let's go."

She whirled and hurried toward Candace's patrol car. The boots proved a hindrance that allowed Candace to catch up to her right away. The argument about who was in charge and when Seth Marner would be questioned grew loud enough that the chief had to intervene.

After a minute or two of his quiet mediation, the three of them returned to where the body lay. Firemen were positioning themselves to help lift the corpse onto a waiting stretcher.

Kara took a few pictures of the group huddled around what remained of Rhett Marner, but she respectfully put her camera down when they put him on the stretcher. I couldn't see much, nor did I want to, but I did notice the brown paper bags covering his hands and secured at the wrists with rubber bands.

The ambulance soon left with its siren wailing and lights flashing en route to the county morgue, a good forty-five minutes away on our rural roads. Mike Baca shook hands with the firemen who had helped. Candace was now on her knees at the makeshift grave ready to assist. Dr. Worthy gave her a dirt sifter and she began working alongside them to hunt for evidence. Morris, I noticed, was standing by the squad car he and Candace used. Or I should say *standing guard*. Lydia marched past him angrily on her way to her county vehicle and didn't give him so much as a glance. She'd been thwarted and was none too happy about it. This seemed to bring out the happy side of Deputy Morris Ebeling. He was grinning from ear to ear as his gaze followed her all the way out of the parking area.

Kara decided her work was done after Mike Baca told her he wasn't ready to release any information. Not all family members had been notified. We stopped at the donut truck to thank Fred Yoder. He offered me a yummy-looking cruller—even held it out close enough to my face that I smelled sugar and yeast and the decadence of at least five hundred calories.

"I have a fitting for my wedding dress later today. If I eat that, I'll have to start all over with the alterations."

Kara took the cruller. "I don't have a fitting. I can't think of a better dessert." She started digging in her bag to pay him.

Fred held up a gloved hand. "As I told the others, Miss Kara, no money. This is a gift to all the people who came here today. I understand it's Rhett they just took away. Such a sad fate, to die like that."

"You knew him?" Kara asked just before taking a bite of the cruller.

"Yes. His family was once part of our community, but his father left the church many years ago. Rhett was related to my wife—a cousin several times removed."

Kara finished chewing and held up what remained of the cruller. "This is heaven, by the way. Do you happen to know who might want to harm Rhett?"

Fred's smile faded. "I wouldn't know. We were no more than acquaintances." He busied himself by wiping the serving window shelf.

"Um, Kara, we should be going," I said.

"I plan to. Morris knows plenty, too, but he'd tell you before he'd tell me."

I laughed. "Why do you say that?"

"Come on, Jillian. You can actually make the man smile just by showing up."

"The feeling is mutual. He's a good guy under that grumpy exterior."

Kara silently typed on her notebook all the way back to the newspaper office, only occasionally interrupting her work to check a picture on her camera.

Her intensity seemed to fill the space around us, making me want to hug a cat or pick up one of the many appliqué projects I had going at the moment. Nothing like a little handwork to ease my worries.

I usually enjoyed being with Kara, but after I dropped her off, I breathed a sigh of relief. She was as intense as Candace. My appointment with Martha for the final alterations was right after she closed the shop around five p.m. I had a couple of hours to relax and check a few more things off the wedding list. With all these preparations coming to a big conclusion in just a few days, I was beginning to feel the city hall route might have been the way to go for this marriage, too.

Syrah, Merlot and Chablis greeted me when I came in through the back door. They did not seem happy that I'd been absent for most of the day. And where was Magpie? After treats were dispersed to my crew, I began calling for the missing kitty. Not that she actually knew her name yet. But cats do like to answer a human voice with a few meows. I was hoping I could track her down that way.

When I heard nothing and couldn't find her upstairs, and knew the door to the basement was always left ajar,

I decided to check down there. Sure enough, Magpie was in Finn's room and when I saw her, I burst out laughing. She had gathered every cat toy in the house, along with a few socks from the laundry basket. She sat surrounded by her treasures in the middle of Finn's bed. There was nothing like cat antics to erase whatever was troubling me. The tension in my neck melted away.

"You've been one busy girl, Magpie." I sat on the bed next to her and stroked her head and the sides of her cheeks. She purred like a fine-tuned motor.

And then I saw something that didn't make me smile. She'd stolen the thread that matched my wedding dress perfectly and basically destroyed it. *Such a shredded mess.* Good thing Martha and I had an appointment. I would buy more today. But I couldn't help fearing the symbolism of this battered spool I now held in my palm. Would my relationship with Tom become a shredded mess, too? Would we be better off leaving things the way they were? My traditional roots, my firm belief that certain things belonged only in marriage, wouldn't gel with us remaining single. Tom loved me and wanted to love me completely.

Maybe I was too old-fashioned, but that raised the question. Were we getting married just to share a bed? I shook my head, dismissing this notion. No way. We wanted to be together forever—because we loved each other. It was right. Case closed. The way I felt about Tom could never be shredded. It wasn't that fragile.

The smaller question confronting me now? What to do about these gathered items? Was Magpie claiming her territory here in Finn's room? It was certainly better than her peeing on his pillow—because cats will do that kind of thing if they want to claim a spot.

I decided to confiscate her collection. Magpie might not be happy, but living with three other feline friends involved certain sacrifices. I had the feeling, however, that she had no room in her kitty world for concessions. She was, after all, a cat.

When I arrived at the Cotton Company close to five p.m., Martha still had one customer lingering. The woman was tiny, no more than four feet ten, and I guessed she had to be in her eighties. Her iron gray hair, fastened in a chignon at the nape of her neck, shined beautifully. I was a little envious and hoped I had hair as thick and healthy-looking when I was her age.

Martha, a fifty-something quilting genius, smiled at me. "Jillian, this is Verline. She's a cat lover and quilter like we are."

Verline's mouth formed an oval, and the eyes behind her lenses gleamed with excitement. "*The* Jillian? The one whose patterns for cat quilts I've copied? I hope you don't mind."

"Of course I don't mind. I'd love to see what you've made sometime."

"Why not right now?" She whipped a smartphone from her giant leather bag—seemingly huge because the woman was so elfin. She beckoned me her way. "Come on, now. No need to stand by the door."

Since quilters these days used sewing machines that were actually part computer, too, I wasn't surprised that she had what looked like a newer-model smartphone. I made my way around an old wash bin full of fabric scraps. A box of small Ziploc bags sat on an antique lamp table next to the bin with a sign that read AS MANY SCRAPS AS YOU CAN STUFF IN THIS BAG FOR $2.

Several bolts of fabric lay on the cutting table in the center of the small store and drew my attention. New patterns for fall. So tempting. I bypassed them and walked over to where the two women stood. I needed to remain focused.

Verline shoved the phone toward me. "That's my Honey. He's partial to anything with half-square triangles."

Honey was exactly that—a honey-coated, long-haired tabby. "He's beautiful and that quilt is stunning." I widened the picture to study the details before looking at Verline. "Your hand-quilting is exquisite."

"Years of practice. I've seen your work here at Martha's store and you're no slouch, young lady."

Young lady? Yes, since I was probably forty years her junior, I suppose I was a young lady to her.

Martha smiled down on Verline. "Besides being an expert quilter, did you know this little woman is a funeral singer? She's got the voice for it all right. Ethereal."

Verline's cheeks pinked up. "You are too sweet, Martha. You know the Marners have already called me to sing. That's quite speedy considering they just found the poor soul buried in the dirt this morning."

I'd never heard of a funeral singer before and I got distracted wondering about it, but the mention of the Marner family had all my attention now. "Really? Did Zoe call you?"

"No, it was Rebecca. She told me she was calling on behalf of Rhett's oldest stepson—Toby Nesmith." Verline leaned toward me, her voice quiet. "Troublemaker, I hear. How a teenager knew about me, I have no idea. He sure didn't waste a second getting himself all involved in the arrangements. What happened to Rhett is a terrible thing to do to a human being, no matter what people thought of him. I've known that man a very long time, mind you. He was in my third-grade class back when I was teaching. Bit of a handful, that one. I heard they might never have found him if not for poor Seth. Now, *there's* a fine youngster."

"I—I was there." My mind drifted back to the scene as I rambled on. "At the building site with Kara this morning." Blinking to erase the memories, I looked at Verline. She'd replaced her phone and now took the paper shopping bag full of fabric that Martha offered. I went on, saying, "I take it Mr. Marner might have had a few enemies? Because you're absolutely right, it was truly an awful thing someone did to him."

"I'll be singing at his funeral, so I best not fill my mind with negative thoughts. I can say this, however. I'm not surprised he was . . . *murdered*." She whispered this last word in dramatic fashion before reaching out a veined hand and squeezing my wrist. "I am so pleased I met you today. We cannot be strangers, Jillian. We have too much in common."

With that, Martha and I slowly assisted her outside. A car idled at the sidewalk and a man, perhaps in his late fifties, slid from behind the driver's seat and hurried around to help Verline into the old Cadillac.

Verline waved a hand at him. "My son, Louis. He's quite a fine singer himself. Louis, this is Jillian—the woman I speak about so often."

The balding man with a gray fringe matching Verline's hair color nodded shyly, said nothing and soon they were gone.

Martha put an arm around my shoulders. "Now, where is your dress?"

"I left it in the van, not sure if you were ready for me. I'll get it and meet you back in the store."

After a half hour of pinning and tucking the bodice and readjusting the cowl neckline so each drooping fold was perfect, Martha said I could pick it up tomorrow. As soon as I climbed back into my van, I checked my cat cam to make sure all four cats were accounted for. The sleeping kitties made me smile, especially Merlot and Magpie entwined together on the sofa. He would miss her once Finn left for his own apartment.

I switched to thoughts of what I had heard from Verline. I wondered if I should tell Candace and decided too much information was better than none. But when I tried her cell it went straight to voice mail. Since I sat only blocks from the police station, I decided to stop by. If she wasn't available—and she most certainly had to be overwhelmed right now—I could leave a message with B.J., the dispatcher.

The police station wasn't a freestanding building in Mercy. It was housed in one wing of the courthouse. The jail was downstairs, but since the public wasn't allowed in the basement, most people waiting for the release of relatives or requiring a pass to have access to the jailer loitered in the hallway outside the police office. Seemed as if more than a few of Mercy's citizens must be locked up today. At least a dozen folks sat on the tile floor or on the worn benches centered in the wide corridor.

I entered the office and to my left, B.J. sat at his desk, phone to his ear. Three young men occupied the chairs that lined the wall and I recognized Seth Marner. His head was down and his body turned away from the other two people. Were these two the Nesmiths? Zoe's boys from her first marriage? Probably.

B.J. covered the phone's mouthpiece and waved a hand toward the corridor ahead of me, whispering, "Break room."

I avoided eye contact with the young men waiting, feeling guilty I was being granted access while they continued to sit on the uncomfortable plastic molded chairs. A swinging gate separated this waiting area from the hall and I hurried through to the end of the corridor. I made a right into the small break room.

Candace's back was to me as she contemplated the tower of Keurig cups. Tom and I had bought the special coffee machine for the few hardworking men and women who often stayed here long past the time when they should be home in bed or with their families. They really could use a couple of extra officers in this town.

Candace made her choice and turned around. She started when she realized she wasn't alone. "Whoa. Takes a lot of quiet to fool me, Jillian." She held up the little flavor cup. "Mocha. Gotta load up on caffeine to get through the rest of the day."

"I know you're busy. I just wanted to stop by and offer my support. I also heard a bit of gossip—not much but a little."

As her coffee brewed, Candace undid her blond ponytail and pulled back her hair to refasten all the loose strands that had escaped. "I'll take anything. We got a cold and calculated killer out there. Can you imagine if Seth hadn't found that shoelace?"

"So you're aware I heard about the shoelace?"

"Lois confessed to being talkative with you and Kara—was worried what she said would get out. I reassured her it wouldn't, and to be honest, I'm glad she spoke to the two of you. It means she's developing trust—something she certainly lacked when she first arrived here last spring."

"I'll bet she had reason to be wary. Anyway, I went to the Cotton Company to get some alterations done and—"

"The *wedding*. It was all I could think about for days, and now with this happening, I sure hope we can find the murderer before your big day." Candace picked up her coffee cup and inhaled the aroma, her eyes closed and a small smile softening her tired features.

"You will *not* miss my wedding, Candace. I don't care if you have to handcuff a suspect to a hymnal rack in the church."

She laughed. "Wouldn't that be something? Anyway, what's the town talking about?"

"About how many enemies Rhett Marner probably had."

"Who's talking?" She sipped her coffee.

"Verline . . . gosh, what is her last name?"

"The funeral singer?"

"You know her?"

"Everyone knows her and she knows everyone. If you sing at funerals for decades, you get to meet a lot of folks—and eat a lot of good food. She name anyone in particular?"

"Toby Nesmith—one of Zoe's sons from her first marriage. Seems he's a bit of a troublemaker, according to her, and awful quick to get the funeral arrangements started. Maybe he's expecting a little inheritance."

Candace grinned. "Could well be. Good timing, by the way. That young man happens to be waiting for me to get my act together and interview him. Morris is taking the other son—Owen. That is, if he ever comes out of the bathroom. I swear the man is taking a power nap in there."

"What about Seth? He looks pretty torn up. Will he have to wait long for his turn?"

Candace tilted her head, looking surprised. "Seth is here? I got his statement and sent him home hours ago. He was exhausted."

"He's back."

Just then B.J. appeared in the doorway. "I tried to call you, Deputy Carson, but you're going to voice mail. Then the phones wouldn't stop ringing. I got tied up, but Seth Marner is here. Says he has to talk to you. Says it's an emergency."

"Hmm. Really? Let's see what this is all about."

The three of us walked down the hall toward the waiting area.

Seth stood as soon as Candace appeared. "Deputy Carson, I—I need your help."

One of the others, either Toby or Owen, spoke. "Wait in line, jerk."

Candace ignored him and waved Seth toward her. "Come on, then."

I muttered a good-bye as Seth and I passed each other, but I overheard him say, "My sister is missing. You have to find her."

# Ten

I left the police station concerned about Lindsey Marner. Maybe she'd been close to her father and was overcome with grief after learning of his death. In times like that, it helped to get away from everyone and everything. That was how I'd felt when John died. I sure hoped she turned up soon.

Before leaving the courthouse parking lot, I decided since I'd planned nothing for supper, I'd stop at the Main Street Diner and pick up burgers. I texted Tom and he said he liked that idea, but I got no response from Finn. He must be helping Shawn with something and couldn't get to his phone, since he usually texted me back right away when my messages concerned food in his immediate future.

I drove the short distance to the restaurant, its attractive green canopy the same as all the storefronts on the main drag in Mercy. But it was the aroma of burgers and fries that had my complete attention the minute I got out of my van. It was amazing how hungry wedding-dress alterations can make you.

I placed my order and stood back near a wall in the retro-type diner with its curving counter and red leather cushioned barstools. That was on my left. To my right were wooden booths, each with its own jukebox. The price for a tune? A nickel. Currently a rendition of Leonard Cohen's "Hallelujah" filled the restaurant, and the beauty of that song might have been the reason for the hushed voices in a usually bustling and noisy establishment.

In a back booth someone sat alone in a black hoodie, head down. The hands that clenched and unclenched on the table were telling. I recognized the nail polish. I'd seen the vibrant blue color when I handed over the key to the donation box yesterday.

Lindsey Marner wasn't missing after all. She just needed to be by herself. Should I leave her alone? Respect her privacy on this most difficult day? But something about those hands, how her knuckles grew bone white as she made those fists over and over, made me move toward her. Seconds later, I slid into the high-backed booth across from her.

She raised her head slowly, but when she saw me, she seemed startled. "Oh. It's *you.* Guess no one knows how to keep a secret in this town."

"I'm sorry. I don't understand," I said quietly as the singer reached the lyric about it being a "cold and broken hallelujah."

"He told you where I was."

Now I was completely confused. "No one told me anything. I just came in to order food and saw you sitting back here."

"You've seen me up close now." Her eyes met mine. "Happy?"

"Lindsey, I am so sorry you've lost your dad. I can tell you're hurting."

"You don't know anything. Could you leave me alone now?" She paused and added a sarcastic "Please?"

"Sure. I understand." I stood and when I turned I nearly ran smack-dab into Finn.

Lindsey seemed to be seething now. "You told her where I was. I asked you not to, Finn. You *promised.*"

Finn locked eyes with hers. He seemed out of breath. "I got Jillian's text that she'd be here and hitched a ride as quick as I could." He looked at me. "You came because you knew we were meeting up, right?"

I shook my head, hoping to clear my brain. "I'm picking up supper. I saw Lindsey sitting alone. That's it." Right now I thought it best not to mention Seth and how frantic he seemed at the police station.

They pondered what I said and I saw the coldness so evident in Lindsey's eyes fade.

Finally she spoke, her gaze on the table. "Okay. I believe you. I just need to talk to my friend right now, Mrs. Hart. Could you leave us alone?"

"I respect that. I'll see you back at the house, Finn."

I started to leave, but he touched my arm and I turned. He hugged me and whispered, "Thanks for understanding."

"If you need a ride home, I'll wait outside. Or come back."

"Lindsey has a car. Thanks again, Jillian."

I paid for my order and picked up my paper sack filled with burgers and fries at the cash register near the door, but the distress on the girl's face had obliterated my appetite. I briefly considered returning to the police station and telling Seth where his sister was, but quickly nixed the idea.

If these young people placed their trust in me and I betrayed them by giving out information, there was no doubt in my mind Finn would forgive but he would never forget. Lindsey was in town, not missing, and hopefully she would talk to Finn, calm down and return home quickly. Her family didn't need any more heartache today.

On the drive to my place, I couldn't help wondering how Finn came to be friends with Lindsey, but he *had* taken a year of classes at the community college last year. Perhaps that was where they'd met. I was certain Finn would explain all when he returned home.

The smell of a meal from the Main Street Diner grabbed the attention of all four cats when I opened the back door. No sitting patiently for treats this evening. Magpie practically crawled up my leg, her nose twitching as she fully captured the aroma. Not to be outdone, Syrah jumped onto my shoulder—something he did when he wanted my undivided attention. He didn't claw me brutally, but he had to dig in to keep his balance. I winced while carefully walking to the counter as he continued his tightrope act. I put the bag of food down, dislodged his paws from my skin and set him on the floor.

"What's with y'all? I didn't go deep-sea fishing and bring you home a big fat marlin."

It was, however, past their dinnertime and I quickly rectified that problem. Tom texted me he would be here in about an hour, so I wrapped the burgers and fries in foil and put them in the oven to keep them warm. They wouldn't taste as good later on, but that didn't matter right now.

As four cats vied over who had the best bowl of wet food, I plopped down on my new microfiber sofa—a fabric cats don't particularly like to dig their claws into because there is no weave. The chaise longue end was so comfortable and designed to be big enough to fit both Tom and me. I leaned into the brown tufted pillow and sighed. I was exhausted. This day had been packed with good and bad, happy and sad . . . okay, those were corny song lyrics, but they sure fit my conflicted mood.

I must have dozed off, because I awoke to the sound of Tom greeting the cats—all except Chablis, who was resting on my legs. I sat up and blinked several times. Chablis jumped down and I stretched as my empty stomach gurgled in protest. I'd had very little to eat today.

"Hey there." I stood and walked into Tom's open arms. "I am so glad to see you. A lot has happened since this morning."

"I heard. It's all over the radio. I have plenty of time to listen to the news when I'm staking out cheating husbands and wives. I got my photos and I'm done with that particular job, thank goodness." He squeezed me tighter and kissed the top of my head. "Are you ready for what are probably dried-out burgers and fries, thanks to me being so late?"

"I am." I squinted at the clock on the stove. "My gosh, it's almost eight o'clock. Where's Finn?"

"He's not here?" Tom stepped away. "Maybe he's still at the shelter."

"No. He's not." Something felt wrong inside. A little knot of fear replaced my hunger.

Tom, being one of the most perceptive people I know, picked up on this immediately. "Jillian, what's wrong?"

"I—I think I made a big mistake."

"What are you talking about?" He sounded concerned, but he didn't appear as worried as I felt.

I told him about leaving Finn at the diner with Lindsey Marner. But then I had to explain who she was, and by the time he understood all the things that had happened today, we were sitting side by side on the barstools by the breakfast counter.

"He's twenty years old, Jillian. And he's a smart kid. Maybe he went to lend her support at her home."

"Could you call him? Don't let on I told you I saw him with Lindsey, though. I don't want him to think I've broken his trust."

Tom rested a hand on my cheek and offered a sweet smile. "Sure. But I think you're blowing this out of proportion. He has a friend who needs him."

"I trust Finn—but Lindsey? That's a troubled girl and . . . I just have this sick feeling in my gut."

Tom pulled out his phone. "I'm phoning right now, okay?" But after listening for several seconds, he said, "Finn, give me a call when you get a chance. We've got some dried-out burgers and withered fries waiting for you and I know you won't want to miss out."

He repocketed his phone and stood. "He might not want supper, but I sure do. Let's see what we can salvage out of this meal."

While we ate, I filled Tom in on everything I'd seen and heard today concerning the murder. Though he tried to hide it, I could tell he was growing more concerned as the minutes ticked by. We moved to the sofa and sat close on the chaise, his arm around me. He left two more voice mails and a couple of text messages on Finn's phone. We played with the cats, watched a couple of TV shows that we couldn't really get into and naturally kept checking for texts and waiting for the phone to ring.

Finally he said, "If you want to go to bed, I'll stay here until he arrives. I promise not to let on that I know everything."

"That's the least of our worries right now. I would never be able to sleep anyway. We need to call Candace. Maybe Lindsey has a history of running away and maybe this time she's taken Finn with her. It's not like he's un-familiar with that way to cope when things get tough." My first encounter with Finn had been after he'd run away from his birth mother's home several years ago in search of Tom.

Tom sighed heavily. "The kid needs his independence, but you're right. This isn't like Finn. Plus, there's been a murder in this town and as far as we know, the killer hasn't been caught."

A niggling of relief eased the knot in my stomach. "Good. I'm calling her."

When Candace answered, she sounded as if she'd been awake for days. "Hey there. Why are you calling so late?"

I could hear B.J.'s and Morris's voices in the back-ground, so they were all still at the station. During a big case, they didn't leave and usually took turns catching naps on the old couch in Morris's office. "I should have called you before, but I was giving Finn the benefit of the doubt and, well, trying to hang on to his trust, but apparently that was the absolute wrong thing—"

"Jillian, what in heck are you talking about?"

I explained how I'd seen Lindsey and Finn together at the diner, and then confessed that I'd overheard Seth's fear that she was missing.

"Do you know where she is now?" Her tone had an urgency that made that tiny seed of fear burst and grow. I started to tremble and couldn't seem to find my voice.

Tom took the phone from my shaking hand. He said his hello to Candace, and then as he listened, I saw his brows knit with worry. Every ounce of guilt at keeping this information to myself transformed to dread.

Tom said, "All we know is that she and Finn were together earlier. If we hear anything, we'll get back to you right away. Finn's a smart kid. He'll make good choices." Once he disconnected, he handed me my phone. "Apparently Lindsey's brother is the only one who's concerned. Her mother told Candace she's been a troubled kid for a long time. What bothers me is that Finn could be swept up in all this—and even if the girl's father just died—"

We both turned at the sound of the back door opening and then Finn saying, "Dad? Jillian?"

Tom and I met him in the kitchen, and right behind him was Lindsey Marner. Her red-rimmed eyes told me either she was very tired or she'd been crying. As soon as she saw me looking at her, she lowered her gaze, the cuffs of her black hoodie clutched tightly in her fists.

"Hey there, Lindsey," I said quietly. "Come on in." I so wanted to wrap her in my arms. Her grief and distress filled my kitchen like a living, breathing entity. Maybe that was why I felt the need to touch her, comfort her.

"Son, what's going on?" Tom's focus was on Finn, his tone gentle.

"Lindsey won't go home. I've tried to talk her into it, but she's a stubborn girl. Could she crash here? Just for tonight?"

"What about her family? Aren't they concerned for her?" Tom asked.

It was Lindsey who spoke. "They don't give a flying flip where I am or who I'm with. It's all about the money now that Daddy's gone." She lifted her eyes and looked into mine. The sadness hadn't left, but I noted a glint of anger, too.

"I'm not sure that's true. Seth appeared very upset that you were missing." This seemed like such a delicate subject to broach with a girl who was a relative stranger. But she needed someone to help her, of that much I was sure.

"What do you know about my brother?" It sounded like an accusation.

"I happened to be at the police station when he came in looking for help to find you."

"Oh. Well, I texted him. Told him to chill and I'd be home soon. He gets it. He knows."

"But what about your mother, Lindsey?" I said. "Even if you two don't get along, I know—"

She cut me off, saying, "My mother hasn't called. She told Seth to take care of the *Lindsey problem*. She's busy comforting *Zoe*." Full-blown anger had now taken the place of sorrow.

"That would upset me, too," Tom said. "Jillian, do you have room for Lindsey here?"

"Of course." I noted relief wash over Finn. I guessed he had worried about what my reaction would be to him bringing Lindsey here. But Tom knew I would never refuse.

"Are you two hungry?" I asked. "I couldn't salvage those hamburgers I brought home earlier, but there's always PBJs."

Lindsey almost smiled. "That would be okay."

While I got busy setting bread, peanut butter and jam on the counter so they could fix their sandwiches, Finn introduced his friend to the four sleepy cats who had wandered into the kitchen from the far corners of the house. Cats' hearing, though not as acute as their canine counterparts', is far better than any human's. They'd heard voices and were ready to offer Lindsey the comfort that I wished I could give her myself.

Then I saw from the corner of my eye that Tom was headed into the other room, phone in hand. I knew who he was about to call and wondered how he would explain this to Finn and Lindsey. Tom was an ex-cop who felt certain decisions just made sense. He probably felt he didn't need to explain. I could hear the phrases in my head he often repeated: "The right thing is the right thing. Simple as that."

But was he calling Lindsey's mother or the police?

# Eleven

Finn and Lindsey were finishing up their late-night meal of chips, sandwiches and milk when Candace's familiar rap sounded on the back door. She often walked right in afterward without waiting for me to come to the door, but not this time. This was not a social call.

But Finn recognized the knock and looked at me with hurt in eyes. "You called her? *Really, Jillian*? You called Candace?"

"I called her," Tom said. I was grateful for this small attempt to rescue me from being labeled the betrayer of Finn's trust. "Lindsey needs to talk to the police. Seth wasn't the only one looking for her."

Lindsey slid off the barstool and glanced around as if searching for a way to escape. But Tom was already at the door ushering Candace into the kitchen. And so were all four cats. Magpie sure fit right in here. All visitors must be vetted.

Candace knelt and petted them while looking Lindsey's way. "I'm Deputy Carson and I take it you're Rhett Marner's daughter. I'm so sorry for your loss."

Lindsey had become a little more animated in the minutes before Candace's arrival, but her anguish seemed to return. "Don't be. I don't need anyone's sympathy." She turned to me. "And I guess I won't be staying *here* after all."

In the calmest voice I could muster, I said, "I hope you change your mind. Candace only wants to talk to you and you're more than welcome to stay." I glanced Candace's way. "You just want to talk, right?"

Candace stood. "Yes, ma'am, that's all. Just a few minutes of Lindsey's time is all I need. It's been a long, rough day."

The girl's eyes narrowed. "I'm not going to jail?"

This seemed to take Candace aback—and she wasn't the only one. Silence hung in the air like a shadow over all of us—and hung for a second too long.

But the girl's next words explained her comment. "Oh, you mean my mother hasn't thrown me under the bus yet? Well, that's a first."

Candace gestured toward my living room. "Why don't we sit down and talk about what happened today?"

But Lindsey had returned to full-blown sullen form. "Do I have a choice?" In true petulant teen mode she swung around and marched into my adjoining living area, shrugging off Finn's comforting hand on her shoulder. She plopped onto a chair facing the sofa, her arms wrapped tightly around her.

Candace sat opposite from her on the sofa, adjusting

a police belt laden by her holstered weapon, a baton and her cell phone holder. "I'm not much older than you, Lindsey. You're nineteen, is that right?"

Lindsey nodded and snuck a peek at Candace's face. I'd never thought of how close in age these two were—Candace was only in her mid-twenties—probably because Lindsey seemed so much younger. She might have been nineteen but could easily have been mistaken for thirteen or fourteen.

"I'm not here to take you to jail or even take you home. You're old enough to decide where you want to stay right now. I need a few answers, that's all."

Magpie suddenly jumped in Lindsey's lap and put her paws on the girl's chest so she could rub the side of her head along Lindsey's jaw. I'd been busying myself by clearing off the counter with Finn's help, but when I saw Magpie go to Lindsey's rescue, tears burned behind my eyes.

The girl's shoulders relaxed and her hands came out of hiding to stroke the kitty. Now that she had Lindsey's attention, the cat curled up in her lap and looked right at Candace.

Lindsey said, "Ask your questions, *Officer*."

"Call me Candace." She glanced at Magpie. "I've met that cat before. Did you know that?"

"Finn told me."

"She's awful sweet." Candace paused, tilting her head, probably hoping to get a glimpse into Lindsey's eyes. But that wasn't happening.

"That's not a question," Lindsey said. "Can you get to the point?"

I tensed and as if sensing my discomfort, Tom put his arm around me.

"Okay, who told you about your father's death?"

Lindsey looked up and stared at Candace. "Why does that matter?"

Candace, her hands clasped between her knees, leaned forward and didn't say a word.

"Okay, okay. First I got a text from my mother, and then Finn called me."

Candace sat back and both Tom and I looked at Finn.

He said, "I can explain. At the shelter, this man came in to pick up his lost Lab and he said he'd seen all these people hanging around that office building construction site and that both Mr. Marner's wives were there and when he saw the other Mrs. Marner—not Lindsey's mother, the new one—anyway, she fainted. Then—"

Candace held up a hand. "I get the picture." She focused on Lindsey again, who had begun to rock ever so slightly. "You haven't talked to your mother?"

"Like I said, she *texted* me. I guess that's supposed to count as talking. And I don't even know how he died—just that someone killed him."

I stifled a gasp, tried to keep my face from revealing my shock. I guessed it hadn't registered when she said her mother texted her about the murder. My Pollyanna brain decided the message was asking Lindsey to come right away. Instead this poor kid heard about her father's death via *text message*? I wanted to wrap her in my arms and hug her, make this better, but I was certain touching her right now wouldn't be received well. Lindsey trusted Finn, and that was about it.

"What she did is not cool," Candace said. "Before I ask a few more questions, would you feel more comfortable if Tom, Jillian and Finn left the room?"

Lindsey's response was swift. "Are you kidding me? These people are normal. They're actually *nice*."

Candace held up a hand. "Okay, I'm fine with it if you are."

I saw Lindsey steal a glance at Finn, noticed her eyes had filled. But she blinked several times and said to Candace, "Do you think I killed him?"

"Did you?"

"I didn't. I wouldn't. Please tell me how he died. Please *someone* tell me." She glanced around at all of us. The tears came then, streaming down her face and making mascara-stained inroads through her makeup.

Magpie awoke, looked back at her. She again climbed Lindsey's chest to rub her own face against the cheek of this sad, sad child. And she was a child. We all became children when someone we love left us forever. I wiped away a tear of my own.

Quietly, Candace said, "He was shot."

Finn left the barstool and knelt by Lindsey, covering one of her hands that clung to Magpie. She continued to cry, shoulders shaking, but she remained restrained by her fear of being too vulnerable in a room filled with people who were practically strangers.

After a minute, Lindsey swiped under her eyes with the heel of her hand, leaving dark-tinted semicircles on her cheeks.

Magpie left her then, leaping onto the floor. She sauntered away with a backward glance as if to say, "My work for now is done."

Finn stayed, gripping Lindsey's wrists and pulling her hands away from her face. "I am so, so sorry."

"I didn't even *like* him, so I don't know why I'm crying." Her tone held a hint of defiance along with the wonder of feeling an emotion she wasn't yet ready to accept—grief.

"Like and love are two very different things," Candace said. "When was the last time you saw him?"

"Maybe three days ago—could have been four. He doesn't come around much. He has a new family. But then you and everyone else know that."

"He came to your house?" Candace asked.

"Yeah, I needed money for a textbook and my dear, sweet mother said that wasn't *her* responsibility."

"He seemed normal? Not upset about anything?"

"In a hurry, and what could be more normal than that?" Her sarcasm had returned in full force, but I noted she didn't pull away from Finn, who now held both her hands in his. That was encouraging, because this girl needed someone to hold on to her.

"Did he say anything out of the ordinary? Anything that seemed different to you? Because you, I can tell, are a very observant person."

Lindsey squinted into the past. "Now that you mention it, he seemed like . . ." She looked straight at Candace for the first time. "Like he'd had too much coffee. Jittery, you know?"

"Talking fast?"

"Yeah. I think he said something about everyone needing money right now." She thought for a second. "Yes. I felt guilty for asking for the money because he said everyone thought he was an ATM."

"And you think he'd had too much coffee?"

"Not really. It was different—and when he hugged me, he didn't have coffee breath like usual, and believe me, my daddy has the worst—" She pulled a hand free from Finn's grasp and covered her mouth. "Oh my God. He's gone and I was such a brat. I pulled away when he hugged me, gave him attitude and—"

This time the tears came with racking sobs and Finn gripped her shoulders, stood her up and wrapped her in his arms.

This kid deserved all the support she could get, so I joined Finn and rubbed circles on Lindsey's back. I was surprised when she threw her arms around my neck and cried her heart out into my shoulder. I was probably about the same age as her mother, after all. I got the sense this release was long overdue.

Thirty minutes later, Candace resumed her questions. Lindsey clutched a glass of water and a box of tissues sat nearby. Finn was cross-legged on the floor next to his friend to offer support, and Tom and I had claimed the barstools. Lindsey still wanted us to stay in the room, which I found touchingly sad. This girl should be surrounded by loving family at a time like this.

Candace's interrogation focused mostly on the day Rhett Marner dropped off the check, and once Lindsey pulled herself together, she was able to pin the time down to five days earlier because of that textbook and why she needed it. She'd lost the one she'd already bought and with an exam coming up she was, in her words, "desperate" after her mother refused to give her the necessary hundred dollars.

Candace wasn't giving much away about her investigation. After being her friend for several years now, I understood the importance she placed on a crime's timeline, and this murder was no different. But then she surprised me by showing Lindsey the picture she had on her phone of Magpie's locket. She asked Lindsey if she recognized it.

The girl nodded. "It sort of belongs to me. Where did you find it?"

"Where did you see it last?" Candace countered.

"I don't remember. My bathroom? My jewelry box? Did you find that with my father's b-b . . ." She halted. Took a deep breath. "With my father?" Her eyes tracked Candace's phone as she replaced it.

"So you think your father had this necklace? Why would he, Lindsey?"

"It's been in our family a long time. Maybe he saw it on the bathroom vanity and didn't think I was taking care of it. He was pretty controlling that way. Or maybe I left it at his new house." She shifted her eyes right and left and right again and took on a nonchalant air. I got the sense she knew much more about that necklace than she was letting on.

But a thought ran through my head and overshadowed my initial conclusion that this was just a teenager being cagey. Candace wouldn't have shown that necklace to Lindsey if it weren't connected to the case.

Did that speck of blood Candace had pointed out before belong to Rhett Marner? The sick feeling in my stomach told me it did.

# Twelve

The next morning, Tom picked me up in his Prius for our appointment with Pastor Truman at the Mill Village Baptist Church. An exhausted Lindsey was still asleep in my upstairs guest room and Finn was taking care of the cats and busying himself with household chores like sweeping and putting plates and silverware away from the last dishwasher run.

*We should keep that kid around forever,* I thought as I left the house. But I was sure he was anxious as he waited for his friend to awake. After she'd gone to bed last night, he told us they were just acquaintances who'd once shared a class at the community college. He was surprised when she reached out to him yesterday. It was so like Finn to help this girl. And she was obviously smart enough to know who she could trust.

Tom stopped at Belle's Beans and picked us both up coffee to go before we were on our way to the far side of town. I sipped my vanilla latte and sighed with pleasure. The Madagascar vanilla Belle used in her recipe, along with the perfect ratio of warm milk to coffee, made this my standard fare. Why change drinks? Nothing could be better than this.

Once we were on our way again, Tom said, "I knew Rhett Marner. Did I tell you that before?"

"You did. How well?"

"I saw how he interacted with people. He turned on the charm for the folks paying him and treated his manual laborers like dirt. I don't appreciate hypocrisy. But he's not alone in how he operated."

"He could have made a lot of enemies, then?"

"Oh, I'm sure he did. That will make the investigation plenty difficult. When I was installing a security system in one of his buildings under construction, I saw two painters get into a fistfight. I broke it up and Rhett came in behind me and shoved both guys against the wall. I don't know what happened next because I walked off the job, told Rhett I wasn't coming back."

"Good for you." I patted his leg.

Tom turned and glanced at me. "I should have called Mike, told him to send a squad car because of the assaults on the part of the painters *and* Rhett. Then I told myself I was a lay person now, not a cop anymore, and it probably wouldn't go any further."

"I heard they had to break up fights at a few of his job sites recently."

Tom nodded. "No surprise. This kind of stuff happens, especially when the boss flies off the handle on a regular basis—and that was Rhett's reputation."

I thought about this for a second before speaking. "There could be dozens of suspects if he fired people regularly or had them thrown in jail."

"Thing is," Tom said, "I believe he used the same crew all the time. Despite his behavior, he paid them well and they did good work. Rhett was a wealthy man who didn't need to be hanging around construction sites in work boots and jeans. He did though, despite the fact that he could have hired a site manager. He was too much of a control freak to—"

"Those were Lindsey's words last night," I interrupted. "Control freak."

"She did say that. Of course Mike and Candace will be looking at the family first. Two wives, two families—there had to be tension."

I explained how Zoe and Rebecca seemed the best of friends but there was no love lost between the Nesmith boys and the Marner kids.

Tom parked in front of the sweet little church where we would be married on Saturday.

"Divorce creates a swath of destruction in its wake. I wish so much of my job wasn't about relationships falling apart. I'm so glad we have more pleasant things to concentrate on right now."

I noted Kara's SUV up ahead. Of course she'd arrived first. Wedding planner was a job that seemed to suit her well.

Tom and I joined hands as we walked up the sidewalk. I felt a quiver of excitement. This place, so peaceful, with huge oaks surrounding it and the old brick-and-stone construction, was absolutely perfect.

Kara, Pastor Mitch and the pastor's wife, Elizabeth

Truman, stood talking at the front of the church. After we exchanged hugs, handshakes and smiles, Kara launched into full wedding planner mode.

"I was explaining about the flower delivery and that I'll be setting out the 'reserved' cards on the pews early Saturday morning. They do have a changing room in the basement, Jillian, so we can dress and put on makeup here. The pastor was telling me there have been more than a thousand weddings in this church since it was built in the early 1900s."

"Perhaps even more." Elizabeth reached out and took my hands in hers. "We are so thrilled you have chosen us to celebrate your marriage."

Tom's smile lit his face. "I'm thrilled there's a marriage to celebrate. This woman is the best thing that ever happened to me."

"I completely agree," Pastor Mitch said. "She's the best thing—"

I held up a hand. "Whoa. Please don't make me get all tongue-tied, though I thank you all."

Elizabeth dropped my hands. "The rehearsal is Thursday night because of a conflict we have—usually we have the rehearsal the day before the wedding and I hope this isn't a problem."

"No problem," Kara replied for me.

I smiled and nodded Kara's way. "If that's what the wedding planner says, then those are the facts."

Kara pulled two folded pieces of paper from her pocket and handed one to Pastor Mitch and one to Elizabeth. "Here's what we talked about as far as timing, music and readings go. The rest is up to you two. Oh, and to the bride and groom."

We all laughed.

I craned my neck toward the paper Elizabeth had unfolded and was reading. "Do I get to see one of those?"

Kara touched my shoulder. "Your list will include all that plus more. Be patient." She turned to Tom. "As for you, you have the easy job. Just stand next to Pastor Mitch and look pretty in your new suit. And you better write down your vows, because you'll forget them the minute you see Jillian walk down the aisle."

More laughter, but it was interrupted by Tom's phone. He looked embarrassed. "Should have muted the darn thing. Forgive me."

"Please, answer it," Pastor Mitch said. "Just remember to leave it in your car on Saturday."

Tom pulled out his phone, which had now stopped ringing. "Candace. Wonder what she wanted."

My phone *was* muted, but I could feel it vibrate in my pocket. "Maybe you better step outside and call her, because now she's trying get ahold of me—or at least I think that's who's calling." I patted my leg.

Pastor Mitch waved a hand. "Go on. The police are absolutely a priority."

Tom thanked him and walked down the center aisle, already returning the call. But before he even reached the double doors that led to the vestibule, he stopped.

Kara looked between Elizabeth and the pastor. "Is there anything I've forgotten?"

Elizabeth smiled. "You seem to be quite organized and very calm. I believe you've covered everything."

Tom called, "Jillian, can Kara give you a ride home?"

I heard an urgency in his voice that troubled me. I walked to where he stood. "What's wrong?"

"It's Mike. He's not answering his phone, hasn't shown up at the station. Candace asked if I'd stop by his house and see if he overslept. She didn't want to seem like she was meddling or overreacting since he is her boss."

"Then I'll go with you," I said.

"Don't you have to finish up here?"

"Kara has this. I believe I will be a guest at my own wedding, and I kind of like the idea."

He smiled. "Okay, then. I'll wait in the car." He waved a good-bye to the pastor, his wife and Kara. I returned to them and explained, asked if I needed to do anything.

Since Kara had things under control, I was free to go. I wondered why Tom seemed so unnerved, but when I slid into the passenger seat of the Prius, he explained.

"Mike, in all the years I've known him, has not once missed work because he overslept. And certainly not when there's been a recent murder. Candace is pretty darn busy right now and sounded so stressed I said I'd help out."

He pulled away from the curb and we drove off. Tom said nothing on the drive, but I knew he was worried.

Mike Baca's house wasn't far from downtown. Yards on this treelined street held autumn's contribution to the landscape. Some lawns were raked, but Mike's was blanketed by brown and gold leaves.

The garage door was closed and the blinds were drawn. Maybe he did oversleep after all. I hurried to keep up as Tom strode to the house, dried leaves crunching under our steps.

Tom pounded on the front door and loudly called Mike's name.

Nothing.

He repeated this two more times. Then, fists on his hips, he turned and faced me. "This doesn't feel right. I'll head around back. You stay here in case he wakes up and answers the door."

Tom never overreacted to anything, but I could tell his cop instincts had taken over—even though he'd left the North Carolina police force years ago. We now shared a sense of urgency. When I heard the sound of glass shattering, I ran around the house and passed through the high wooden gate to the backyard.

I caught sight of Tom's foot as he was climbing in through a broken window. I'd been in this house before and I was pretty sure he was going into Mike's office.

"Tom? What's wrong?"

He didn't answer.

*What made him break that window?* I didn't want to know and yet I *had* to know.

I approached slowly, repeating Tom's name.

But before I reached the window, Tom called, "Phone Candace. Tell her—tell her . . ." His voice was laden with emotion. "Tell her Mike is dead. GSW to the head. I—I can't make that phone call."

My breath seemed to leave my lungs in a rush, leaving me unable to speak . . . to think. *This can't be. He's wrong.*

I didn't step closer to the window. Instead I pivoted and faced the other direction, slowly took my phone from my jeans pocket. He wasn't wrong. My brain knew what my heart could not accept.

When I heard Candace's voice, tears slid down my cheeks, into my mouth, salty proof of life in this place of death.

# Thirteen

I huddled in the passenger seat of Tom's car listening to approaching sirens scream their approach. This felt like a safe place amid the horror of what Tom had found in Mike Baca's office.

When we first met several years ago, when I was new to this town, Mike and I hadn't exactly started off on the right foot. He suspected me of murder and I suspected him of being clueless and uncaring. None of it was true. First impressions can be right or they can be oh so wrong.

I still had no idea what had happened in Mike's office. Surely no one would shoot Mike. Maybe he hit his head after suffering a heart attack and Tom just thought it was a gunshot wound. I understood after watching my late husband die that one minute you're alive and laughing and the next minute you can drop like a stone. Mike worked long hours and ate too much junk food. He also had personal issues in the past that no doubt caused him stress. Those are the killers most people never suspect and they'd probably claimed a good and generous man today. Not a gun. Not a gunshot wound to the head. No way.

Candace arrived first, her squad car screeching to a halt at the curb. She came running to Tom's car and I opened the door, fell into her arms and wept. She gripped my upper arms and sat me back down. Her eyes sparkled with tears and sadness and more. Eyes like hers tell the truth.

"Are you okay?"

I nodded. "Window broken in the back. Go be with them—with him and Tom. They need you."

She ran full on toward the gate, no other words needed. No questions. No worries about evidence. Just fear. Yes, that was the last thing I'd seen in her eyes.

The entire working police force arrived one by one until Mike's street resembled the county courthouse parking lot. The fire truck and the ambulance's tragic sirens died when they stopped in the street. They all ran. As if running could change the past or affect the future. The memory of Tom's voice, his command for me to stay in the car, told me different. There was no changing this outcome. Tom spoke the only truth that mattered: "Mike is dead."

I pulled out my phone and watched my cats play, watched them find the sunniest spots near the windows to watch the birds, watched Magpie dragging socks toward the basement door and then returning for more treasure. My smile was lost somewhere deep inside, but I calmed as I watched them. I wanted to be in their world, at my house, not here in this car.

But when I saw Marcy, one of the paramedics, walking

Tom through that gate grasping his forearm with a bloody bandage beneath, I came back to the awful world, to the real one, and scrambled out of the car. My turn to run.

"It's nothing," Tom said before I reached them. His voice was flat, his face ashen.

Marcy spoke as I stood in front of them and stared at the blood leaking between her gloved fingers. She said, "He needs a few stitches."

"I don't. Put that glue on that they use for cuts. Hell, find some superglue and stick the skin together. I'm not leaving."

Marcy looked at me, her stare pleading for my help.

"What about pressure? Will that work?" I asked.

Marcy shook her head, her lips tight.

"Then get the damn doctor to come here and fix it, because I am *not* going anywhere. My friend is dead and he did not kill himself." Tom's voice rose. "He didn't. He wouldn't."

"Kill himself?" I glanced between Tom and Marcy. *"Kill himself?"*

She looked down, avoiding my stare.

"I can prove it if I don't have to stay at some stupid hospital for hours." Tom seemed to calm when he turned to me. "You always have a needle and thread with you. Can you sew this up?"

I made eye contact, touched his face. "We came in your car. I've got nothing with me. Besides, I can't. That wouldn't be good for you." I turned to Marcy, glad to talk about this rather than what had happened in Mike's house. "Do you have sutures?"

She didn't answer, kept staring at the battered, dead leaves at our feet.

Just then I felt a presence behind me and turned to see Mayor Harley Kenyon closing in, grim-faced, shoulders slumped, gray hair uncombed.

He, too, would rather focus on Tom's bloody arm than on the bigger truth, because he said, "What happened?"

"Broke the window to get in. Cut myself. It's nothing."

"Doesn't look like nothing. You need to get that taken care of."

"I'm *not* leaving. He was my friend."

The mayor looked at Marcy. "Can you repair that so he can stay?"

She shook her head. "He needs sutures and I am not qualified."

Tom jerked to look at her. "Not *qualified*? Does that mean you don't know how?"

She hesitated. "I know how. But I'll get in trouble if anyone finds out and—"

Mayor Kenyon said, "Let me worry about that. Besides, y'all can keep a secret and so can I."

I stayed with Tom in the ambulance while the mayor went to where everyone else still was—with what remained of Mike. The small space felt like a safe haven with all its clinical cleanliness, its shelves neatly packed with items of rescue, items to help and heal. But it was all a worthless truckload of stuff as far as Mike Baca was concerned. *Worthless.*

I held Tom's free hand while he sat on the stretcher and Marcy cleaned the two-inch gash on his left forearm with Betadine. She didn't numb the cut—he told her not to—and once she was sewing his skin together, he never flinched. It was as if no pain could match what he'd just discovered in the house.

I rested my free hand on his shoulder and he looked at me, really *looked* at me, for the first time since Marcy had walked him out through that gate.

"There are no words, Tom. No words."

His eyes glazed and he swallowed hard, fighting back the tears successfully. "He didn't kill himself, Jillian. He didn't. I know it."

I nodded, smiled sadly. Grief is the great distorter. Grief is the Grand Master of Deception. I was all too familiar with that trickster Grief.

The back door to the ambulance burst open and Marcy stopped her work, caught in the act. But it was Mayor Kenyon, our confidant.

"Tom, you will say yes," he said. "Okay, I can't make you, but I need you. *We* need you."

"What?" Tom's one sluggish word began to tell the tale of a man coming to terms with the unthinkable.

The mayor sucked in a wheezy breath caused by years of backroom cigars. He let the air rattle out slowly before he spoke. "I'm having the town council appoint you temporary police chief."

"Me? I've been off the job for too long. I—"

"You've been consulting with this police force for several years on cases. Don't tell me you're not capable. No one is more qualified. You know these officers and they need your leadership."

"Candace could do it. She's headed in that career direction." Tom's tone remained flat, unaffected by this request for help.

The mayor spoke quietly. "She's too young. Besides, she wanted me to ask you."

I caught Marcy nod her agreement as she tied off the

last suture. She placed a square of nonstick gauze on the wound and rolled fresh gauze around his forearm.

"Temporary, right? Solve Mike's murder and—"

"*Murder*? He killed himself, Tom." Mayor Kenyon was playing the soothing father now, presenting reality to a man stricken by the death of a close friend.

Tom shook his head. "No, he didn't. He wouldn't. Not Mike. So I guess you have your answer. I'll do it." Tom released my hand and pointed at the mayor. "You don't say a word about suicide. Not one word to anyone. No one on this scene will, either. So I guess I need to start acting like I'm in charge and make sure they know what I expect of them."

The mayor, Marcy and Tom left the ambulance. When I didn't come with them, Tom stopped and turned. He beckoned me to follow.

I had been about to leave, thinking I could drive Tom's car back to my place, but I couldn't go, couldn't abandon my Tom or my friends at a time like this. So I joined them all in Mike's backyard.

But when I saw Lydia Monk pull up in the coroner's van before I made it to the back gate, I wanted to become invisible.

For the first time, however, I saw a side of Lydia I'd never known existed. Though the hair and the makeup and the jewelry were as over-the-top as usual, her confident walk was gone and her gaze was on the ground.

"I want to see him." Her voice, so often strident and demanding, held none of that. She sounded profoundly sad.

I nodded. "I was just headed back there myself."

We walked side by side, unspeaking.

The sliding glass doors that accessed the living room stood open now, but the officers, firemen and Tom stood close together, some with their arms resting on the shoulders of the person next to them, a solemn gathering that brought fresh tears to my eyes.

Lydia joined them while I hung back near the gate.

The mayor spoke. "This tragedy will affect all of you, probably forever. You need a captain for your ship right now so you can get on with this terrible business. I have asked Tom Stewart to take over as temporary police chief. Tom?"

Tom, his face still pallid, left Candace's side to address these responders.

My gaze locked on Candace, and I saw her close her eyes briefly, saw her lower lip tremble, but I also saw what I knew to be determination and defiance. She was angry along with being hurt—angry at Mike for leaving Mercy by his own hand, angry at what had happened here.

Tom cleared his throat. "I know all of you. Each and every one. I grew up in this town. You might not know that Mike and I were friends in high school before we took the same career path in different places. You are aware I was a cop for many years, but that doesn't mean I won't need everyone's help to bring Mike's killer to justice. Yes, I said *killer*."

There was a murmuring among them, a shaking of heads, looks of confusion.

"I know what you're all thinking," he went on. "Tom is grieving. He's lost his mind. But I'm asking you to be cops and inquirers now. Ask yourself this: Why was every blind and curtain in this house closed except for the window where I could see his body lying on the floor? I'm asking you to never say the word *suicide* in the same breath with Mike's name. He *didn't* commit suicide."

Candace spoke. "The curtains must have been left open because he—because *someone* wanted him to be found."

"Exactly. Next question. Was Mike Baca left-handed or right-handed?"

Morris's gruff voice broke the momentary silence. "Left-handed."

"No." It was Lydia. "He used both hands."

Tom went on. "Correct. On the rare times you saw him in uniform, where was his gun strapped? Anyone?"

Morris squinted as if picturing Mike. "On the right. Always on the right."

"Where was the .22 that killed him planted? A .22, *not* his service revolver."

Candace almost smiled, her voice filled with relief. "In his *left* hand."

"Mike Baca was murdered by someone who thought they knew him and believed he was left-handed. And I don't want a word to leave this property that we know the truth. Some jerk is out there thinking he got away with this—and we want him believing he's a criminal mastermind. We will get that person. We will make sure whoever it is pays for this."

Tom went on, directing everyone to handle specific jobs to secure the scene. He also told me what to tell Kara when she came, because she would come—in fact, I was surprised she wasn't here already. He directed Lydia to wait while the scene was photographed, the evidence was collected, the house dusted for prints—all the many things that had to be done. Then she was to follow

Marcy and Jake's ambulance with Mike's remains to the morgue and not leave his side. "Trust no one, Lydia. Say as little as possible, even to the doc who does the autopsy. And I want a tox screen—both an initial and the one that for some damn reason takes forever. There was no struggle here. Why not? My guess is, he was drugged or he was drunk. And Mike never got drunk alone."

Lydia nodded.

As folks scurried to do their jobs in morbid silence, Tom came over to me, took my hands. "You can tell Kara the truth. I can't make her keep the facts out of whatever story she chooses to run. I can only ask for her help. Perhaps she could omit the suicide nonsense by calling this a *serious incident*. I want whoever did this to wonder and worry why we're not saying he took his own life—why we're not saying much of anything. Can you explain that to her?"

I nodded. "She'll help. And thank you for trusting her. What about Finn?"

Tom shook his head. "Nope. Not a word other than it's all being kept quiet, that we don't know much. Each person who learns the truth is a potential leak, even Finn."

Mayor Kenyon joined us and told Tom he had been amazing. Tom handed me his car keys and said good-bye to both of us. He wanted to return to his new job and he did. A fellow officer taken down has a profound effect on the police.

The mayor and I left the yard together.

"I'm sorry I didn't give you two time to discuss my . . . *job offer*. But Tom is the right man for this, as we both just witnessed. I understand you're getting married, and in my house, we'd talk something like that over first. Circumstances didn't let — "

"Of course they didn't," I interrupted. "But if we had discussed it . . . well, you're right. Tom *is* the right person to handle this tragedy."

"Glad you understand. Never get on the wrong side of the missus, I always say."

I clicked the remote to unlock Tom's car, and the mayor opened the door for me.

"I gotta gather the town council to vote on what I've already decided. Should be no problem. But first, I want to thank you for being here, Ms. Hart. Thank you for all you've done for our town. It's not gone unnoticed."

Before I slid behind the wheel I gave Mayor Kenyon a hug. "You absolutely did the right thing," I whispered.

# Fourteen

Before I maneuvered around the police cars and the ambulance, not to mention the fire truck with its lights still spinning garishly in the morning gloom, I called Kara and explained the situation. She was already headed to Mike's house after hearing scanner broadcasts and agreed to run the "serious incident" story without hesitation.

"That's exactly what it is," she'd told me.

I felt relieved as I drove toward home, but sorrow hung over me, heavy and tight. Tears came again, rolling down my cheeks. How I wished I could have said goodbye. How I wished I'd had the courage to look in that window and—

*No. That is not how you want to remember him, Jillian. You were lucky not to see what Tom did.*

I pulled into my driveway about five minutes later and once inside I sat on the floor in the kitchen, cats surrounding me, loving me, as I dealt with the pain of losing a friend.

"Why are you crying?" It was Lindsey, her hair wet from a shower. She was wearing a too-big T-shirt and baggy jeans that obviously belonged to Finn.

I wasn't even aware I was still shedding quiet tears. "Tough morning. A friend passed." I couldn't keep the emotion out of my voice even though I tried. This girl didn't need to hear about more death.

Lindsey joined me on the floor and Chablis immediately climbed onto her crossed legs. "I'm sorry. Can I help?" She stroked Chablis, not making eye contact. This girl, who put a shield of sarcasm and hostility up against the world, was having a hard time being herself. And I believed that her special *self* was just as hurt and alone as I felt right now.

"You sitting here with me and being close to the cats helps." I smiled at her as she peeked up at me.

"Okay. I can do that."

"Where's Finn?"

"He went to the shelter. I let him take my car. But I have a class I can't miss, so he promised to be back by noon."

"He'll be back, but it's not Halloween yet, so you can't go dressed like a hobo. Let's check my closet."

Though Lindsey was shorter than I was by several inches, I had boyfriend-style jeans that fit her perfectly and a tunic sweater that looked far better on her than on me.

She asked to borrow a hair dryer and after I gave her mine, I promised to wash her clothes. But she said to point her in the right direction and she'd do it herself. We didn't talk about how long she would stay with us or about my friend Mike. She had her own grief to deal with and I guessed she was still a little bit in denial.

"I have a few things to take care of in my sewing room," I said to Lindsey. "You can join me. We can listen to music."

"No, thanks. I need to read a few documents online for my class. Finn said I could use his computer."

I pointed out the laundry room and noticed Finn had left his laptop on the small table in the kitchen that overlooked the lake. The two of us, with death shadowing our lives, retreated to our separate spaces. It didn't feel right, but Lindsey obviously needed her privacy and I respected that.

The cats and I—all except Magpie, who I'd seen slip into my bedroom, no doubt hunting for bounty—went to the sewing room. Chablis, Syrah and Merlot found their spots and curled up. It was way past their naptime. Chablis had to be close, right next to me in the big overstuffed chair and I was comforted by her warmth.

I picked up an appliqué square that was part of a Christmas quilt and tried to work. But my fingers wouldn't cooperate. The handwork remained in my lap, my hands folded on top of it. My mind seemed to have been wiped of anything but memories of Mike, how he'd interrogated me not long after I first moved to Mercy, back when Syrah went missing and terrible things happened one right after another. He'd been a good police chief, but when it came to the women in his life, he hadn't been quite as smart. He was divorced, had been dating Lydia for a time and then had a disastrous relationship with another woman.

Yes, women—or rather choosing the wrong ones—were his Achilles' heel, he always used to say. Lately he hadn't talked about who he might be seeing, if anyone, so I assumed he was taking a break from dating. He'd been burned badly and seemed all the more dedicated to his job.

Yes, the man who once suspected me of being a criminal became my friend. And now he was gone. He wouldn't be there for Tom or me at the wedding. We might be having his funeral that day instead. If so, that was fine. Tom and I had time. Mike's had run out.

As it closed in on noon, I finally left the quiet room, where all the cats were sleeping, even Magpie. She'd dragged in the T-shirt I'd worn to bed, dropped it at my feet and made her own little bed. Finn wasn't back, and I found Lindsey pacing on the back deck.

I joined her outside. "Did you call Finn and tell him you needed your car?"

"I did. Voice mail. I texted him, too. Got no answer."

"You want me to take you to school and have forgetful Finn pick you up?"

"Would you?" There seemed to be a desperation in her demeanor that seemed, well, *off*. As if she had to move, get away, perhaps run from the truth of her loss. I understood.

But just as I grabbed my keys and we were about to leave, I heard a car honking over and over.

I saw Lindsey smile for the first time—what a transformation. She was a lovely girl. "That's my car. That's him." She ran out through the back door and to my surprise they left together, Finn barreling back down my driveway way too fast. We'd have to chat about that.

I waved to them and saw them speed off, just as Rebecca Marner's SUV appeared. They went by her without slowing down. I had a bad feeling about this, and it only got worse when Rebecca pulled into my driveway all the way up to the back gate. She was the last person I wanted to talk to right now.

Her inscrutable expression didn't help me figure out how to navigate this awkward situation. She seemed calm, however, when she said, "I'm glad she's safe." She glanced back at the road in the direction they'd left.

"Would you like to come in?" I asked.

"I'm planning a funeral, so I don't have much time — but yes."

She followed me through the gate and up the stairs to my back door. Before we went inside, I told her I had cats — lots of cats.

"I always keep a lint roller in my purse. It's no problem."

I'd been more concerned about allergies, but she was worried about cat hair. I should have known her charcoal suit and gray silk blouse would be her first concern.

She refused my offer of sweet tea or coffee. We sat at my dining room table after she said she'd prefer to stay away from upholstery where the cat hair clung and would transfer to her clothes.

I needed sweet tea, if only to have a glass of *something* to hang on to. I feared this would not be an easy conversation. She was Lindsey's mother, after all, and deserved some sort of explanation.

"You are a kind and caring person, Jillian. I am rather . . . *difficult* to get to know. But I have one friend and she could use your help. Zoe."

I tried to manage my facial muscles to tame any look that would be interpreted as stunned. But I was. No mention of her daughter? She was here about her former husband's widow? I couldn't wrap my mind around that one. "I—I thought you came here about Lindsey. I—"

She waved a dismissive hand. "Lindsey can take care of herself. She's an independent girl like her mother. I have no worries there. No, it's Zoe. She's quite incapable of dealing with all this funeral business."

I sipped my tea, wanting to hide my face with the glass so she wouldn't see how confused I was. What the heck was happening here? But then I remembered something. "I understand someone arranged for a funeral singer, so is she—"

"That was me. Right now I just need a volunteer to sit with Zoe while I collect what she needs for the funeral, create the obituary, make calls to out-of-state relatives, make sure when Rhett's body is released that we are all in agreement on what he should wear. There's so much to do, and no one seems to be stepping in to help her manage."

It all sounded so cold, almost like a grocery list. Plus Verline said Zoe's son called her, not Rebecca. I felt a little sick then because my thoughts went to Mike. Who would make those arrangements for him? Certainly not *his* ex-wife.

"I wish I could, Rebecca. But there's been a serious incident involving a friend of mine. I need to focus on that right now."

But Rebecca wasn't about to take no for an answer. "You can squeeze in an hour for another friend. She's done so much for the community. She'll be alone and she shouldn't be."

I closed my eyes and remembered Zoe in that parking lot, how devastated she was. I *had* planned on picking up a rotisserie chicken and deli salads and dropping them off for Zoe and her family before . . . before Mike's death.

"I can only spare an hour, Rebecca. But I'd be glad to help her." There. Helping out when I was feeling so devastated would certainly be the right thing to do for Zoe and for her family, and might help relieve the pain of Mike's loss that sat like an icy, heavy stone on my heart.

"Good. I knew you would be the right person for the job. Be there at three o'clock. You have the address?"

I didn't, so she whipped out a smartphone from her Michael Kors bag and rattled it off, not even waiting for me to grab a pencil and paper. I made her wait while I took a magnetized pad with attached pen from the fridge door. Then I had her repeat the address. I was beginning to feel like one of the servants in *Downton Abbey* and I didn't like it one bit.

She left without asking anything more about her daughter, how she was dealing with her grief, what she might need in this terrible time. I might have been angered by her callousness, but it only triggered a wave of sadness once Rebecca drove off. What was wrong with people like her? *What in the heck was wrong with them?*

# Fifteen

No one called and no one showed up in the time between Rebecca's departure and my trek to Zoe Marner's house. I was hoping to hear from Finn, thinking maybe he needed a ride back from the community college. I finally decided he was waiting for Lindsey to finish her class. He'd seemed to have taken her under a protective wing, and that was a good thing.

I didn't expect Tom or Candace to call in the aftermath of Mercy's loss—not to mention the other murder they still had to solve. I totally understood, but I thought Kara might phone me. She didn't, though, and I assumed she was preparing a special edition of the *Messenger*. Tom might stay at work until the day we were married, which right now could well be delayed. That was okay. Our time would come.

Close to three p.m. I pulled in front of Zoe's house. Another stone-and-brick minimansion typical of a Rhett Marner development loomed on a slope with its manicured lawn and sculpted landscape reminiscent of a botanical garden. This attempt at perfection unnerved me in this far-from-perfect world. Maybe on a different day I wouldn't have found it quite so ostentatious.

I saw no cars in the driveway, and the isolation here reminded me of the other house I assumed Rhett Marner once owned—the one where I'd first met Lindsey. Then I heard water trickling over rocks to my right as I walked up the winding pebbled path to the front door. *Must be a ravine over there,* I thought. *That's nice. Very soothing. Maybe this place isn't so bad after all.*

I rang the bell and heard it chime inside despite the heavy oak double doors. Zoe answered and immediately wrapped her arms around me, her sobs interrupted by "thank you for coming" over and over. I couldn't return the hug because I held the grocery bag of chicken in one hand and the salads and dessert in the other.

She finally composed herself and drew back, staring down at what I had in my hands. "I'm so sorry for throwing myself on you like that, but I'm grateful you've come."

I'd always thought she seemed surprisingly young for a woman who had two teenage boys—and they had to be older teens from the few times I'd seen them at the community center when they came to see Zoe there. Big, burly boys who dwarfed their mother.

Now that I had a moment to notice, I was surprised by her appearance. She was dressed in pressed khakis and an expensive-looking designer blouse. Her makeup showed little wear despite this recent bout of tears. Did they make waterproof makeup as well as waterproof mascara? Probably. Her blond hair, with its reddish lowlights, was recently washed and styled. I recalled how I'd had to force myself to shower after John's death. But fix my hair and put on makeup? Forget it.

Zoe, however, belonged to a different crowd than I felt comfortable being around. Appearance was everything for them. If you looked flawless, then you were flawless—that was what I'd come to understand they believed. Apparently it was a way to cope, and even if I never would take that route, plenty of people like Zoe and Rebecca did. We all had our way of navigating through life.

She invited me in and thanked me again for coming. We went through an expansive foyer, a winding staircase in its center. Then we moved down a short hall, past a formal dining room with a table set with gleaming square white plates on pleated green place mats. A huge bowl of red and yellow mums surrounded by golden fall leaves sat in the center. A matching arrangement graced the polished sideboard against the wall.

We ended up in a gigantic gourmet eat-in kitchen with a granite-topped island and chef-quality stainless steel appliances. Cakes, pies, cheese plates, baskets of fruit and platters of cookies sat on a long counter flanked on one side by a row of barstools. There was certainly no shortage of food and I felt a tad embarrassed at my store-bought offering.

I smelled fresh coffee, and knowing I wouldn't be getting much sleep tonight with so much on my mind, I figured caffeine this late in the day wouldn't matter. I accepted when Zoe offered. Then it dawned on me I was here to take care of her, not vice versa. I insisted I fix a mug for both of us and encouraged Zoe to sit down.

"Are you sure?" she said hesitantly.

"Sit. I can manage coffee and put this food I brought in the fridge. Thank goodness you have much better offerings than grocery-made stuff." I couldn't help wondering where any of the people who'd brought all this food were. Why was I, not much more than an acquaintance, here instead? What about her family? Where were her kids?

"Jillian, my boys will scarf up that chicken and potato salad before anything else. You're practical and thoughtful. That's what makes you so special."

I felt a blush heat my face. "Trust me. I am the most ordinary person you'll ever meet."

A few minutes later, we both sat at a white-painted table in an alcove overlooking the pool and patio. Turquoise water shimmered in the late-afternoon sun. A stone fireplace surrounded by upholstered patio furniture and a giant stainless steel barbecue grill completed the magazine-worthy picture. The backyard alone, with its rolling lawn and shade trees, must have cost a fortune to landscape.

I felt awkward and at a loss for words, but Zoe launched right into troubled territory. "I wasn't kind to Rhett the last time we spoke. We argued and now I feel so guilty. It was over a stupid party he'd accepted an invitation to—a birthday party for one of his employees. I thought he was angry with me for being stuck-up. I—I thought that's why he was gone—that he was staying with one of his hunting buddies. And all the time he was probably . . . *dead*."

That explained why he hadn't been reported missing sooner. "You've convinced yourself that the argument made him stay away, but that's probably untrue. Something happened when he left, something the police will surely know soon enough. Please don't feel guilty."

"You lost your husband suddenly, right? I mean, that's why Rebecca thought it might be good for me to talk to you. You know what I'm going through."

I nodded. "I do know. It's like a sucker punch to the gut. One day you have this life, this routine . . . and the next day, it's changed completely and forever." I placed a hand over her balled fist.

"I heard you were there yesterday right after they . . . *found* him." She stared into her mug. "Were people saying anything? I mean, I know he was shot, but I wasn't notified right away and all these people were already there by the time I got to the site."

"You do know he wasn't identified immediately, right? That's probably why you weren't notified. But I thought Candace would have explained that when you spoke with her. You did speak with her, right?"

"Oh yes. But I—I don't remember what I said, much less any questions she asked. She probably told me about the delay in calling me and I blocked it out. Did you know they took me to the emergency room and gave me a shot of something to calm me down? The medication messed with my brain and I feel kind of hungover today."

"No wonder you don't remember," I said.

"Did they say who found him? She probably told me that, too."

*Or not,* I thought. I wasn't about to start spilling anything I knew. It wasn't my place. "I'm sure Candace will want to speak with you again and you can go over everything. It's tough being fuzzy on the details, but that's part of grieving. Your mind will let you remember when you're ready."

Zoe smiled sadly, blinking hard. "Rebecca was so smart to have you come, to send someone who knows how hard this is."

"It took me a long time to rejoin humanity after John died. Many months, in fact. Only with the help of lots of people and most of all my cats, I'm doing fine. I didn't come here to talk about me, though. Tell me about you. How long had you and Rhett been married?"

"Five years. He was so good to take on a woman with two young sons. They needed a father." Her voice caught. "And now they've lost him."

"Is their biological father in the picture?"

"He wants to be. But the restraining order keeps him at a distance, thank goodness."

This fell into the "too much information" category for me, or TMI as Finn would say. An awkward silence followed as I realized that a man who was under a court order to stay away from his sons—sons who obviously became well off when Zoe married Rhett—might be of interest to Candace. Oh, and to the new police chief, Tom Stewart, as well. But they probably knew this family's history already—and no doubt half of Mercy was aware, too.

Thank goodness the back door opened, because I'd run out of things to say. I was beginning to feel more and more as though there was some other reason I'd been asked to come here—perhaps as a source of information to Rebecca as to what was going on with the investigation, since I was friends with almost everyone on the police force.

Two teenage boys rumbled in, one shoving the other and laughing about something. Zoe rose and went to greet them.

I was introduced to Toby, the taller of the two. He wore a bright green letter jacket from Mercy High School with "football" embroidered beneath the school logo.

Next I was introduced to Owen, who had a baby face, flushed from laughter. I guessed he was probably a couple of years younger than his hulking brother—but he had time to catch up. They had identical gray-green eyes and reddish blond hair.

Teenagers, especially those who've lost the father figure they've had for the last five years, do not act like adults. I decided their behavior—laughing, being a tad cocky and seemingly nonplussed that a stranger was in the house with their mother—was probably normal. Grief the Trickster at work again. Or maybe they, like some of the young men who'd worked for Rhett Marner, hadn't cared for their stepfather. In this age of blended families I wouldn't be surprised.

The two of them didn't linger in the kitchen and offered nothing in the way of acknowledgment of their mother's distress. They did check out the fridge, grabbed the chicken and potato salad I'd brought and retreated for a room, probably as far as they could get from this kitchen. In this house, that could be a long way off.

Zoe smiled apologetically. "Sorry. They don't know what to make of all this. But I told you that chicken would be appreciated."

Now that the boys had arrived home, I figured it was okay to leave. But before I could even get any parting words out of my mouth, the front doorbell chimed. I pulled my car keys from my pocket and decided I'd follow Zoe when she answered. Then I could say good-bye once she had someone else to distract her.

But getting out of here wouldn't be that easy, I soon learned. Rebecca Marner stood on the stoop along with Lydia Monk. When Lydia saw me, the truth I'd seen in her eyes, the sad person from this morning, was gone. Totally gone.

"What are *you* doing here?" That was her usual greeting for me. Those lacquered eyes—her mascara so thick I swore it was actual paint—bored into me.

"Oh, I forgot to tell you, Lydia." Rebecca pulled Lydia by the arm into the foyer and shut the door. "I asked Jillian to come over—you know, to keep poor Zoe company until I could get things rolling as far as paperwork and other necessary evils that accompany a sudden death. There is no extended family in town yet, and a wife in mourning shouldn't be left alone."

"But Jillian asked you to come here, right? Hinted around?" Lydia hadn't taken her eyes off me and Zoe shrank back, probably wishing she could disappear.

"Actually it was my idea." Rebecca sounded dismissive, might as well have added, "*End of discussion.*" "Now, where's that paperwork for Zoe to complete? She'll need her death certificates as soon as possible. Bank accounts are frozen when something like this happens, and she'll have to prove he's dead to gain access to funds to feed her family."

*Feed her family?* I thought. There was enough food to

feed an army in the kitchen. I turned to Zoe, rested a hand on her upper arm. "If you need anything or just want to talk, please call me."

I didn't even get a chance to handle any awkward good-bye with Lydia because Rebecca was already herding her and Zoe toward the back of the house.

The tightness in my neck that always started after an encounter with Lydia disappeared the second I closed the door behind me. But the tension actually started before she'd arrived. I truly hoped I wouldn't get any calls to come here again. This whole meeting with not only Zoe, but with her sons, with Lydia and of course master planner Rebecca, almost seemed frenzied. I had to learn that every request for my help didn't have to be answered immediately—especially with death and weddings and flowers and funerals all mixing together in my head like a lethal cocktail.

The minute I climbed into the van, I pulled my phone out. This time, I engaged the chat feature on my new cat cam. The speaker on only one camera was turned on so it would draw the cats to me. I called all their names and added an "I love you." Sure enough, soon four sets of cat faces stared up at me in the kitchen. Merlot warbled in response and Syrah stood up on his back legs and pawed the air in the direction of the camera as if stretching toward my voice would allow me to pet him. Chablis lay on the tile and rolled on her back. Though I couldn't hear her, I was sure she was purring. Magpie, to my amusement, had a big fat button in her mouth—she'd been in my sewing room again hunting for treasure. But when she saw what Syrah was doing, she dropped the button and it bounced away. She, too, stood on back legs to hear as I talked to them about how I would be home soon.

But my dose of cat therapy was interrupted by an incoming call and I had to say good-bye. I switched off the cat cam and answered. It was Finn.

"Um, Jillian, we could use a little help. I know my dad is super busy, I can't find Gramps and we're kind of stuck out here."

"You and Lindsey?" I jabbed the key in the ignition.

"Yup. I took her to Shawn's shelter because . . . because there's no better place to be than at the Sanctuary when you're down. Someone dropped off a sick batch of puppies with Shawn, and since his wife is gone for her internship at that vet hospital in North Carolina, he's alone and needed help. But we ran out of gas on the way home. At least I think that's all that's wrong with her car."

"I can fill a gas can and be there right away. Tell me exactly where you are."

Twenty minutes later, Lindsey and I watched as Finn added the gas to her BMW.

The girl seemed in a terrible mood. Not that I blamed her. Her father was murdered, she'd left her home to stay with strangers and now this small event—running out of gas—was probably the last straw.

I rested a hand on her shoulder as she stared at Finn filling up her car. "I didn't mind coming out here."

Her shoulder tensed beneath my touch and I withdrew my hand. Maybe she needed space.

She turned to me, her eyes apologetic and angry at the same time. "It's not *you*. I called my mother and she wouldn't pick us up. Now, if it had been one of her committee members who called? Or the mayor? Or even a stranger off the street? Oh, she would've answered their plea for help just like that." She snapped her fingers. "But my daddy, the guy everyone loved to hate? He'd never leave us out in the country like this. If he couldn't come, he'd send someone. He'd complain all the way and call me stupid, but he'd come."

As soon as she'd mentioned her dad, emotion filled her voice and those sly, unpredictable tears struck again. I didn't care if she resisted me. This girl needed a hug.

I gathered her close and told her how sorry I was. She relaxed into me, finally wrapped her arms around me and put her head on my shoulder. "Why did this have to happen? Why am I always her scapegoat?"

These tears weren't about her dad. They were about Mom.

Finn finished his task and faced us. "Let me check if we're good to go."

The car started right up.

"I am so dumb," Lindsey mumbled as she started for the passenger side. "Can't even check a fuel gauge."

She stopped halfway to her destination and looked back at me. "Thank you."

"I'll follow you two back to my place. Or are you headed home and Finn should ride with me?"

"I can go home if you need me to leave. I know I'm pretty nasty company."

"Absolutely not. You stay as long as you want. And I'll put you to work washing china for the wedding reception my stepdaughter is having later this week." There was no china to wash, of course, and right now it was a *maybe* wedding reception. But it felt like the right thing to say.

Lindsey must have picked up on my expression and misinterpreted what I was thinking. "Oh, that's right. Finn said you and his dad were getting married. I should get out of your way."

"No way. You are welcome in my home. End of conversation."

I caught the hint of a smile before she joined Finn in her car. He pulled out and I followed. This road between here and town was a deserted stretch, but not a minute later, I saw Finn's right blinker come on and he pulled over. Maybe running out of gas wasn't the only problem with this car. Maybe we'd have to call a tow truck.

But when I saw Finn get out and hurry into the dry ditch bordering the road and head up into the heavy brush, I wondered if he suddenly needed a pit stop. Curious, I slid from behind the wheel and waited for him to reappear. That happened only seconds later and he waved me toward him.

When I reached his side, he pointed at a rusty, sea green pickup truck.

"I see. Someone dumped a truck," I said. "You thinking of calling Ed to retrieve this old thing?"

"No, Jillian. I was afraid someone was in it, that they might be hurt. Look at the tread marks from the road to here." He pointed at the ground.

He was right. I could see the path this truck traveled when it went off the road. It couldn't have been that long ago. I drew closer, saw the driver's-side door was open and the tailgate down.

Lindsey joined us. "What's happening? You got a thing for old trucks, Finn?"

I stepped closer, thankful I'd chosen jeans and shoes today. They would protect my legs and feet from whatever lived among these bushes and nearby trees. Lindsey's shoes weren't quite as nature-friendly.

But it wasn't the truck itself that had me pulling my phone from my pocket. It was the streaks in the truck bed and the drip marks on the bumper. I can tell rust from dried blood—and this wasn't rust.

# Sixteen

I stayed about ten feet from the truck, feeling as if I were guarding Fort Knox. It could be animal blood, but I wasn't taking any chances—not this close to where that sofa had been dumped. Finn took Lindsey back to her car after I pointed out that she had sling-back flats on and could get bitten by ants or something more lethal— like a snake. He was good at reading me and knew I wasn't *really* talking about her shoes.

Tom and Candace arrived ten minutes later. Soon Candace, hands on hips, was taking in the tread marks and the path the truck had taken. Finally she said, "This truck wasn't here two days ago. I surveyed this road up and down looking for something exactly like this—a clue to how a bloody sofa ended up next to that box. It could very well have arrived in this old thing."

"Traffic here picks up at lunch and suppertime," Tom said, "but it's not all that busy unless you're adopting an animal from the shelter or stuffing the charity box with discards. Finn sure has a sharp eye, because the truck's almost completely hidden."

"It's no surprise he spotted it." I smiled. "Finn might not be your blood relative, but he lived with you as a boy—what was he? Twelve when you married his mother?"

"Yup."

"You were the best thing that ever happened to him. He admires you, Tom, and has modeled himself after you. He questions, observes and works hard. Nope, no surprise he noticed that piece of the bumper at all."

Tom squeezed my shoulder. "Let me ask Finn a few questions and y'all can be on your way."

I went with him to Lindsey's car and stood next to Tom by the rolled-down driver's-side window.

"Hey there, Dad," Finn said. "What are you doing here?"

"Helping Candace out." He bent, nodded at Lindsey and said, "Heard you two ran out of gas. What were you doing out this way?"

"We came to help Shawn—right after Lindsey finished her class. And he sure needed us. We took care of cleaning the cattery, feeding the dogs, stuff like that while he helped these cute premature puppies. We were on our way back to Jillian's when we came to a surprise stop."

"That's my fault," Lindsey offered. "Too preoccupied to even notice the gas gauge."

"Happens to all of us at one time or another. Glad you noticed the truck, son. We're on this and I appreciate you being so observant." Tom straightened, ready to help Candace. She was taking pictures of the truck, the grass and probably every leaf, stone and shrub in the vicinity.

Finn knew something was up and he wasn't letting Tom off the hook that easily. "It's just an old truck, right? I mean, you have a lot more important things to handle than this. You're obviously consulting with the police again."

"Can we talk about this later?" Tom said. "Time for you two to be on your way."

Finn got the message and they took off. Too late I shouted, "Stop at a gas station on the way home."

Tom said, "You worried Lindsey saw the blood?"

"I don't think she got close enough."

"Good. We're on this now. Go on home and say hi to the cats for me. I'll probably crash at the station, especially now with this possible new lead. Could be deer blood in that truck for all we—"

"It's human," Candace called, erasing any doubt. I turned her way and she was holding up the swab. "Bagging this as evidence and I hope we can speed up the DNA test. I'm betting it belongs to Rhett."

I kissed Tom good-bye, but as I was starting toward my van, a white late-model pickup pulled up behind it. Since the squad car Tom and Candace arrived in was in front of my vehicle, I was pretty much stuck here for now. An older gentleman wearing carpenter's overalls and sporting two days of gray stubble approached me. Tom, who had joined Candace, did an about-face and started back in my direction.

"You know what's going on here?" the man asked.

Tom reached us and held out his hand in greeting. "Tom Stewart. Mercy PD."

"You ain't dressed like no cop."

"No, I'm not." Tom smiled.

He probably didn't want to reveal his new job quite yet, so he left it at that.

This seemed to make the man uncomfortable and he shifted from one foot to another, saying, "This here is my property. Got fifteen acres between here and my house. I want to know what's goin' on."

"Ah. Maybe you can help us identify this truck we found abandoned. Seen it around?" Tom gestured toward where Candace was using tweezers to pick up fibers in the truck bed.

"Seen it? Son of a gun, that's *mine*." He started toward it, but Tom put out an arm to stop him.

"We're collecting evidence right now, Mr. . . . ?"

"Strickland. Wilbur Strickland." He kept staring at the truck and Candace's activity.

"Mr. Strickland, did you leave your truck here?" Tom asked.

"Leave it here? Why would I do that?"

"I don't know. That's why I'm asking."

I was about ready to leave them to do this verbal dance without me and wait in my car, but I was curious. I wanted answers almost as much as Tom did. I stayed right where I was.

Mr. Strickland, still avoiding the question, said, "That truck, even with three hundred thousand miles, runs just fine. When I got a messy job—dead animals in the woods that need proper buryin' or a slaughtered wild hog I need to carry back to the house—I use it."

"Pretty well taken care of, I have to say," Tom said.

"You can't leave blood and guts in a truck bed and not expect to draw critters out in the country. Even bobcats. I keep that baby clean, inside and out. Why do you think it's lasted twenty years?"

"Point taken," Tom said. "Why is it out here, then—and *not* being *taken care of*?"

Mr. Strickland scratched his salt-and-pepper crew cut. "Don't know."

But if even *I* could read deceptive body language—no eye contact, fidgety behavior—Tom was already aware this man knew something he didn't want to share.

"Yes, you *do* know." Tom's voice was quiet, but confident.

The man sighed heavily. "Okay, my nephew's been known to take the truck out for a ride, 'specially if he fancies a girl. But the truck's on my property and I won't be pressing no charges, so what's the big deal?"

"I can't tell you that right now, but trust me, it *is* a big deal."

Mr. Strickland turned to me then, probably to change the subject. "And who are you? Another cop without a uniform? 'Cause I know that pretty Deputy Carson up there messin' with my property, but the two of you? What the heck is goin' on here? It's a dumb old truck, is all."

I held out my hand. "I'm Jillian Hart and it's kind of a long story why I ended up here, but I'm glad to meet you."

Mr. Strickland's eyes widened. "You that quilt woman? The person my wife wants to become?" He grabbed my hand and shook it vigorously. "I can score some major points with her today sayin' I met you." He smiled broadly. A few teeth were missing, but that smile transformed him into a far less suspicious and ornery person than he'd first seemed.

From the corner of my eye I caught Tom's grin, the

little shake of his head as if to say, "There she goes again, making friends out of strangers."

"You the one who found my truck, then?" he asked. Tom had suddenly become invisible to Wilbur Strickland.

"Um, yes." Not exactly the truth, but it didn't matter at this point. "And I called the police. I was sure it belonged to someone, and the discovery needed to be reported."

"You sure saved me a bunch of trouble, little lady. I was gone for the past couple days—looking to buy a few milk cows up toward Anderson—and I come home to find the truck gone. Did the missus notice? She says no. But I'm sure my brother's boy took it. He mighta had a little too much to drink and drove it right through this here ditch. It's not like the truck's worth much to anyone but me, so I ain't got round to callin' up and askin' him what he's been up to."

"What's his name again?" Tom's eyebrows were raised and I could tell he was trying hard to remain patient. This had been one of the most difficult days in his life, and remaining calm surely couldn't have been easy.

"Bo Strickland. But don't go runnin' over to my brother's place and rouse him. Kid sleeps all day. Works graveyards at the Stop and Shop. Guess that's why when he has a night off he don't sleep and sometimes comes round here and takes my truck."

"He doesn't own a car?" I asked.

"Nope. Says he's savin' up. Sure. That'll be the day. Anyways, he gets his sister to drop him off here so he can take the truck and meet up with the latest girlfriend.

Desperate, I guess. Sister's not fool enough to lend him *her* car. She's actually got a lick of sense."

I smiled and nodded. And I could tell Wilbur Strickland had a lick of sense, too—well, almost.

Tom asked the question that was now on my mind. "How did he get the keys to the truck if you weren't around?"

"No doubt Floretta, the missus, gave 'em up. Big softy. The kid smiles at her and she runs to the kitchen to make him cobbler or cookies. We couldn't have kids, so she wants Bo to keep comin' round." Wilbur looked at me. "She would so love to meet you, ma'am. Pick your brain about your ideas. See, we got ourselves about eight semi-feral barn cats. I take them from Shawn whenever he asks me to. Hard to find homes for cats like that. There's nothing better at killing the rats and mice that love my chicken feed than a cat that won't come indoors for nothin'."

Wilbur sure loved to talk, and the mention of cats and his obvious love of country life were almost soothing after this difficult day. This must be the couple Shawn had mentioned the other day—just two days ago, but it seemed like a decade.

I was then surprised when Tom came up with an idea, which of course served his police purposes.

Not that I minded.

# Seventeen

The Strickland house and barn sat alone back from the road. This small farm was located several hundred feet past the spot where I always turned off to head to the Animal Sanctuary, so I'd never noticed it before. A fenced area, as well as the cattle guard Tom and I rumbled over in my van, kept the cows I'd spotted grazing in the field, and not out on the road. It was almost time for them to lumber back to the barn. Days were getting shorter.

We'd followed Wilbur here, leaving Candace with the squad car. She was still collecting evidence from the truck, and Wilbur told me—not Tom—that he didn't mind one bit, that she could even tow it off to check it more thoroughly, but he "sure as heck" wanted to know what they were looking for. Tom dodged the question again—for now. At some point he would have to explain, but that wasn't my job, thank goodness.

Tom told him he wanted to see where the truck had been parked and also talk to Mrs. Strickland, the keeper of the keys in her husband's absence. I was guessing a visit to nephew Bo would be on Tom's agenda in the near future.

The white farmhouse, tinted amber by the setting sun, might have been old, but it was freshly painted. The barn seemed in pristine condition, its rusty red color brightened by light from the west. I'd caught a glimpse of the garage when we made a slight turn and parked on the gravel drive in front of the house. What I saw of the shabby garage did not seem to match the house and barn.

Wilbur pulled his truck under a carport next to the house. As soon as our vehicle doors slammed, three cats raced from the barn toward us—two tabbies and a tuxedo.

I crouched and extended a hand palm down, made a chattering noise. The tuxedo came right up and butted against my knees.

Wilbur joined Tom and me and said, "Simpson ain't never done that. Not ever. He'll let me and the missus pet him but not no one else—until you."

The tabbies hung back, but they didn't seem frightened. I wished I had a few treats in my pocket to tempt them. Cat love was the absolute best and I needed all I could get today.

Tom cleared his throat. "Can I have a word with Mrs. Strickland?"

Wilbur had been staring down at me as I stroked Simpson. The handsome boy was rubbing his face on my knee and thigh, leaving his scent on me, owning me. I smiled and told him he was beautiful.

Tom repeated his question to Wilbur, who was taking in Simpson's behavior with wonder.

"Oh, sure enough, but Mrs. Hart, my wife won't never forgive me if she don't get to meet you."

I stood, brushing dirt off my rear. "I want to meet her, too. And please call me Jillian."

A few minutes later, Tom and I were sitting on a sofa with a floral chintz slipcover while Floretta Strickland hustled to make us sweet tea. Tom understood that in South Carolina, if you greeted a person in her home, you first had to be polite and usually accept tea or coffee. Floretta, a kind-eyed woman with large bones and rough, reddened hands that had seen all kinds of work in her life, wobbled on her feet and went wide-eyed when she met me. Her husband had to steady her.

I was by no means a celebrity, but a kitty I fostered had been. The cat and I had made the national news together, and folks in Mercy do not forget things like that—especially the cat lovers. My quilt orders skyrocketed afterward, too. So, as we sipped tea, Floretta's questions centered on the quilts I made for cats. She was one of the many quilters in this region, and wanted to learn how to make them. I usually had a few in my van but didn't today. I had pictures on my phone, though.

Tom saw this as a perfect opportunity to have Wilbur show him the garage where the truck was always parked. While they were gone, I displayed photo after photo of my quilts to Floretta. She nodded and smiled and said she could easily make these for her own cats, particularly for the kitties who slept on the screened back porch when it got chilly in winter.

She was about to refill her tea and was ready to see my kitties on the cat cam when Wilbur burst in through the back kitchen door and into the living room.

"Honey bear," he said to his wife in a voice not exactly dripping with sweetness, "did you go and sell that old sofa I keep out in the garage?"

"Why, whatever are you talkin' about, Wilbur Strickland?" She stood, walked past him and Wilbur followed. So did I.

As I went through the screened porch and down the outdoor steps to the garage, I noted it was being repainted to match the house's fresh white exterior. The sun, now almost in full retreat, offered only enough light for me to notice the painting was about half-done. It wouldn't be shabby much longer.

I had to almost run to keep up with Floretta and Wilbur.

A lone bare bulb lit the interior of the garage. Tom had his phone flashlight on and was examining the oil-stained concrete where the truck usually must have been parked. Floretta started to walk right across the garage, but Wilbur grabbed her by the back of her housedress.

"The man's workin,' Floretta. He said I should only walk around the sides and that's what you should do, too."

She turned. "I don't need to go no further. I can see it's gone." She seemed to study the space for a while, as if the sofa might magically reappear. "Now, who would up and steal an old thing like that?"

Suddenly I realized what they must be talking about. "What color was that sofa—and was it small? A love seat, maybe?"

Floretta was staring beyond Tom, but the light was so poor, it was difficult to see. "It was brown. Ugly old brown and not worth the space it took up." She turned to me. "And yes. How did you know it was a love seat?"

"I don't know. I was just asking." This was Tom and Candace's area to explore, not mine.

"I kept it 'cause the cat liked it," Wilbur said. "Pretty little thing, she was. She loved that old couch. That one wasn't like the others. At one time that baby musta been someone's house cat. She'd sneak inside any time you weren't careful enough goin' in and out of the house."

"A cat stayed in here?" I glanced at Tom, who'd stopped sweeping the flashlight and was listening to this conversation.

"Yup. That's my Wilbur. Keeps a sofa 'cause a cat liked it, a cat who'd probably steal the breath from his lungs if she could." But the smile she directed at her husband was a loving one.

"What do you mean by *stealing his breath*?" I asked.

"Cat was a thief. Hauled stuff here like she owned it—but what cat needs a pair of socks or a scarf?" Floretta laughed and then stopped abruptly and squinted, seemed to be pondering something. "You know, I ain't seen that cat since about the time you left, Wilbur."

Tom finally spoke. "And when exactly was that?"

"Saturday last. I come back yesterday," Wilbur said.

"You haven't seen the cat in four days?" I asked.

"Nope." Floretta nodded, sure of this. "She may have been sweet, but she sure did like to collect trash. I figured she'd found some way to get in that donation box 'cross the road. Course, a few times, I did catch her tryin' to steal from our house when she snuck in. Had one of my bedroom slippers once, don't you know?"

And yes, that would be Magpie. But what sent a chill up my neck to tingle my scalp was the realization that perhaps Rhett Marner died here—in this garage—and the lone witness besides the killer was our new family member, Magpie.

Tom shone his light where Wilbur and Floretta said the sofa belonged. I caught a glimpse of a small pile of what looked like the kinds of things Magpie collected— a small teddy bear, a pencil—but that was about all I could identify for certain before Tom spoke.

"Folks, I'm truly sorry, but you'll have to leave the garage. I'm getting my forensic officer over here. Do you know Deputy Carson, Mrs. Strickland?"

"I do, but I know her mama better. We go to the same church." She punched Wilbur's arm. "The same one he should be attendin.' But what the holy-oh-heck is happenin' here, Mr. Tom Stewart? Are you really a policeman? 'Cause I never seen you before today."

"I guarantee you I am an officer, ma'am. Now, if y'all would go back in the house, I'd appreciate it." He was ready to make the call to Candace.

"All right," Wilbur said. "Not that I like it one bit. Floretta's right. We need to know what's goin' on."

"I understand." Tom walked toward us, as if to hurry us along. "I promise to fill you in when I have all the facts. Just know that your truck and your missing sofa are important to an ongoing investigation."

Floretta, sharp as a tack, it would seem, came back with "Is this about Rhett Marner dying? 'Cause that's the only thing I know of that's happened in this town and is important enough to have you here tellin' us what to do."

Tom nodded indulgently. "This is frustrating, I know. You've been so helpful and I want to thank you for that."

"Come on, Floretta." Wilbur tugged her hand. "Let's go to the house. We'll find out soon enough."

I hung back for a second and when they were gone I said, "Should I tell them anything?"

"Probably not yet. But I'm betting Mrs. Strickland would tell you all about this nephew Bo with a little prompting."

"Shouldn't you or Candace be the ones to bring that up?"

Tom closed his eyes. "Sorry. You're absolutely right." I got a peck on the cheek before he told me to keep them in the house if at all possible until he could get Candace here.

Turned out, however, that Bo Strickland might have been the apple of his aunt's eye, but his uncle? Not so much. When I walked in the back door after a cursory knock, Wilbur was shaking his finger at Floretta.

"You coddle that boy and now look what he's gone and done. Got us all involved in something we shouldn't even know about."

The two of them didn't seem to notice I was standing in the kitchen with them.

"He didn't come to me for the truck, Wilbur. Never asked me for the keys." Floretta's high cheekbones bore red circles of heat.

"Then how'd he get them keys?" Wilbur shot back.

She looked at her scuffed house shoes. "I may have left 'em in the garage."

"Oh, ain't that fine and dandy? You knew he'd come here the minute I rolled out of town."

I cleared my throat.

They both turned and embarrassment sent a flush from Wilbur's neck to his skull. "You heard all that. And I hope you heard what she went and done."

"I—I didn't hear much at all—and I'm sorry for intruding. I can't leave until Deputy Carson gets here, though." I supposed I could. But something told me I should stay. "Sounds like Mrs. Strickland had good intentions, though."

"You've heard about the road to hell, right?" Wilbur directed this at Floretta, but when tears filled her eyes, her husband melted. He clutched her to him and told her he was sorry.

I breathed a sigh of relief. These two reminded me of the way my grandparents interacted. They would speak their mind, but they always ended up comforting each other at the end of the day. And thinking of my grandparents gave me a start. "Oh no," I muttered.

Floretta looked at me. "What's wrong, Miss Jillian? You okay?"

"I forgot something I needed to do. Excuse me while I make a phone call." I stepped out onto the porch where the signal was likely to be the best and called Martha's home number. I apologized for forgetting to pick up my dress as promised.

"Just as long as you don't forget to marry that man, it's all fine. The dress is at the shop and you can pick it up tomorrow."

We said good-bye and I disconnected just as I caught headlights sweep the landscape to my left. Candace must be here. I stepped out into the early-evening air so thick with cool humidity my skin felt clammy. I walked around to the front of the house to catch her before she made it to the front door.

"This place is where the sofa came from?" she whispered. "What's the connection to Rhett Marner?"

"I don't know. We did learn the nephew's name—Bo Strickland. And get this. Mr. Strickland kept that sofa for Magpie. The kitty used to hang out here when she was scouring the surrounding area for treasure."

"So we have a definite connection even without DNA. But I've never heard of a Bo Strickland. He hasn't been in our jail that I know of. But I'm about to get to know him, that's for sure."

She seemed energized by this lead and perhaps this would put thoughts of Mike's death aside for at least a little while.

"Is it okay for me to leave now? I don't think I want to be here when you start putting crime scene tape up around the Stricklands' garage."

"Are they being difficult?" Candace asked.

"No. But they're understandably concerned. And I don't think they're used to any attention from the police. They're nice people, Candace."

"And I'll be as nice as I am capable of being back to them. But this hasn't exactly been the finest day of my life."

"I'll introduce you to Floretta."

After they let Candace inside, I said good-bye and Floretta gave me a bear hug, saying how proud she was to have met me. I was embarrassed and said I was the one lucky enough to have met such a kind couple so willing to welcome strangers into their home.

Then I drove home to join the kitties and the two special young folks staying with me. I wanted to comfort both Candace and Tom, but there would be little chance for that right away. They would be far too busy. Instead I'd been offering solace to Zoe Marner and wasn't sure

I'd done one bit of good there. And what was Lydia's real purpose in showing up at Zoe's house? She made people come to her office to fill out forms. She didn't hand-deliver them. And was the autopsy even done yet so the death certificates could be issued? I doubted it. One thing I didn't doubt was where Magpie had been before Finn adopted her. How I wished she could talk.

# Eighteen

When I was feeling down, there was nothing better than coming home to fur friends who greeted me at the door with enthusiasm and of course the expectation that treats would be doled out immediately. But it was also nice to find Finn and Lindsey sitting at the dining room table, apparently having a conversation. They both said hello as I tossed lots of treats on the floor. Even Magpie, who'd been hesitant about treats at first, gobbled up as many as she could.

"You were gone a long time," Finn said.

"Yes. Things got a little more complicated after you left. But I'm home now and I'm hungry. What about you two? Pizza okay?"

"Sure. Will Dad be home soon?"

I cocked my head, smiled at him. "Your dad probably won't be here or going home at all tonight. Could you call in a pizza order? Then I'll fill you in on what's gone on today."

After hanging up my coat and bag, I joined them at the table, but I was having a hard time containing the emotions filling me after the events of the day.

Lindsey's expression turned to concern and then she became guarded. "Is this about my father? Or is it something just between you and Finn? Because I can leave the room."

"There's no reason to leave and it's about the friend who passed—the one I mentioned before," I reassured her.

"What friend?" Finn's voice was leaden with dread. "Who are you talking about? Is it Gramps? Did something happen to him and—"

"Sorry. I didn't mean to scare you. Mike Baca died this morning."

Finn sat back in the chair, his surprise evident. "But wasn't he something like forty? That's young."

"Doesn't matter how old he was. He died suddenly and I can't say anything more. There's an investigation. They're calling it a *serious incident*."

"An accident? What? Tell me Jillian. You know we have history and I liked that guy."

When Finn first came to town, he'd spent a little time at Mercy PD explaining his unexpected arrival after crashing Tom's car.

I said, "What you need to know right now is that the mayor asked Tom to take over as interim police chief. That means he'll be awfully busy."

"Okay," Finn said. "That's about the only thing you've said that makes perfect sense. That's why he went with Candace to check out that truck."

"Exactly," I replied. "He planned to tell you, but it's

been a tough time for everyone—first Lindsey and her family. And now Mike's death leaving so many unanswered questions."

Lindsey slumped back in her chair and she spoke in a monotone. "Chief Baca talked to me yesterday, asked me questions about my daddy. He's always been so nice, but I was a total idiot. Practically cursed him out." She looked across at me. "I can't say I'm sorry now. Can't say I'm sorry to my daddy, either. I don't deserve to be treated so nice by you two when I've been such a bitch to everyone in my life."

"I understand, Lindsey," I said. "There's no need to apologize to us."

Finn piped in, too. "I wouldn't want to help you if I didn't think you were a decent person. But you don't believe it's true. I was that way. I blamed everything bad that happened in my life on myself. Jillian and my dad helped me trust again, helped me like myself. You'll rock it one day. Totally rock the planet."

A few tears escaped and she quickly wiped them away. She had a faraway look that I didn't quite understand. Maybe Mike's death reminded her that she'd lost her dad forever. That's a hard thing to understand at age nineteen.

The food arrived and we all must have been ravenous because we ate in silence, totally focused on the pizza and the side of hot wings Finn added to the order. Lindsey and Finn drank sweet tea, but I expected to have trouble sleeping as it was, so I couldn't risk another load of caffeine.

We played with the cats for a while and sure enough,

Magpie was a total toy hog. No wonder she'd stolen them all and taken them to Finn's room. Syrah was peeved that she tried to catch the mouse on a string before the others and after that, pushed him out of the way to get to the red laser dot first. We all needed the light moments the cats offered.

When the cats tired of playing—and it was always they and not I who decided when it was over—we all sat in the living room. An awkward silence filled the space. What was there to talk about except two men dying? Nothing seemed important compared to that.

But then the sound of the back door opening let us all breathe easily again. We needed another distraction, and this time it was Tom.

"Dad?" Finn stood. "Jillian told us you wouldn't be here tonight. And that you have a new job."

The dark circles accenting his blue eyes told me the man was exhausted and the sadness he must be feeling seemed to be breaking through in his drawn face and slumped shoulders. "Glad she told you. Listen, I can't stay long. I just wanted to ask Lindsey a few questions. Is that all right?"

"I guess," she replied. "I told Mr. Baca—I mean the police chief—all I knew, but . . . well, maybe he didn't record it or take notes?"

"He did record it. It's not about that. I figure you're about the same age as Bo Strickland."

"No way. He's four years older than me."

"Okay." Tom plopped down on the sofa next to me. "But you recognize his name, so you do know him."

"Know *of* him. Mercy only has three schools—for the

small, the medium and the large kids. We ran into each other at times, maybe during my first year in high school, but we were never friends."

"What's this about, Dad?"

"The truck. I have to speak to this guy Bo about it, but before I do that, I was hoping to get some info about him. I hate going into interviews cold."

"The truck belongs to him?" Finn asked.

"Can't answer that right now. Just trying to get a bead on this man—who I thought was a kid."

"What kind of info are you looking for?" Lindsey asked. She seemed intrigued.

"Who he hangs with. What kind of guy he is. Did you ever hear about him getting into any trouble?"

"No, but I don't hear much about anyone from my high school days. My friends have all gone to college— you know, the big expensive ones with their parents footing the bill. My gossip grapevine dried up when they left." A bitter edge had returned to her voice. It might take a long time for her to react less defensively, find the truly sweet girl who resided beneath her hard shell.

"Sorry. Just thought you might know something. Gotta get back to work." Tom kissed my cheek.

But Lindsey apparently wasn't satisfied with Tom's explanation about a random guy she might have known. She was too smart for that. "If this has to do with my father, I have a right to know."

"No, you really don't, Lindsey," Tom said wearily. "I'm still investigating and if you want me to be honest, I believe you're holding back. Kids don't get as angry as you are without good reason. Why aren't you at one of those expensive schools in a sorority and partying every weekend at football games? What's going on with your brother? He's a wreck since you took off. He cares about you and yet you left your home to stay here."

She stood, fists at her side, her back stiff, anger making a poor attempt to disguise the fear I saw in her eyes. "You want me to go home? Is that what this is about?"

Tom stood so that now he was above her. "No. In fact, I don't think you should go anywhere near your house right now. You can be yourself with Jillian." He glanced down at me. "She brings out the best in people and, Lindsey, you have plenty of the best."

His words punctured Lindsey's bubble of protection. She sat down, deflated. "I'm sorry for giving you attitude. I'm so sorry about the police chief. And I'm sorry about Seth. I'll talk to him tomorrow after my classes. It's my busiest day."

Tom was on an emotional roller coaster and he took a deep breath before saying, "Like I said, you need distance from your mother and her busy life right now. Go to school as usual. Call your brother, though. Keep in touch."

His patience might just run out if he stayed here any longer. Here he was, bending over backward to help a girl who was obviously wearing on him. That was Tom being Tom and another reason I loved him so much.

He turned to leave and I followed him to the back door. What did he know about Lindsey that I didn't? What did he know about Rebecca? Were they suspects in Rhett Marner's death?

He hugged me when we reached the back door, but we were interrupted when Magpie appeared out of nowhere, crawled up his pant leg and leapt onto his shoulder.

"What the hey?" He went to pet her, but she quickly stole the pen from his shirt pocket and was off and running.

He grinned. "That cat is hilarious. Good thing Mercy PD has no shortage of pens."

After he left, I rejoined Finn and Lindsey.

Her first words once I sat down were "I'm a selfish idiot. Poor Seth has been left to deal with Mom alone. That's a cruel thing to do to anyone, much less my own brother."

I wanted to agree with her but decided Lindsey had perfected her skill at hiding behind a facade. She'd learned from a master, after all—her mother. Plus, she didn't need another hit to her self-esteem even though I did believe she was being a tad selfish.

I said, "This will all be resolved soon. Tom and Candace will find out who killed your father."

"My dad is the best person to do this, Lindsey," Finn said. "You have to trust him."

"Why was he asking about Bo Strickland? What's he got to do with this?"

She was looking to me for answers I couldn't offer right now. "Maybe he worked for your father?" That was the only diversion I could come up with.

"You think? Daddy and I never talked much about his work." Her expression became more intense. "Did Bo kill my father, Jillian?"

I closed my eyes briefly, trying to think my way out of revealing anything about the truck, the blood, and any of the other evidence connected to this case. It was giving me a headache.

I felt two front paws touching my leg and glanced down

to see Chablis's sweet face and blue eyes. She jumped into my lap, sensing I needed a little help right now. I scratched between her ears and she began to purr. "I'm not sure the police have any idea who killed your father. But then, they don't share everything with me."

"Nice try." Lindsey got up and abruptly left the room, her "good night" tossed out over her shoulder.

"She's used to drama, I think," Finn said in a low voice.

"Oh, don't you know it. I've met her mother."

# Nineteen

Lindsey was gone when I awoke the next morning, but she'd left a small overnight bag on the neatly made guest room bed. She and Finn must have picked up a few things at her house yesterday, because she'd had nothing with her when she first arrived. That bag meant that for now, at least, she wasn't returning home and I felt relieved. As Tom had said last night, home wasn't a good place for her right now.

When I got to the kitchen, Finn confirmed she would be back later on. "I fixed her breakfast and while we were eating, she said she feels super guilty about the way she acted last night and for leaving her brother to deal with her mom. I haven't met Mrs. Marner, but she sounds like she could own a few flying monkeys."

I doled out four dishes of wet cat food while my fur friends surrounded my ankles like sharks circling in the water. I said, "Rebecca's not that bad. Well, almost. Her priorities aren't where they should be, that's all. A flawed human. Imagine that."

I washed the fishy smell off my hands once all the critters were chowing down.

Sitting at the breakfast bar next to Finn, I put an arm around his shoulder and pulled him to me. "You're a great friend to Lindsey. You should be proud of yourself."

He grinned, but the smile faded quickly. "Will Dad be okay? He didn't say anything about the chief dying. He's got to be feeling awful."

"Tom is the strongest person I know. This has been a terrible blow, but he's determined the best way to honor his friend is to find out who killed him." I wanted to grab the words back as soon as they left my mouth because nothing got past Finn.

Finn pulled back, staring at me in silence for a few seconds. "He was murdered, too? Wow." More silence before he said, "I'll pretend I don't know, because obviously Dad doesn't want me to—but this is huge. No wonder he looked like he could be a cast member in *The Walking Dead* last night."

"Tom's pretty shaken. By the way, remember not to ask me to keep any secrets. My mouth tends to spit out what my brain is focused on. Let's change the subject. What are your plans for today?"

"I wanted to stop by the Swap Shop and visit Gramps. He said he'd keep Yoshi until Magpie is more settled, but I miss that little guy. Think I could catch a ride?"

"Sure. I have an errand to run in town anyway." I wouldn't forget to pick up my dress again, but I felt ashamed for even thinking about the wedding. I needed to talk to Tom about a delay, but I was certain that no matter what turmoil swirled around us, he would want us to go ahead — because that was what Mike would have wanted, too.

Once I had an apple and some yogurt under my belt, we took off. The first stop, however, was Belle's Beans. The morning was still chilly despite the sunny skies, and a latte was in order. The place was crowded this morning, but sweaters and jackets must have provided a sort of insulation. It seemed extra quiet.

Finn had taken a liking to coffee since going to college, and as we waited in line, I saw a *Mercy Messenger* lying on a table nearby. Looking at it, I realized the front-page headline might have more to do with the hushed atmosphere than gearing up for a cold day.

It read Police Chief Dies Unexpectedly.

Mike had been well liked and respected. Losing a good man like him in a small town would of course send ripples of sadness through the whole community.

The line moved slowly, perhaps because the Belle of the Day was someone I'd never seen before. When it was our turn, I smiled and said, "You're new here. I'm Jillian and this is Finn."

"What can I get you?" She wasn't the friendliest of baristas, something that could get her fired if the actual Belle saw her being borderline surly. She looked about my age, mid-forties, with weary eyes and a beaten-down presence. Her demeanor struck me as odd in this setting because Belle always hired cheerful types, be they old or young, male or female. She said the face that greets customers is the one that should keep them wanting to return. This lady did not fit the bill.

I gave her our order, paid and stepped aside to wait. As she made our lattes, I asked her what her real name was.

"Lucy," came her curt reply.

Maybe Lucy was another reason why Belle's place seemed so subdued this morning.

We left not long after, but before we reached my van, Belle came hurrying up the sidewalk and nearly ran right into us.

She offered one of her famous smiles—and since she was wearing her glasses, her lipstick was directly on her lips where it should be. "How's she doing? Because she's new and wasn't supposed to be alone, but one of my other Belles is sick, so—"

"She's fine. Seemed to know what she was doing," Finn piped in. He took my coffee and said he'd wait in the van.

I was guessing he feared I might say something less than pleasant about Lucy—which of course I would never do. I hadn't even said anything to him, but he knew me well enough to guess what I'd been thinking about the woman.

Belle glanced at the door to her shop. "I know she's not as . . . *perky* as maybe she should be. But she's got a little girl to raise and really needed the job."

"She's doing amazing, Belle. I'd be pulling out every strand of hair if you asked me to make a half-soy double-shot anything."

Belle laughed and then grew serious. "What exactly happened to Mike? No one seems to know."

I couldn't lie to Belle but couldn't tell her anything, either. "I don't want to spread rumors. I'm sure the police will give a statement soon."

She put her hands on both sides of my face. "I heard Tom took over for him and I know how hard this must be for all of you, especially Candace. Us folks don't need knowing what we shouldn't be knowing." She hugged me and said she had to get inside to help Lucy. How I wished the world was filled with people as wise and wonderful as Belle Lowry.

Knowing Ed wasn't a fan of "fancy coffee" as he called it, we hadn't brought him any. He usually had his own pot brewing early in the back room. Yoshi was so excited to see Finn that he nearly knocked Finn's coffee out of his hands. I took the take-out cup from him so Yoshi could jump into Finn's arms and kiss him.

"Sad thing about Mike," Ed said, gesturing me back toward the little kitchen area.

"I'm taking Yoshi out to play with his Frisbee," Finn called.

"Good. Dog needs to run off some of that energy," Ed said.

We sat at a small round table in what had once been the kitchen of this crowded little house Ed had turned into a shop. Ed's mug of coffee was steaming and he took a tentative sip. Mine had cooled down enough that I could have slugged the whole thing down, and I was tempted, since I was that much in need of caffeine. As expected, I'd spent a fitful night.

"You know about any arrangements for Mike yet?" Ed asked.

"I don't even think the autopsy has been done yet, so no. I understand there's just a sister and she doesn't live in town."

"Suppose the county morgue is backed up what with

two deaths right out of Mercy in as many days and who knows how many are comin' in from other places. Seems like Rhett Marner finally crossed the wrong person."

"You knew him?" I was tempted to tell him about the sofa, how it was connected to Rhett, but I couldn't.

"There's a word for men like him—quarrelsome. Always had to be right. Always had to argue about every little thing. Rubbed some folks the wrong way and then one of them just rubbed him right off the face of the earth."

"You know his family?" I asked.

"Know his boy Seth the best. He comes in here every now and then lookin' for fishin' gear. He's an odd one, but I like him. What teenage boy goes fishing alone? So I took him out on Mercy Lake a couple times, taught him a few things. He was polite and grateful, but a quiet kid. Sensitive type. Reminds me a little of Finn."

"That's so kind of you to take the time with him, but I'm not surprised."

"Any excuse to go fishin'." He offered a wry smile. "Rhett left his first family for the younger woman and you know kids suffer 'cause of that sometimes. Especially boys. A boy needs his daddy to show him the way."

"Are you saying he had an affair with Zoe before he divorced his first wife?" I was almost finished with my coffee and decided to warm it with some from Ed's pot.

"He sure did. She worked out on his site trailers and in his office. Did the books, kept track of equipment, paid the bills. Nice enough herself, but she has those two hellions. Used to come in here with them to look for video games. Maybe the good Lord decided her boys needed a daddy more than Seth and the older girl did. Don't seem right, though."

I sat back down. "Did you know the girl, too?"

"I did. Leslie, maybe? No, that's not right."

"It's Lindsey," I said.

"Yup, Lindsey." He tapped an arthritic finger on the table. "Smart as a whip, that one."

"You seem to know them pretty well, Ed."

"Guess I know more than I thought. In this business, I see everyone at one time or another. Miss Rebecca was always callin' me to haul stuff from her house to sell here in my shop. She never donates the most expensive stuff to the charity store. She likes cash in hand—even though she never got near enough for whatever I took on consignment. She's one of those ladies who has to 'change things up' about every year. New tables, new chairs, new rugs. If I had room in my truck, she'd ask me to take the shabbier things to that charity store she's all involved with."

"Did you know her even before the divorce?" I asked.

"No, right after. That's when she decided to redecorate her big, old house—and it seems like she can't help herself, 'cause every year like clockwork it's out with the old and in with the new."

"When was the divorce again?" He'd piqued my interest, that's for sure.

"Maybe five or six years ago. You know, I remember one time, I came back to give her consignment money for a table I sold of hers—maybe five hundred bucks. Anyways, she had some babysitter livin' there with Seth. She said Miss Rebecca had to take Lindsey to a special school. Told me Miss Rebecca would be stayin' in a nearby rental for a couple of months while the girl got what she needed. The sitter for Seth was old Mrs. Handler, good friend of

Tom's mom. Mrs. Handler blamed the whole special-school thing on the divorce. Said it tore Lindsey up."

"I'm sure you're right." So the scars that Lindsey covered with sarcasm and rude behavior dated back that long. Why should I be surprised? "What about Seth? How did he do?"

"That's about the time I started takin' him fishin.' He never went with his dad anymore. No better time to get a boy talkin' about how he feels than when he has a fishing pole in hand."

"And did he say how he felt?" I was beginning to feel a buzz from the high-octane coffee Ed liked to make.

"He was worried about his sister. Said she was mad about stuff. And the last time I spoke with Seth — maybe six weeks ago he come in here for a lure I'd called him about — he told me it ain't got no better. The girl was mad at the world."

"I know her — in fact, she's Finn's friend — and Seth is spot-on. She *is* mad at the world. But now I understand her a little better. So thank you."

"With Mike's passin' so sudden, you still marrying in a few days? 'Cause I can't wait to see you two hitched."

"I should have mentioned this the minute I walked in. With Mike dying suddenly, Tom took the police chief position — just an interim thing. Rhett's murder has to be solved, too, so the mayor thought someone should step in immediately. The wedding could be put off." I hadn't let the truth slip out about Mike's death this time, thank goodness.

"Oh, Karen and me know all about the police chief job. Tom came rushing over with Dashiell last night so Karen could care for the cat. He said he'd be way busy the next few days and you already had a houseful of cats, but Dashiell needs his insulin on time. Karen will take good care of him." Ed leaned closer. "She'd keep that tabby if Tom would let her. Loves him almost as much as she loves me." He laughed and I joined him.

Karen loving a cat was a good thing. She and Ed were such special people. I was so glad that I would officially become part of their family soon.

Finn and I took off after about fifteen minutes, once Ed and his unofficial grandson spent a little time talking. Finn's last visit to the Swap Shop had been cut short after we removed Magpie from the bloody sofa.

After Finn came back inside with a panting Yoshi, we all agreed the little dog missed Finn. Dashiell's blood sugar might spike from the stress of being anxious because Tom wasn't around. Dashiell was certainly used to Yoshi, but under these circumstances, the dog's high energy level sure wouldn't help Dashiell stay as calm as he should. We agreed to pick Yoshi up later today at Karen's house. Though Ed loved that dog almost as much as Finn did, it was time for Yoshi to get acclimated to a house full of cats. We'd have to ease Dashiell into his new living situation once Tom and I were married and he moved in.

At Finn's request, I dropped him off at the community college. He hoped to meet Lindsey when she had a break between classes. I was beginning to believe those two might become more than friends. Finn would sure be a great influence on Lindsey. He'd been through plenty living with his mother and could help Lindsey.

I arrived to pick up my dress after taking Finn to the college and found Martha teaching a quilting class, so I had to wait a few minutes for her to finish. In the meantime, I texted Tom and asked if he wanted me to bring lunch for what were probably some very tired and hungry police officers. I suggested sub sandwiches like the ones we'd had the other night, and he texted back that it would be great if I had time to pick several up. I had plenty of time and a little information on Rhett that he might want to hear.

Twenty minutes later I stood staring into the full-length mirror in Martha's office. She told me she'd brought it from home. The creamy satin felt soft against my skin. The long sleeves had old-fashioned loops for a finger on each hand and using them pulled the sleeves down perfectly. The back of the dress mirrored the front and I realized I would have to wear a special bra, since the one I now wore showed beneath my shoulder blades—and it wasn't a pretty sight.

The small train might be difficult to manage, but its curving flow behind me had me picturing my grandmother walking down the aisle to greet her groom, my dear grandpa. My eyes filled. How I wished they were here to see me honoring their marriage by wearing this dress—because that really was what this was all about: love that lasted forever.

"Don't you go spilling tears on this dress, Jillian." She handed me a tissue from her skirt pocket. "Had a feeling you'd get a little emotional when you saw yourself, so I brought some clean tissues along. It's a beautiful dress and you'll make a beautiful bride."

I dabbed at the corners of my eyes. "I have something old and something borrowed wrapped in one package."

Martha smiled and began examining the seams, the

hooks in the back, the seams at the hips. "Seems right to me."

"It's perfect. How much do I owe you?"

"You don't owe me a red cent. This was my privilege."

Once I took off the dress, Martha carefully folded it into its large box. We both were aware that plastic bags or boxes were not good for fabric—especially old fabric. The chemicals in plastic disintegrated the fibers, and I didn't want that to happen.

Though rain was in the forecast, I was grateful the true cold front we expected hadn't arrived yet. The dress made it safely to the back of my van and I was off to the sub shop, mentally calculating how many sandwiches to buy. There was a small fridge in the break room at the police station, and anything left over wouldn't go to waste, so it was actually a mental calculation to occupy my mind. But it couldn't erase how selfish I felt getting ready for a wedding while Mercy was preparing for two funerals.

# Twenty

When I walked into the police station with my grocery-size bag of sub sandwiches and gallon jug of tea, the place felt different. I understood Mike was gone, but until that moment, the loss hadn't totally sunk in. He was no longer down the hall in his office. Someone had taken him away from the people who cared about him. Their resolve to find his killer was something I now completely understood.

B.J., sitting at his desk close to the door, cleared his throat. "Jillian? You okay?"

I'd been so taken by the change in the place that I'd forgotten to say hello. "Hey there, B.J. I brought sandwiches."

"Great. Go on down to the break room."

"I hardly ever see you leave your desk. Promise me you'll take time to eat?"

"I'll try."

This wasn't the animated B.J. I knew, but then probably everyone here was doing their best to act normal and carry on while struggling to make sense of Mike's death.

As I walked down the hall, I heard the familiar sound of Tom's voice behind a closed office door. Not Mike's office, though. His door was open and flowers, cards, trays of cookies, pumpkin breads, stuffed animals and more sat on his big desk. All this was to help out a grieving police force. The town had loved and respected Mike, and they wanted to show how much they cared for those left behind.

I turned into the break room and saw Candace with her head resting on folded arms at the table. How long could everyone go without sleep?

I put the sandwiches and tea in the center of the table.

When I rested a hand on Candace's back, she lifted her head and mumbled, "Just a little catnap."

"You need more than a nap. Everyone must be exhausted."

She blinked away the fatigue and stretched. "First forty-eight is no lie. You gotta get a break with whodunits and—"

"And we just got one. No, two." It was Tom, standing in the door, holding two pieces of printer paper.

Candace tucked loose hair behind her ears. "Ballistics?"

Tom nodded. "As soon as the pathologist removed the bullet from—from *Mike*, they compared it like you suggested to the bullet you found in that sofa and *bingo*." He shook the two reports and uttered a ferocious "Yes."

"Didn't the sofa bullet have Rhett's blood on it?"

Candace nodded. "It sure did. But now they need to compare the gun that was in Mike's hand to Rhett's bullet so we've got all our ducks in a row for a future murder trial."

"They're doing it now, but this connects the two deaths. Now we know why Mike had that gun in his dead hand." Tom nodded, glancing between Candace and me.

"You're saying someone tried to frame Mike for Rhett's murder?" I said.

"You bet they did," Candace said. "Mike supposedly kills Rhett and then commits suicide. Does this murdering turd believe we fell off the stupid truck?"

Tom came to the table and sat, pulled a sandwich out of the bag. Candace followed his lead, hunting for her favorite—the kind I'd been sure to include in the order.

After Tom took a giant bite of a turkey club, he said, "Now we can start asking questions. Why *him*? Why Mike?"

"That's what's been driving me crazy." Candace unwrapped her buffalo chicken sandwich with the bleu cheese dressing she loved. "Why this victim? Why did he have to die? Why now?"

Tom gestured her way with his sub. "Exactly."

"Since Lois knew Mike the least amount of time, I asked her to look into his personal stuff. I know you asked me to do it, Tom, but I couldn't. It felt like I was prying."

"That's fine," Tom replied. "I shouldn't have asked you. Glad someone is thinking straight around here. Lois is good at her job. She'll get what we need."

I contemplated what they said and knew there had to be a reason someone wanted Mike dead. What was it? What would the investigation uncover? I had a bad feeling about this.

Candace, whose sandwich was already half-gone, stopped eating for a second. "Preliminary tox screen done yet?"

"Oh yes. Another lead to follow and I'll take this one. Small amount of alcohol, big dose of flunitrazepam."

"Huh? What the heck is that?" I said.

Candace said, "You might know it by its other name. Rohypnol."

I blinked a few times, stunned. "The date-rape drug? Wow. Surely the person who killed Mike would know you'd find it in his system."

"Only if we looked for it," Candace said. "The killer assumed this would be ruled a suicide and probably no autopsy would be done. See, that's why we had Lydia come to the scene—even though it was the last call I wanted to make. A coroner can rule that no *living person* caused the death and therefore no autopsy is required. That's the law in South Carolina. Lydia took the evidence about Mike always using his right hand to shoot straight to her boss, and the cause of death was ruled homicide immediately and an autopsy ordered."

"I had no idea the coroner held so much power. And he's not even a doctor, is he?"

"Not in our county," Tom said. "Elected, remember?"

"I forgot. Despite all those election billboards I pass on the highway to Greenville."

Tom grinned and it was so good to see his smile. "Aren't you older than me? Does that explain the memory malfunction?"

"By six months. Doesn't count."

Lois, looking less tired than her colleagues, appeared in the door of the break room. "Not much on Mike that I can find. He did eat out a lot and from the credit card bills I've looked at, he wasn't eating alone. Or he had one huge appetite."

Tom looked at me. "You want to go out to dinner tonight?"

"What? You need to work and—oh, I get it. We're headed to wherever Mike ate, right?"

"Lois, if you get me a list of those restaurants Mike went to, I'd appreciate it."

"You got it, sir." She disappeared before I could tell her to grab a sandwich.

Tom mumbled, "I'm not a *sir*. I don't ever want to be called sir." The intensity was back, the pain in his eyes evident. Tom was just helping out here, determined to find a friend's murderer. He didn't want to be their boss during this difficult time. He simply wanted to lead them in the right direction.

Candace said, "Can I go out to dinner, too? And give you the bill?"

"I think everyone should go out to dinner. Let's make that happen. Spread out to different places and talk to people who might have seen Mike and any dinner companions. Show the wait staff and hosts or hostesses a picture of Mike and maybe we can get a description of who he was with."

I stood. Time for me to—oh, wait. I came here with a little history concerning Rhett Marner's family. Ed knew plenty about the Rebecca Marner family and I had to share it. I summarized what I'd learned about Seth, Lindsey and Rebecca and said, "That divorce seems like it was pretty traumatic for the kids. So why are Rebecca and Zoe so buddy-buddy?"

"Same social circle?" Candace was hunting in the bag

for another sandwich. This time she chose a Philly cheesesteak and grabbed a cup from the counter for some of the Milo's Sweet Tea I'd brought. Almost as good as what I made. *Almost.*

I considered Candace's hypothesis. "Could be the reason. Maybe the two women wanted to avoid any awkward tension when they're around other people. It certainly wasn't to avoid inflicting any further pain on Lindsey and probably Seth, too. She doesn't even seem to care that the girl is staying with us."

"Good line of inquiry," Tom said. "How do Rebecca and Zoe truly feel about each other? Maybe the ladies who volunteer at the charity store have thoughts on that. I know we won't get the truth out of the other kids."

"What other kids?" I asked.

Candace said, "Toby and Owen. Everything is a joke to them, even their stepfather's death. Of course, I don't think there was any love lost between them and Rhett from what I could tell after interviewing them."

"And then there's Lindsey," I said. "What do you make Lindsey being sent to a special school?"

Tom looked at me. "What kind of special school are teenage girls sent to?"

"Oh." My brain really must be on overload. "Why didn't I think of that? She got pregnant."

"Exactly," Candace said. "Might be worth following up on, but I don't see how a pregnancy from five years ago could be related to our murders. You've been getting to know Lindsey. Why not just ask her?"

"Are you kidding?" I paused, knowing I sounded way too protective. "Talking to her should be as gentle as possible. The girl has her guard up all the time. If she gets upset, she'll shut down."

Tom put a hand over mine, the one now clutched tightly around a napkin. "You have the finest set of kid gloves I know. Why not handle her with those?"

"I—I can't. Her trust in everyone is so tenuous and I've worked hard to try and be a friend to her. If she believes for a second that I'm probing into her past— and that means judging her—she'll clam up completely."

Tom's voice was calm. "Take your time and if you don't feel comfortable asking her about this, then don't. Like Candace said, it could be a lead, but we have a lot more pressing clues to pursue. Bo Strickland alibied out, however. He was at defensive driving school, and then he and his mother went out of town after a cousin died. So he didn't take the truck. Seems like he's in the clear."

Candace wiped a napkin across her mouth and sat back in her chair. "I thought we might have something when we found out about his love for borrowing that truck. I've been interviewing laborers since early this morning. Zoe Marner seems to be the only person on this earth who cared about Rhett."

"Lindsey cares," I said. "But she's conflicted, doesn't know what to do with her grief."

Candace balled up her two sandwich wrappers and threw them at the wastebasket. They landed inches shy. "After my talk with Seth, I'm thinking he cared, too, but that kid is a mess. The person he cares about the most is his sister and she abandoned him. Even so, he's not angry. He's worried about her."

"She promised to talk to him today. She's consumed

with school and I'm guessing she uses her studies as a shield, just like she uses sarcasm and hostility. Her head is down and she's plowing forward, not wanting any help."

"If anyone can get to her, it's you," Tom said. "But you might be opening a Pandora's box. She's held in a secret for a long time—and for a reason."

"Shame. Guilt. Those are gigantic issues for adolescents. I mean, she was *fourteen* when she went to that school if my math is accurate." Though Finn could talk to her about anything else, a pregnancy might be more in my wheelhouse. I paused and realized this might not be her truth. "You *are* speculating about a pregnancy, though. You don't have any records or anything, right?"

I was met with two skeptical stares.

"Okay. Maybe I'm being naive. And it's time for me to leave so you can get back to solving these murders." I stood. "Please make sure everyone knows about the sandwiches. Especially my good friend Morris. Y'all need to feed your minds and come up with answers."

Candace rose, too. "Morris went to the bank with a subpoena so we can look at records for the construction business as well as the families. And I'm expecting a guy to come in for a second interview right about now. Marner fired him only a couple days before our victim went missing. His first interview did not go well. The guy was still pissed and said he was glad Marner was dead. Doesn't he know you don't say that kind of stuff to the police?"

Once Candace left the room, Tom took me in his arms and hugged me tightly. "Thanks for coming here. You made this day easier to handle. And don't forget we'll be eating out tonight. Where, I don't know yet. I'll text you with the time and place so you'll know the details."

As I left the courthouse, Candace's words stayed with me. How could this man she was about to interview be glad someone died violently? But I was being a Pollyanna. Some people did feel that way about their family or coworkers. Candace had drilled into me that most folks know their killer, that they are often related. Mike probably knew his murderer, too. He'd been drugged and you have to get up close and personal to drug your victim.

As I was driving away, I noticed the new barista walking down the sidewalk. Her shift must be over. Beside her, holding the woman's hand, was a child who looked to be four or five years old. What was the lady's name again? Lucy. Maybe they needed a ride.

I pulled over and rolled down the window. "Hi, Lucy. Remember me?"

She stopped. "What do you want?"

"You look tired. Can I give you a lift somewhere?"

"No, thanks." She started walking, but the little girl didn't move and tugged at her mother's hand.

"It's a long way, Mommy. Can we get an ice cream first?"

Lucy crouched and talked to her daughter, something I couldn't hear. The result was a full-blown, fall-down-on-the-sidewalk tantrum.

I pulled to the curb, got out of the car and approached them, but stopped a few feet away as the child continued to wail and kick.

Lucy stood watching her, looking helpless.

I said, "I don't mind a crying little girl. Pick her up and let me take you wherever you need to go."

Lucy didn't refuse this time. She glanced my way and said, "Only because I don't want someone to think I abused my child and that's why she's acting like this."

She swept her daughter up while I used the remote to open the side door of my van. I stood back as Lucy strapped in the suddenly calm girl. She was so cute, with big brown eyes and long lashes. Even her pouty little mouth was endearing. No booster seat, of course, but these two needed help and I figured the car seat police were all rather busy. I'd get these two safely to their destination.

On the drive to a neighborhood not far from Ed's Swap Shop, I learned the little girl's name was Amelia and their last name was Rucker. Lucy wasn't as irritable as she'd been once we were on our way. She apologized for her attitude saying she was simply exhausted. They'd only moved here from Charleston a week and a half ago. Amelia wasn't sleeping well and that meant Mom wasn't, either.

Turned out they would have had a considerable walk. Lucy lived in a tiny clapboard home that looked pretty darn old. Since Amelia had fallen asleep within seconds of her being belted into the backseat, Lucy carried her while I took her bag, found her keys and unlocked the front door.

Lucy whispered, "Please come in. And excuse the mess."

The house seemed dark, probably because of the paneling and deep brown wooden floors. Boxes were stacked in one corner of the small living room, and a leather sofa faced a flat-screen TV. There was no other furniture if you eliminated the pile of toys to my left. It included a play kitchen set and small table and chairs for tea parties. An American Girl doll in a pink faux leopard print outfit sat in one of the chairs. Nice stuff in a tiny, musty old house with a parent who worked a job that didn't pay well. The contradictions confused me.

Lucy returned to the room after putting Amelia down. "I don't have anything to offer you besides water, and that seems like a meager thank-you. I hope to get a car soon and we won't have to walk so far. Not much public transportation in this town."

"I'm glad you accepted a ride. Amelia needed it and so did you."

"It's been a difficult few months. My husband died suddenly. Heart attack, they said. He just dropped dead at work."

"We have a lot in common." I swallowed down the lump in my throat that almost kept me from speaking. "The same thing happened to my husband about six years ago." Here was another person in mourning. And this dank, gloomy house surely made things worse for the poor woman.

"I'm sorry." She rubbed away her tears so quickly and with such force I could feel her resentment at being robbed of someone she loved. I knew the feeling only too well.

"Do you have family here?"

She hesitated. After seeming to struggle to find what should have been an easy answer, she said, "No, not really."

"I'm asking too many questions. Forgive me." But I still wondered why she'd moved here at such a difficult time.

She replied to my unspoken question by saying, "It's less expensive to live here than in Charleston."

"You chose a good place to relocate, then. Belle is a fine woman and she'll help you any way she can."

"She's been wonderful. And so are you. Thank you again for helping us out. I'm just a little overwhelmed right now."

"With good reason, but you—" My phone rang. I glanced at the caller ID and saw it was Finn. I let it go to voice mail so I could offer a polite good-bye. I'd forgotten all about picking him up so we could get Yoshi. "Anyway, we're glad to have you in Mercy. Take care."

She thanked me again and I was glad to breathe fresh air when I left the house.

# Twenty-one

The first thing Yoshi did when we arrived back at my house was race around the backyard that sloped down to Mercy Lake. He acted as if he'd just gotten out of jail. Finn and I watched from the deck and had a good laugh. I needed a laugh after all I'd heard and seen today.

But as I disarmed the alarm and we entered the house, thoughts of Mike took their sobering toll again. I felt guilty for laughing, for enjoying a moment—and then banished that guilt by reasoning with myself. Remembering his life was far more important than selfish reflection on my own emotions.

Finn held Yoshi in his arms as we entered. It wasn't as if I could sit down and have a talk with the cats about how the dog was coming to stay with them again, and they had to be on their best behavior.

But as soon as Yoshi saw Syrah and Chablis sitting in their usual spot waiting for me to greet them, he squirmed loose and leapt out of Finn's arms. He jumped over the cats and ran like a wild animal around the kitchen island, out into the other room and then back.

Syrah's ruff stood on end, but Chablis couldn't have cared less. She was waiting on treats first and she'd worry about the dog later. Yoshi stopped abruptly in front of Syrah, front paws down, butt in the air. It's the play position for dogs, and Syrah was having none of it. He offered Yoshi an openmouthed hiss. But Chablis seemed to think Yoshi might be the bearer of treats so she arched her back and rubbed up against him. This sent Yoshi off running again.

"Let the chaos begin," I said.

Finn was watching all this with amusement. "I think Ed was putting energy drinks in his water."

I smiled. "No. He's simply happy to be back with you."

Syrah retreated to sulk on the windowsill, but Chablis readily accepted a couple of treats. But even the rattle of the treat jar didn't bring Merlot and Magpie out from wherever they were at the moment. I pulled out my phone and checked the cameras while Finn refilled the water bowl Yoshi had just sloppily emptied.

What I saw on the camera feed in my craft room made my heart sink and I hurried to stop what was going on in there. One wall had a set of open shelving where I kept my fabrics folded and sorted by color group. Either Magpie or Merlot had pulled down fat quarters, and what had been neatly folded yards of fabric. They were all mixed together on the floor like a circular crazy quilt. Merlot, looking quite proud of himself, was curled up in the middle of the bed he'd made—no doubt with the mischievous Magpie's help.

But where was Merlot's partner in crime?

I checked the camera feeds on my phone again. I didn't see her, and the bedrooms had no cameras. I started toward my room at the end of the hall, but the guest room door was open and there she was, sitting on the bed. Somehow she'd gotten Lindsey's bag open and the second she saw me, she grabbed a few items and took off. This girl was more than a little shrewd, not to mention fast.

I followed her toward the living room, expecting her to make a run for the basement, where she kept her stash, but a dog in her path stopped her dead. She looked at Yoshi, standing next to the breakfast bar blocking the way into the kitchen and the basement door. She glanced up at me and decided I was the safer option. But this time, I was ready for her. Before she could get by me, I scooped her up.

She continued to hold on to her latest steals, so I took them from her mouth—a sock and a tiny little leather folding object—maybe for a driver's license or ID card?

Magpie squirmed free and ran down the hall toward the bedroom, probably to join Merlot in their freshly made bed of fabric.

Finn was grinning from ear to ear as he came toward me. "What did she find this time?"

I looked down at the small wallet. "Could be Lindsey's ID. Shouldn't she have this with her?"

"Let's find out." Finn grabbed it before I could protest.

He appeared confused after he opened it and said, "Oh. A baby picture. Weird." Then he turned it to show me. "Guess I'll return this to her room."

"Wait." A flutter in my stomach gave me pause. I wanted a closer look, but this belonged to Lindsey. It was her business.

"What's going on, Jillian?"

But I did look closer. And I was right about what I'd seen. "I recognize this picture."

He telegraphed more confusion by staring at me as if I'd lost my mind. "What are you talking about? Did you see the same picture at her house?"

"I was never *in* her house, Finn. But I did see this same picture inside that locket. And this baby looks familiar."

He stared at the tiny face for a few seconds. "That's because the baby looks like Lindsey. It's her. Same chin."

"As of right now, I can't explain why this bothers me, but it does."

"She's got her baby picture. It means something to her." He closed his eyes. "Uh-oh. The locket. The blood. Her father's blood, right?"

"That's part of it, yes. And what young person carries around her baby picture, Finn?"

"You're right. So I'll ask her." Finn closed the picture holder and started toward the hall to replace what Magpie had stolen.

"Let me talk to Candace about this first, okay?" I sounded as if I was pleading—and maybe I was.

"She didn't do anything to her father, Jillian." He sounded upset as he left the room.

"I'm not saying she did," I called after him. How I wished I could share what I knew. But that was Lindsey's secret to keep or to share.

Finn took Yoshi to his basement bedroom and after

about thirty minutes he came back upstairs carrying Magpie. Yoshi was at his heels. Finn hugged me and said we were "cool" and he was sorry for being a little *argumentative*, as he put it. But I heard no promise that he wouldn't talk to Lindsey about the picture and I wasn't about to bring it up again. Finn would do what he thought was right.

Tom picked me up at six p.m. wearing a freshly ironed blue shirt and a tie under a beige cardigan.

"You look . . . preppy, Dad." Finn then looked at what I'd chosen, wool slacks and a sweater. "You two going to a frat party or something?"

Tom petted the exuberant Yoshi as well as the cat crew. "We *are* preppy. And yes, that's exactly where we're going."

"Then be home by midnight and no pot smoking." Finn offered a droll grin.

Earlier in the day, he'd texted me the name of the place we were going, Hagerty's. Once in the car, I told him that from what I'd seen from pictures of the restaurant online, he could lose the tie.

"Really? Because from the credit card statement I saw, Mike dropped a small fortune at this place. I figured it was fancy enough to pull the tie out of mothballs."

"It's a nice place when you're used to pizza and Main Street Diner fare, but the customers I saw in the online pics weren't all that dressed up and the ad line read 'Casual Dining and Award-Winning Chef.'"

"Best news I've had all day. Loosen this thing for me, would you?" He pulled at the tie. "I hate ties. What are they for, anyway?"

I wiggled at the knot while he kept his eyes on the

road. "The male equivalent of panty hose, maybe? No, panty hose are far worse. And don't get me started on Spanx."

"What are Spanx? Sounds intriguing." He grinned.

"You don't need to know." I freed him from the tie and we continued on for almost an hour to Jones Hill, a more upscale town than Mercy and on the way to Columbia.

Hagerty's Restaurant welcomed diners with a pleasant and dim atmosphere. I smelled good things like fresh bread and grilled fish the minute the hostess greeted us. After seating us, she gave us menus and handed Tom the wine list. "Nora is your server this evening and she'll be right with you."

She turned to leave us, but Tom stopped her with a "Pardon me, ma'am."

"Yes, sir?" The hostess couldn't have been more than twenty, with dark waves framing her ebony face. She was stunningly beautiful and certainly not of the "ma'am" age yet—but this *was* South Carolina.

Tom had his phone already opened to a picture of himself and Mike together taken at our engagement celebration this past summer.

"Has the man in this picture ever been in here that you can recall?" Tom widened the picture to make Mike's face bigger.

She stared at the photo and shook her head. "I don't remember him, sir." She started to leave but turned back, her curiosity getting the better of her. "May I ask why you want to know?"

Tom pulled his sweater aside to reveal the badge on his belt—his brand-new shiny gold shield.

The hostess's mouth formed a circle and she said, "Oh," followed by "Anything else I can help you with?"

Tom thanked her and she hurried away, but I had the feeling that word would travel through this place about the cop sitting near the window as fast as Yoshi could lick a dish.

I, for one, was not here to work, so I took the wine list from Tom, who was paying absolutely no attention to it. He was scanning the room. On the job. I wondered if he knew something about the people working here that I didn't.

"To honor one of the smartest cats I know, I'll have a glass of the house wine—which happens to be Syrah. What about you?"

"Can't drink tonight."

I sighed. "That's right. Well, once we're married, we need to come back for a date night. We will have date nights, you know."

I had his attention then. "Yes, we will." He smiled. "My guess is, you've had thoughts about postponing the wedding because of all that's happened this week. Don't even go there. We will be at that church and you'll be my wife in a couple days. We've waited too long already. Mike would curse me out from heaven if I said we were too busy solving murders to take time out for what will be the best day of my life. But it's a good thing we're waiting until spring for our honeymoon. That might well have gotten lost in this murderous shuffle." He reached across the table, palms open, and I put my hands in his.

"It promises to be the best day of my life, too. Besides, who am I to argue with a man wearing a badge?" I said. "And when did you get that, by the way?"

"The mayor came and swore me in right after you left the station. Got the badge then."

Nora arrived at our table with a basket of warm bread and little sculpted pieces of pale butter on a china plate. She looked thirty-something, with tied-back tawny hair and a small starched white apron over her black clothes. After we'd placed our orders, Tom showed her the photo.

"May I?" She gestured toward the phone and he handed it to her.

She moved the phone under the Tiffany lamp above our table. "Was he a police officer, too? Because you seem to be friends with him."

I was right. Everyone knew a cop was here.

Tom said, "He was police. Have you seen him?"

"I have. Mr. Baca, I believe. Very nice man."

Tom smiled, a smile that lit his eyes and diluted the dark circles of fatigue beneath them. "Was he alone?"

"Never." She returned Tom's smile and hers was a knowing one. "I don't want to get anyone in trouble, so if—"

"Mr. Baca—*Police Chief Baca*—is dead. You can't get him in more trouble than that. Do you know who he was with? Or did he come here with more than one person at different times? See, we know from his credit card statements this was a favorite place for him to dine."

She glanced around, lowered her voice. "It was always the same woman. But I don't remember him saying her name while I was at the table, so I can't help you with that."

"But you can describe her." Tom didn't state this as a question. He expected she would know, and she did. She gave a very detailed description.

I was left reeling because I knew exactly who she was talking about. Tom kept his reaction to himself until she left to get our drinks. I would need that glass of wine and I was sure Tom wished he could share it with me, because the person Nora had just described was Rebecca Marner.

# Twenty-two

Once we were on our way home, stuffed with bread, delicious fish grilled to perfection and a shared sliver of cheesecake, Tom said, "I never would have put Rebecca and Mike together. Okay, maybe I would, but why the heck didn't she show up and ask what happened to him once the story broke that he died?"

"I'm not surprised. The word *narcissist* comes to mind when I think of her. I mean, she doesn't even seem to care about her own daughter."

"Mike never found the right person. How could such a smart guy make mistake after mistake when it came to women?"

"We all have a story, one that stays with us from childhood to the grave," I said. "It was Mike, it was part of his story and we can't know why he made the choices he did."

Tom glanced at me, his face half illuminated by the blue and white dashboard lights. "You're right. Unfortunately this particular choice might have gotten him killed."

"I guess you'll be bringing her in for more questions right away."

"You bet. This evening, as a matter of fact." The set of his jaw told me anger was setting in. Rebecca Marner had withheld important information—but why? Was she embarrassed about her relationship with Mike or was there a more sinister explanation?

"I'll probably be seeing Lindsey very soon. Should I say anything about what we learned about her mother tonight?"

"I have no idea what Lois, Morris and Candace may have learned when they went to their respective restaurants. What if Mike was seeing a string of women? Maybe Rebecca Marner's involvement with him was just a fling among flings? Her daughter certainly wouldn't want to hear about *that*."

"No, she wouldn't." A thought came to me. "But Lindsey might know something about Mike, might have seen him at her house."

He seemed to consider this. "True. You could ask her, but from what I've heard from you as well as others, that girl is super quick to anger. And even though I understand you've taken her under your wing, remember she's considered a suspect until we can nail down the timeline and see if she has an alibi. See, we don't know exactly when her father died. The stomach contents are our best lead right now—but we have to find out what he ate and when. That line of questioning was derailed by Mike's death. We asked the coroner to get us the complete autopsy report today but they are backed up."

"Tom, that girl did *not* kill her father." I sounded like Finn now. "And you shouldn't spoil memories of a wonderful meal by talking about autopsies and stomach contents. Yuck."

He patted my knee. "Sorry. That's my focus right now, but I'll try to be more sensitive in the future."

"There is something interesting that Magpie showed me today that might be helpful."

"The cat showed you something? *Really*?" I caught his grin.

"Did Candace mention the baby picture in the locket?"

"I vaguely remember she'd bagged the jewelry and photo as evidence."

"Lindsey brought that same picture with her to my house—and she brought so few items it has to be important. Probably her baby, right? Born when she was fourteen?"

"You're accepting the most logical explanation now? That the special school was indeed a *specialty* school for pregnant teenagers."

"Maybe, but gosh, she was so young."

"Trouble is," he said, sounding serious, "if the baby picture was so important to her and a necklace with the same picture ended up in contact with her father's dead body, what do those two things mean? Was she there when he died? Had he been kept in the dark about the pregnancy? Did that lead to an argument? Looks like I'll have to pull her in for another interview sooner than I thought."

"Why bring her to the station? She's probably at my house right now and seems to feel more comfortable with Finn and me present. Talk to her tonight."

He didn't say anything for what seemed like forever, but it was probably more like thirty seconds. "Maybe."

I changed the subject and asked Tom if he'd had time to pack his stuff yet for the big move. He told me no but had decided that since he had no need for his old furniture, he'd donate it to the charity store where Rebecca was in charge. Maybe with the furniture as an excuse he could persuade a volunteer or two to talk about Rebecca and her relationship with Mike Baca.

So much for changing the subject. I told him I was betting the volunteers knew plenty and I'd be happy to head there in the morning on the pretext of seeing what procedures they had for getting furniture from his house to the store. He agreed this might be a good idea, since the workers might be more candid with me than with the new police chief.

After Tom pulled up to the back of my house, he hesitated and stared at Lindsey's car parked near the garage up ahead. "Lindsey might open up if we do talk here. From what I understand, she didn't say much at all when Candace questioned her right after her father's body was found. But it was a very brief conversation. Can't blame the kid for being upset after hearing about her father's death via text message. No matter what, she was already on the list for a more extensive interview."

"Y'all have been so overwhelmed. I don't know how you've accomplished as much as you have."

Tom let us in the back door, saying he was pleased Finn had engaged the alarm and locked up. "Someone murdered two people in town this week—and one of them was Lindsey's father. If she's innocent but knows something she's failed to mention, she could be in danger."

"Who's in danger?" Finn was waiting right there in the kitchen with the cats, ready to greet us.

I sure hoped Finn had only heard the danger part, because he wouldn't have appreciated the "if she's innocent" remark.

Tom smiled, probably thinking the same thing. "I can tell you who's not in danger. *You*. Thank you for locking up the house."

All four cats and the dog became the welcoming committee and it took several minutes for us both to give them all an adequate greeting. Tom then patted his chest and held his arms open. Yoshi jumped up into them.

Lindsey sat curled in one of the big living room chairs, a textbook open on her lap. She smiled briefly and offered a quiet hello.

"I asked her about the baby picture," Finn announced.

Deep down, I knew he would. I just wished he'd waited.

Tom and I sat on the sofa across from her and Finn took a spot on the floor next to Lindsey's feet. He looked both protective and anxious. That body language was all Yoshi needed to join him and rest his head on Finn's crossed leg.

He said, "Lindsey, you want to tell them or do you want me to explain?"

"I can speak for myself." She looked straight at Tom. "I had a baby, gave her up for adoption. End of story." The wall was up, a hostile shield that seemed even more impenetrable than the first time we'd met at her front door.

"Okay." Tom's voice was gentle. "Stuff like that happens. And it's not easy. It's also none of my business—our business really." He gestured at me and then Finn. "What *is* my business is solving your father's murder. A locket was found. That locket has your father's blood on it. I'm told the picture inside is the same as the one you brought with you here."

"So?" She lifted her chin. "That means I killed him, right? Because he had my locket?"

Tom was steady and calm in response to her defensiveness. "Why do you believe your father had this locket?"

The question seemed to throw her off, and a bit of her guard went down in her confusion. "I—I don't know. Because it was found where he probably died—on that sofa Finn told me about?"

Tom glanced at Finn before his next question. "When was the last time you saw the necklace?"

"That's the thing. I lost it. And I have no idea where or when that happened."

Tom nodded. "I believe you. But we need your help, Lindsey. Can you think on this? Try really hard to remember anything about the last time you saw it."

"Like *right now*?"

"No. It's late. You're tired. We're all tired. And this has been a terrible time for you. We need your help, though. Just try to remember. That's all I'm asking."

She nodded, lips pulled in, eyes cast downward. Magpie jumped in her lap and she pulled the cat close. "This little thief obviously wants me to remember, too."

Tom left then, and I was certain he would be calling Rebecca Marner—and maybe a list of other women depending on what Candace, Morris and Lois found out this evening. I sure hoped they'd enjoyed as good a meal as we had. They probably had, since it seemed as though Mike knew where to wine and dine the women in his life. Or *woman*.

"Lindsey?" I said.

She didn't look at me right away, just kept petting the cat.

When she finally met my gaze I apologized. "I am so sorry. Like Tom said, this is your business and you can be certain none of us will share it."

"Can we stop talking about it now?" Her stare skidded away and she seemed as tense as when we first met.

"Absolutely. I'm tired after a night out on the town." I stood. After the baby picture discussion, there was no way I could ask her who her mother was seeing. Besides, Rebecca Marner's history seemed like treacherous territory to explore at any time.

I asked Finn if he'd fed the cats since I'd been gone, and he had. There were no dishes in the sink to take care of, so I grabbed a glass of water and said good night.

Three cats tailed me to my room and began to claim each of their little quilts at the foot of the bed. Magpie already preferred to sleep with Finn. Cats know who they own, I suppose.

As I undressed, I couldn't get that necklace off my mind. I didn't believe for a minute we knew the whole story. Why would an adolescent keep a picture of a child she'd given up for adoption? At that age, especially as young as Lindsey had been, she'd want to forget. But Lindsey was no ordinary girl. At some point in her life she'd been free to share and laugh and be herself, but something had happened. Someone hurt her or threatened her and she'd decided that if you didn't let people in, they couldn't hurt you. She kept secrets and if I knew her whole story, I'd probably know exactly why she felt compelled to keep them locked away inside.

# Twenty-three

The next morning I made the trip to Kara's house on the outskirts of Mercy. Her home was less than a year old and sat on a beautiful, wooded piece of land. She wanted my final approval on the setup and decoration for the wedding reception. Though I told her everything would be perfect because she had great taste and style, she'd insisted I come. Once I was finished at Kara's, the charity store visit was next on my to-do list.

My jaw dropped when I saw that she'd lined the path to the house with containers of pink wild roses. A vined archway studded with more roses framed the front door. If the outside looked like this, I couldn't even imagine what she'd done with the inside of the house.

When she let me in, the glimmer in her eyes and the warmth in her smile turned on the waterworks. Tears spilled down my cheeks—but these were joyful tears. It felt so good to let the emotion flow out of me. I couldn't believe how much trouble she'd gone to and how much beauty she'd created.

Because of her two cats—Pulitzer and Prize—certain things would have to wait until the last minute, Kara explained. Things like huge vases of pale pink peonies, the containers accented by satin ribbon that matched the favors we'd already picked up. She had those closed away in the pantry for now. The staircase, she told me, would have vines and roses wrapped on the railing. But I noticed she'd added lots of small tables everywhere—dark wood with crocheted lace doilies on top and covered by protective glass.

As she started toward the hall leading to the bedrooms and she beckoned me to follow, I asked, "Where did the tables come from? And those beautiful doilies?"

"The caterer had the tables and I bought the glass. Caterer Supply has this huge warehouse full of stuff. I could have spent all day there. Anyway, the crocheted pieces? My mother gave them to me. They were made by my grandmother." Kara's mother would be here in spirit—a woman who died too young and who John had always said would have been happy if he remarried.

"Have you hidden more stuff from the cats?" I asked.

"Oh yes. The stemware and flatware we rented. Got them separately and not from the caterer. It cost less."

"So not only are you the perfect wedding planner, but you find the best deal. I can't thank you enough for—"

"Jillian, stop thanking me. This has been the most fun I've ever had. If the newspaper folds, I have found my calling."

"You know that won't happen. Not in this town. Folks

here do not like to read the newspaper on a computer screen."

The guest room was decorated in shabby chic style. The furnishings included an iron bed, a chenille spread with lots of floral pillows and an antique dresser. That, too, came from Kara's maternal grandmother and always made me feel like saying "I love this" every time I walked in.

Kara shut the door and pointed at several boxes on the floor in the corner.

I knelt and lifted a champagne flute out of one carefully packed box. "These are gorgeous, Kara. But I want to make sure I gave you enough money for all—"

"Oh, please. You gave me plenty."

I smiled. "Just making sure. I'm glad the caterer will be taking care of all the food, because you'll be busy helping me stay focused on the big day. But I have to ask. What would happen if we had to cancel at the last minute?"

"We aren't canceling anything. Tom already called me and said you'd probably be worried. He said to tell you nothing will be postponed or delayed in any way."

"He called you?" I said.

She nodded and sat next to me on the floor. "He knows you, Jillian. I was worried about it, too, what with Mike dying so suddenly and all. But Tom's got this. You found an amazing guy who, it seems, can actually read your mind."

"He is amazing. But I'm still worried he might have to chase a killer down the day of the wedding, and that will take priority—and it should. Have *you* heard anything this morning about the case? Or should I say the cases?"

Kara shook her head. "The deaths have to be connected, right? I mean, two murders in less than a week? What was Mike onto that got him killed?"

I explained about the locket found with Magpie, the one that had Rhett's blood on it. Then I told her about the kitty's other find—the picture Lindsey kept with her, that little wallet with a photo of an infant that looked an awful lot like the girl who was fourteen when she gave birth.

Kara shook her head sadly. "That must be a terrible secret for a kid to have to keep. I guess they won't ask about the baby daddy unless it becomes important to solving the murder."

"Gosh, I never even thought about that. But how could it be important five years later?"

"Depends on who it is," she replied. "What if someone raped Lindsey? And even worse, what if that person was *related* to her?"

"You're talking about Rhett?" I swallowed. It was hard to even consider that a father would do such a despicable thing to his daughter. "You think Lindsey was so angry with her father that she shot him?"

"I don't know, but the fact that the locket was close to the bleeding victim at some point tells me something. And don't think for a minute Tom and Candace aren't thinking the same thing."

My shoulders sagged. I didn't want to believe that Lindsey could ever kill anyone. "Mike probably figured this out somehow. I mean, he was drugged and—"

*"Drugged?"*

"I probably shouldn't have mentioned that." I explained about the Rohypnol.

"Mike was sedated and *then* shot? That sounds too premeditated for a girl not even out of her teens yet, no matter how angry she was. But if Mike figured it out and was about to arrest her, I suppose that's motive."

I shook my head vigorously. "No. This is all too complicated. My gut says there are secrets we don't know about. But Lindsey as some criminal mastermind? I'm not buying it for a second. Her mother is a different story."

"You mean Rebecca Marner, Queen of Mercy Society?" She paused. "And it's a very small kingdom when you think about it. Anyway, that could make sense, Jillian. She finds out what her ex did to her daughter and kills him, then gets worried Mike knew something that would embarrass her and her daughter, so—"

"That doesn't make sense. Rebecca doesn't seem to give a flip about Lindsey. The girl is staying with me at a terrible time in her life—and I'd never met her before this past week."

"Okay, if we remove the whole baby angle, would anyone else in the family hate Rhett enough to murder him? Because it's usually someone close."

"I have no idea. Lindsey says very little about her family. Obviously the whole story hasn't come out yet, so I'm counting on Tom and Candace. Just so you know, Rebecca was seeing Mike. There could be personal issues that we don't know about."

"*What*? Seeing him? As in, like . . . you know?"

"That's what we think." I told her about last night's trip to the restaurant and what Tom had learned from the waitress.

Kara put her hands up by her head and made a gesture with her fingers like I'd just blown her mind.

"I know," I said. "Mike and Rebecca Marner were apparently a couple. It's crazy, but it was his pattern to get involved with difficult women."

"This will make quite a story once all the facts are in. Special edition, here I come." Then she switched gears. "You need to stop focusing on all this and remember you're getting married in a few days. Have fun with it — because I sure am enjoying this week. Did you bring those favors we picked up?"

I nodded and we went out to my van to unload them. The gray skies worried me — there was rain in the forecast — but it was supposed to be clear and sunny on the big day. I hoped those weather people were right.

After we stacked the boxes in the guest room, I wanted a peek at Pulitzer and Prize. They were sleeping on Kara's bed and looked so cute all curled up together. Pulitzer was an orange-and-white boy and Prize was a calico girl. They'd been with Kara since they were babies and I couldn't resist petting them both before I left.

After I hugged Kara good-bye, my next stop was the Charity Thrift Store. I remembered Kara's words and knew she was right — a joyful day loomed in the near future and changes would come. Wonderful changes. I turned the radio to an "oldies" station just in time to hear "Good Vibrations" by the Beach Boys. Funny how some songs just make your heart happy.

By the time I reached the thrift store, the rain started. I grabbed an umbrella from the backseat and noticed the wind had shifted and a wintry chill surrounded me on the walk from my van to the store. It was located in a nearly abandoned strip mall. The only other business was a Chinese restaurant.

I didn't have a jacket with me and my cotton sweater and jeans weren't adequate against the sudden change in temperature after a day that had begun with mild temperatures. I shook my umbrella out before I entered the store. My hands were cold and my feet were wet from the short run to get inside. The place smelled musty despite what I assumed was an air freshener with a tropical scent plugged in somewhere in the store.

*At least my hair is still dry,* I thought, as I closed up the umbrella. When I looked toward the glass display cabinet where the cash register sat, I was surprised to see Zoe Marner standing there. *What in the heck is she doing here? Shouldn't she be . . .* anywhere *but here?*

*Wait. You're judging her, Jillian. That's wrong.* We all deal with grief in our own way. Just because I acted like a cloistered nun for way too long after John died didn't mean everyone reacted the same way. Zoe probably needed to keep busy.

I approached her with a smile, and the wan expression she offered in return tugged at my heart. The joy I'd felt earlier on the drive here evaporated.

"Hi, Jillian." A pile of girls' clothes lay on the counter in front of her—probably recently donated—and she was folding them carefully, her fingers smoothing each wrinkle and crease as best she could. "I'm so glad you stopped by so I could thank you again for spending time with me."

Owen Nesmith appeared from a hallway in the back

of the store carrying a large cardboard box and yelling, "Where do you want this stuff, Mama?"

He was only about twenty feet away, so I wasn't sure why he had to shout.

Her response was to just stare at him with a blank, dull look. But he seemed to understand whatever she meant. He dropped the box and nearly ran into Toby as he left. Toby also carried an overflowing box of clothing.

Toby looked at me and said, "Oh. You again," plopped the box down and turned around to head back down the hallway to what had to be the back entrance. Candace and I had brought the bags from the donation box there the other day—the day that seemed like a hundred years ago.

"I'm sorry about their manners." Her tone was flat, devoid of emotion. "They didn't feel like heading back to school right away, so I asked them to help me out here."

"Good of them. It must be so difficult."

She walked around the counter and hugged me. Even though we'd shared tough emotional issues at her home, the hug she gave felt forced and wooden. I felt so sorry for her and it seemed those two boys of hers would be no source of comfort. But they were teenagers who probably thought they had to be strong and unaffected. I understood.

She pulled away and offered me a weak smile. "Is there anything I can help you with? I understand you're getting married and we do have plenty of 'something olds' here." She made the little joke with a mirthless and flat delivery.

I forced myself to return the smile and asked about the procedure for picking up or delivering furniture. I wondered how much they could handle in the store. There seemed to be room toward the back, since clothing—racks and racks of clothing—took up most of the area in the front. If not for this case, Tom probably would have given the furniture to Ed to dispose of, but delivering it here might offer him insights he wouldn't ordinarily get. He'd be coming as a donator rather than a cop.

"We'll accept anything and if we can get a volunteer to pick it up, we often do that. For some folks it's difficult to deal with heavy items, and a few of the ladies who volunteer have husbands willing to help."

"I'll bet Rhett helped out here at the store—not to mention those boys of yours. They've got plenty of muscle."

She nodded, pressing her thumb and finger on the bridge of her nose. "Yes," was all she seemed able to manage.

I'd wandered into sensitive territory. "Tom and Ed can use Ed's pickup and bring the furniture here themselves. You know Ed, right?"

That seemed to brighten her mood and she smiled. "Everyone knows Ed. Tell them to pull the truck around to the back entrance when they come. Stuff like couches and appliances usually won't fit through the front door."

The boys appeared again, this time carrying an old dresser. They set it down by the boxes.

"Mama? Where?" Toby sounded downright rude. Was this how they always treated their mother? Or was their attitude disguised tension spilling out over losing their stepfather?

"Sorry," I said. "You obviously have work to do. Tom will bring the furniture next week sometime."

I left, thinking, *So much for finding out anything about Rebecca Marner's male friends. I can't ask Zoe. Not right now. She seems so out of it and who can blame her?*

As I opened my damp umbrella under the eaves, I heard a familiar voice.

"Is that you, Jillian?"

I raised the umbrella and saw Rebecca striding through the parking lot toward me. Her son, Seth, was trying to keep up. He was getting soaked, while she wore a belted charcoal raincoat and carried a large red umbrella to protect her ever-perfect hair. It would have been large enough to keep Seth from getting wet, too, if she'd been willing to slow down.

She smiled when she reached me. "Did you come to volunteer?"

Now I felt embarrassed. "Maybe after the wedding," I said quickly. I glanced at Seth as he arrived next to his mother seconds later. I smiled at him. He had a cherub look—pale skin, round cheeks bright from the cold, large brown eyes, the lashes bearing tiny drops of rain.

"Oh, that's right, the wedding." Her features seemed tight, as if she were holding back emotion that might seep through every pore if she didn't stop it. Perhaps she was missing her daughter or her ex-husband after all. Or maybe her reaction had to do with Mike. I still couldn't picture those two together.

Seth said, "Is Lindsey okay?"

*Finally someone who can say straight-out what's on his mind.* When I answered, I looked first at Seth with compassion and then straight into Rebecca's eyes. "She is holding up."

Seth's chin quivered. "Tell her I miss her."

Rebecca glanced at her son and then back at me. "Do you have time for coffee? Maybe we should discuss exactly what my daughter has told you."

"I have time," I said. "Let's go." But I wouldn't be sharing any confidences with Rebecca Marner. Not if I could help it.

"We'll meet you at Belle's place in five minutes. I'll text Zoe and tell her Seth and I will be late to take over for her." She turned and tugged at Seth's elbow. She held on, this time shielding him from the hard, cold rain as they walked back to her SUV.

Five minutes later, I parked in front of Belle's and discovered that the weather front that had so unexpectedly swept into town also swept a lot of folks inside for some coffee.

Rebecca arrived right behind me and pointed with her umbrella toward the back of the café. "Seth, grab that table before someone else does. I'll bring you something to drink."

We stood in line, not speaking until Rebecca insisted on buying my vanilla latte. She bought a double-shot mocha latte and ordered hot chocolate for Seth.

She said, "He's not working nights anymore—all Rhett's construction sites are shut down—and he's trying to sleep regular hours again. No coffee for him."

Her words suggested she was a tad concerned about his welfare, and certainly more than she was with Lindsey's. *Why?*

Soon we headed to where Seth sat alone, voices surrounding us in the crowded café. Guitar music played from the overhead speaker. I took a chair next to Seth, and Rebecca sat across from us. We all put our hands around our cups to warm them. It had gotten really cold outside in a hurry.

"I should have talked with Lindsey," Rebecca said. "I suppose you think I'm a terrible mother. In fact, I'm sure she's even *told* you I'm a terrible mother."

I kept my voice as quiet and even as possible, though I was a little put off that she actually believed that my opinion of her had anything to do with this. "Whatever has upset Lindsey is between you two."

"Come on, Jillian. What exactly has she said?"

Was she wondering about the secret pregnancy or something else? I had no idea and remained silent. Women like Rebecca want to control everything, even conversations. I wasn't about to become a middlewoman between her and her daughter.

Surprisingly Seth spoke up. "Mom can't talk about Dad's murder, Mrs. Hart." His voice held a tremor. "She won't talk about anything. That's why she's focusing on Lindsey."

"Seth." Rebecca's eyes flashed at her son as she practically hissed his name.

"Mom, this lady is helping Lindsey. She can help you, too. Let her."

"Sometimes," I said, "a public place like this is just the right spot to say what's unbearable to think about."

Seth's forearm touched mine, almost like a nudge for me to keep talking.

Rebecca leaned toward me and whispered, "And sometimes a public place is where every word is overheard and passed on." She glanced around. "I had no idea it would be so crowded in here."

"Would talking about the tragic death of the father of your kids be the worst thing that could happen?" I gave a sideways glance in Seth's direction. "You love your children, right?"

"Of course." The tightness around her mouth was beginning to crack, and for the first time I saw that she was actually fighting tears.

"They need you to teach them how to grieve. They don't know how. They *need* their mom."

She shook her head. "No, they don't. No one needs me anymore."

"Her boyfriend apparently needed her, though, and now he's dead, too." Seth said this so matter-of-factly I was at a loss for words. "She hasn't cried about *him*."

Rebecca spoke again, her whisper harsh now. "Seth, you need to *stop talking*. People will hear you."

"Like Mrs. Hart said, would that really be so bad?" His gaze didn't waver from his mother. Could this young man—who couldn't be more than eighteen—be the most mature person sitting at the table?

Rebecca sat back. It was as if someone had touched her with a branding iron, the pain was that evident on her face. She hung her head as if to hide.

"He's talking about Mike, isn't he? You loved him." If Seth could be honest, so could I.

She nodded, not lifting her head. It seemed so strange to see this confident and abrasive woman so vulnerable. "How did you know?"

"That's not important. You need to talk to Tom about

him, about what you know. They have to find out what happened. Candace, Tom, Morris—they all loved Mike, too."

She jerked her head up, and the fire in her eyes had returned. "What I *know*? I don't know anything about what happened to him. And that is extremely difficult to bear."

I believed she was having an *extremely difficult* time. In a gentle tone, I said, "Sometimes you think there's nothing important to share, nothing significant. But that's because you're blinded by grief and denial. You need to go straight to the police station and talk to them. Let them decide what's important. You could have answers they need."

"You know something I don't. I can tell. What is it?" Rebecca asked.

"Talk to the police. Help them and they'll help you."

No one had touched their drinks, but my last sentence seemed to have a calming effect on everyone. Seth picked up his hot chocolate and sipped.

Rebecca put her bag over her shoulder, picked up her umbrella and coffee and stood. "Let's go, Seth. I suppose I have to get this over with now that at least one person in town knows about Mike and me. Probably Lindsey said something—and who knows what else she's told people?"

But Seth balked. "I don't want to step inside that place ever again." He turned to me. "Can you take me to see Lindsey?"

"That is *not* what you need to do, Seth," Rebecca said. "She'll say things you won't want to hear."

Seth smiled. "That's what I'm hoping."

I realized then that Rebecca was afraid Lindsey would tell him about the baby. But how could he not know already?

I rested a hand on Seth's. "I'm not sure if she has class today, so—"

"She doesn't. I texted her on the drive over here. She's at your house right now."

I looked at Rebecca, who in turn was staring at her son. "Go. Talk to her. But I want a full report."

Leaving us sitting there, she stormed out of Belle's Beans, wearing her shield of anger, the same one Lindsey had inherited. But unlike Lindsey, this woman seemed like . . . a *bully*.

"Thanks, Mrs. Hart." Seth's soft voice helped me let go of the confusion and distrust I felt toward his mother.

I smiled. "No problem. Come on. Let's go see your sister."

On the way out, I saw that because of the burgeoning number of customers, Belle had called in extra help. Lucy was busy behind the counter working with the other Belle of the Day. I caught her eye and waved hello, and she smiled briefly in return. I put two ten-dollar bills in the tip jar before we left, one for each of the baristas.

# Twenty-four

Thank goodness the rain had been reduced to just a drizzle, but the cold lingered. I might have a winter rather than an autumn wedding if this kept up.

As soon as we got in my van, I took out my phone. But first I told Seth what I was about to do. "I'm texting Tom—he's the new police chief. I want to tell him that your mom is coming in to talk."

"*If* she shows up," Seth said. "I wouldn't count on it."

"Are you saying she lied about heading over to talk to the police?" Why was I surprised?

"She lies all the time—even to herself. But I couldn't say that in front of her. Then she'd be even more upset with me than she is right now. But I figured the stuff about Chief Baca would come out. The police aren't dumb, even if she thinks they are."

I sighed. "I'm texting him anyway—just in case she does show up." And just in case Tom or Candace wanted to track her down. She'd admitted she and Mike were involved, and they needed any information she could offer.

After I was done with the rather lengthy text, we took off for my house. Seth mentioned how much Lindsey liked all my cats. "She wants to be a doctor, but she said after staying with you, she might want to become a vet. She really likes you, by the way. That's why I figured you were the right person to talk to my mom."

"You and your sister are close, I take it." I recalled how upset he'd been when he feared Lindsey was missing.

"We are. She's not as mean as most people think she is. Neither is my mom. I guess it's complicated."

"You go to school?" I asked.

"No. I didn't get my admission papers in on time. My bad. But I've been accepted to South Carolina starting the end of January."

"And why is Lindsey at community college and not enjoying the big school experience?" I made the turn off Main onto the more rural road that led to the lake.

"She didn't tell you? She missed a year of high school—got sick or something. No one told me what was wrong. I'm pretty much the last person to know anything, and Lindsey won't talk about it. Anyway, her grades went south. She dropped out."

"Wow. I had no idea." But I did have an idea about the "sickness" that kept her out of school.

"When she finally got tired of my mom ordering her around the house like she was the maid, she got her GED. But man, is she bitter about losing out on going to Duke or Clemson. She's sure smart enough to go to those schools."

"You're saying Lindsey's attitude is about missing out on college? Do you truly believe that's why she's so angry all the time, Seth?" I asked.

"I'm not sure. It's this love-hate thing with Mom. We both have it, but she shows it. I keep it inside and smile."

I glanced at him and he *was* smiling.

He went on. "I can see why Lindsey likes you. You're easy to talk to. Just direct and genuine."

"I find that a lot of people have trouble being honest. Lindsey is spending a lot of time with Tom's son, Finn. Tom is Police Chief Stewart now. It's strange calling him that. Anyway, Finn tells it like it is, too, and he's taken Lindsey under his wing. He's helped her more than anyone."

"She told me about him. Says he's pretty cool."

"And smart, like Lindsey. Like you." I glanced at him.

"Thanks, Mrs. Hart. My dad was real smart. But he wasn't a nice guy. I don't want my sister to end up like him or like my mom."

"What's in your future, Seth? What will you major in?"

"I don't know yet. I like to write. It helps me stay even-tempered rather than getting all nasty like Lindsey and my mom."

I nodded. "Yup. You're very smart."

I turned into my driveway and Seth craned his neck in the direction of the lake.

"I'll bet you like living by the water. Do you catch fish for your cats?"

We stopped right behind Lindsey's car and I was recalling how Ed said he'd been fishing with Seth several times. "I never have enjoyed fishing. The hooks, dragging them out of the water—none of it appeals to me. I do like to sit on my dock and watch the fish swim by, though. There's geese, and eagles and a big blue heron that like to hang around here, too."

"Bet that's a good time to be alone and think. Sometimes there's so much noise around me it's hard to think. Fishing helps me."

Lindsey met us at the back door holding Magpie. Once we were inside, she handed the cat to me and hugged her brother tight, murmuring "I'm sorry" over and over.

Seth's silent tears left wet patches on the shoulder of Lindsey's T-shirt.

Meanwhile, my three amigos and Magpie sat waiting for their turn to meet Seth. Seconds later, he and Lindsey were sitting on the floor playing with them. I left them in the kitchen so they could have some private time to talk about their father's death—or at least I hoped that was what they would talk about.

I took out my phone and decided to call Tom rather than text him, since I'd heard nothing back from him about Rebecca.

He answered right away with "We've got her in an interview room. How did you manage this, Wonder Woman?"

"Rebecca needs a friend. Not servants or volunteers she can order around, just a friend. I told her the truth, which is what friends do. I said she should talk to the police and tell them what she knows."

"She's still pretty arrogant, but at least she's here." Tom lowered his voice to a near whisper. "The gun that killed both men was registered to Rhett. I'll ask Rebecca, but maybe you could see if Lindsey or Seth knew where the gun was kept. Rebecca Marner says Seth's with you, right?"

"He's in the other room. Nice kid."

"Anyway, Rhett had a ton of money, two houses, site trailers and an office. Plenty of places to keep a weapon. Now Candace is chasing down a lead on *another* property he might own. Seems he just bought a house, but we're thinking he planned to tear it down and build a strip mall or a parking lot. That's the kind of thing Rhett Marner would do."

"The family money could be motive, right? Do you know who inherits what?" I asked.

"Not yet. Getting our hands on a will that's locked up in a bank—which seems to be the case—is not all that easy. We found that out the last time there was a suspicious death in Mercy. But we'll see who gets what eventually."

"I'll let you get back to work. Seth was certain his mother wouldn't show up to talk to you, and now I can tell him she kept her promise."

I disconnected and Finn stumbled up the stairs sleepy-eyed just as I walked into the kitchen. Yoshi came up the stairs, too, tail wagging, ready to greet everyone.

"Get your twelve hours of sleep in?" I asked.

"I don't sleep much when I'm at school, so last night was heaven." He glanced at Seth and Lindsey. "Hey, man. You Lindsey's brother?"

Seth stood and extended his hand to Finn. They did some kind of handshake that included a half hug and a shoulder bump. Being around young men was certainly an interesting cultural experience and I was pleased they had this neat greeting.

It was a grilled cheese and tomato soup kind of day, so everyone helped fix lunch. Finn had slept right through breakfast and was starving.

Cheese was a cat favorite at my house, and everyone took turns feeding one kitty or another small strings of cooled melted cheese, which they all gobbled up with gusto. Poor Yoshi only got leftover crusts of bread, but he didn't seem to be unhappy.

As we were cleaning up, Finn told Seth how sorry he was about his father's death. I also told him that his mother had shown up at the police station.

"Really?" He nodded his approval. "Glad she proved me wrong."

I decided it was now or never to ask about the gun.

I looked at Lindsey. "Did your father own a gun?"

"Why?"

I knew that expression. Her guard was up.

"He did," Seth answered. "More than one. He kept one at home and had others at his office or the trailers. They had a lot of thefts—tools, copper pipe they dug up doing jobs, wiring, cables and more. My dad fired a lot of guys over stealing stuff like that. Guess he thought he needed protection because some of them left the job pretty upset."

This seemed to surprise Lindsey. "Really?"

"Yeah, really," Seth replied. "Was he killed with his own gun?"

"He was," I said solemnly. "What about your mother?"

"No guns for her." Lindsey looked at her brother. "Unless you know something else I don't."

"She does have one. Keeps it locked up in the bedroom," Seth said.

Lindsey looked shocked. "Whoa. Maybe I've been more absent from my own life than I thought."

"I'll pass this along to the police." Maybe a gun that wasn't where it was supposed to be would be helpful—but it would seem a lot of people had access. Even Seth.

Finn, who hated guns, apparently wanted this discussion to end. He suggested they all have coffee and they took their cups to the small table by the window. Finn and Seth sat in the chairs and Lindsey settled on the window seat. Yoshi curled by Finn's feet. The cats, all except for Magpie, stayed close, hoping for as much attention as they could garner from these people.

Where had Magpie gotten to? My search didn't take long. I found her in my closet in the hamper, ready to steal something, I was sure. But she apparently hadn't taken anything yet. I removed her from my closet and, realizing my wedding dress was still in the box Martha had packed it in so carefully, I panicked. It had to be hung up, something I'd meant to do the minute I brought it home. I couldn't show up in a massively wrinkled dress on the big day.

I shut Magpie out of the closet so I could do this and carefully slid the dress onto its satin-padded hanger. I then carefully opened the door, but only as wide as I needed. Sure enough, Magpie was waiting right at the crack to sneak back in. I thwarted her with my foot, slipped out and quickly shut the door.

This miffed her and she ran out of the bedroom and down the hall, no doubt to find another place where she could pilfer something.

I texted Tom about the guns and then decided I needed a little time alone, since we planned to each write something that we would read at the ceremony. I closed the door to my bedroom, something I hardly ever did, and settled on the bed with pencil and paper. I got lost in the words, in rewriting them so I would say exactly the right thing. I had just finished when someone knocked lightly on the door.

As soon as I answered, four cats raced in as if they were storming the Bastille. A closed door was unheard of, and completely unacceptable. Finn laughed as they all jumped on the bed and began to vie for space to curl up in. It was nap time.

Finn told me Lindsey took Seth home. "She's hoping to talk a bit with her mother, but she's not ready to stay home yet. Can she crash here for another night?"

"Of course. She and Seth are close, aren't they?"

He nodded. "He misses her. But the time she's spent here has helped her think about her situation more clearly. She needed the distance from her mom for a while."

"I'm glad staying here has helped her. Did Lindsey by chance tell you her mother was involved with Mike?"

"She didn't offer it, but Seth brought it up. We've been talking about it for the last half hour. Seth seems to think his mother feels guilty about Chief Baca's death for some reason—but he's sure she didn't hurt anyone. Says she's all bark."

"Seth is a pretty observant young man. Maybe he

should talk to Tom about what he saw and heard between Mike and Rebecca, but that might be difficult. It
could implicate his mother in murder, no matter what he
believes about his mom."

"You think she did it? Killed her ex and then killed
the chief?"

"I don't *want* to believe that, Finn. But I don't think
any of us know what's happened yet."

# Twenty-five

When Shawn called asking Finn to help him out at the shelter a few minutes later, I drove him out there right away. Finn, of course, couldn't have been happier and told me he'd call for a ride or Shawn would drop him off at home later on. When I made the turn onto the main road to go home, I was surprised to see Floretta Strickland walking a collie. I didn't remember seeing a dog the night we'd visited that farm.

I waved at her and was about to continue on my way when I saw her gesture almost frantically for me to stop. Maybe she wanted to chat about quilts again. She seemed like such a nice lady, so I pulled over.

"Can you come in for coffee?" she asked when I rolled down my window. "I'd like to talk to you for a spell."

She had something on her mind and I got the sense it had nothing to do with cat quilts. She seemed worried.

"I'd love to." I opened the side door for her dog and

gestured in the direction of the passenger seat. "Get in, and I'll drive us back to your house."

"But it's been raining and Betsy might mess up your van."

"Nonsense," I said with a laugh. "A dog sat in that very seat not too long ago. Mud is not a problem."

On the short drive I mentioned I hadn't seen Betsy when I'd met her, and she explained that the dog brought the cows in at night, so she hadn't been around the house then.

"Ah, that makes sense. She's a herder."

When we pulled in her circular drive, I noticed her husband's truck wasn't in the carport. "I guess Mr. Strickland isn't home."

"Nope, and that's why this is a perfect time to have a little heart-to-heart about somethin' that's been on my mind. And let me tell you, seein' you on the road was the sign from God I needed."

I opened the back door and Betsy leapt out and raced for the barn.

"She's fast," I said.

"Betsy prefers cows to people. Which I guess isn't so odd. But she prefers them to other dogs, too."

Once in the house, Floretta made a fresh pot of coffee while I sat at her kitchen table. I was intrigued by her desire for what she called a "heart-to-heart." Did she know that perhaps nephew Bo's alibi wasn't quite as tight as he'd apparently claimed when he talked to Tom? Maybe he'd skipped out on that class he was supposed to be attending. In truth I had no idea, and it didn't seem that I'd get an answer soon. She'd begun chattering about how she'd already cut the pieces for a quilt exactly like one of mine.

With coffee, cream and sugar in front of us, as well as a plate of banana bread, Floretta got settled at the table with me. Then she abruptly fell silent, staring at her coffee as she stirred it and clearing her throat several times.

I added cream and sugar to my mug, patiently waiting to hear whatever it was that she felt the need to tell me.

Finally she said, "I was gonna call that new police chief once I got up the courage, but I need to come clean right away and you're my messenger."

*Come clean?* Had this seemingly sweet lady committed a crime? Surely not. "Go on, Floretta. I'm all ears."

"You remember the other night when y'all were here?"

I nodded.

She tapped her mug with her index finger and stared into her coffee. "Seein' as how Wilbur was present, I didn't exactly speak the entire truth. I felt so bad about it that I went to church last night and prayed on it. God spoke to me and said I was wrong and should make it right."

She was obviously nervous and I tried to reassure her. "Whatever it is, I'm sure it'll be fine. Just tell me."

"I *did* consider givin' away that old sofa. Called up the charity store and everything."

"So they came and took it?" *Or did she somehow manage to get it into the truck and drive it there herself?*

She shook her head. "Nope. I left a message with some lady who answered the phone and I told her how I wanted it gone before Wilbur came back in town. She told me they'd come by. But they never did."

"Could they have come while you were out and simply taken it?" I asked.

"I s'pose, but wouldn't they leave a note or sticker on

my door? Besides, I mentioned my bingo night to the woman I spoke to, said not to come by that day since I wouldn't be home. She said she'd give Mrs. Marner the message and that was that."

"Mrs. Marner? You're sure?"

Floretta nodded. "I must say I was shocked when y'all came out and Wilbur called me to the garage and that sofa had gone and disappeared. I thought, 'Have you lost your mind, Floretta? Did they come take it and you just plain forgot?'"

"You don't seem to have a memory problem." I sipped my coffee, staying calm despite the uptick of my heartbeat. I just took in this information, trying to make sense of it. "You didn't want your husband to know you made that call to the charity store, so that's why you didn't mention you'd actually made an effort to have it hauled off. Have I got that right?"

She smiled. "I knew you'd understand. But then I thought God might be angry with me for deceivin' my husband. You have a thought about doin' something you shouldn't and then, bam." She clapped her hands and startled me. "A strange thing like this happens to bite you. I gotta admit I was scared the other night. But now that I've prayed on it, I'm certain somethin' evil happened in our garage. I have to speak about it."

"You did the right thing. But you have no idea when the sofa or the truck disappeared? You didn't hear anything? See anything?"

She shook her head. "I can only think it musta been in the middle of the night. I wear earplugs 'cause a speck of dust droppin' on the floor is enough to wake me. Isn't this sofa business the strangest thing, Miss Jillian?"

I had to agree, but the connection to the charity store bothered me. This could be important and Tom and Candace needed to know. "Would you feel comfortable talking to one of the officers about this?"

"I'd be happy to talk to Candace. Remember, I'm friends with her mama. I know that child."

I wasn't sure if this was something Floretta needed to report in person, but it was important. A phone call would be the quickest way to get this information to the police, and Candace could decide if Floretta should make a formal statement. I pressed Candace's speed dial and thank goodness she answered.

"Hey there, Jillian. I'm super busy with—"

"Candace, I'm with Mrs. Strickland and she has something to tell you. Can I put her on?"

"Where *are* you?" Candace sounded confused.

"At her place. I'll explain later." I handed the phone to Floretta.

She repeated everything she'd said to me, answered a few questions, asked about Candace's mama and then abruptly shoved the phone back to me.

"Candace, you there?" I said.

"Writing it all down as we speak. She says she didn't recognize the voice of the person she spoke to. Could have been anyone who volunteers at that store. It doesn't mean this involves them—the message Floretta left could have been forgotten. But I'll be getting a list of those folks who answered the phone in the last week and a half. We'll see if Rebecca ever got this message—or perhaps she took the message and didn't want Floretta to know who she was speaking with."

She disconnected before I could mention that Zoe

Marner could also have taken the call. There were two Mrs. Marners who stayed busy in or around that store, after all.

I said good-bye to Floretta not long after. She seemed brighter, relieved of her burden. As I drove back toward town, I wondered how this new piece of information fit into the puzzle—if it fit at all. This seemed like a case that had too many leads, and most of them pointed nowhere—or everywhere.

I was surprised when, before I reached home, Belle called. Belle hardly ever called me, mostly because I saw her almost every day at Belle's Beans. I switched on the Bluetooth and answered.

"Hey there, Belle," I said.

"Hey there, Jillian. You still got Rebecca's girl staying with you?"

"How did you—oh, I forgot. You know everything that goes on in Mercy." I laughed. "Yes, she needs time to make sense of losing her dad so suddenly and—"

"Listen, I know there's no love lost between Lindsey and her mama and that's why she's with you. They had a set-to right here in my place not two weeks ago. This isn't about that. I'm wondering if she'd like to make a little extra money."

"At Belle's Beans? I thought you just hired Lucy."

"No new baristas needed, but it does involve Lucy. See, she's been bringing that child to work until she's back on her feet—got money troubles—and I've let her girl play in my office, made sure she stays away from the equipment and the customers. But that's not exactly working too well for me. She's a precious child, but I can't get a lick of work done."

"You need a babysitter?"

"Exactly. I'll pay her, but I don't want Lucy to know this minute. If Lindsey agrees, we can say we've got this young woman who's volunteering, loves kids. Could you ask her?"

"She does have classes at the community college and I don't know her schedule—but it can't hurt to ask. If she can't do it, perhaps Seth would be willing to help out."

"Oh. Okay. He's a nice boy, but I wouldn't want that little girl around Rebecca Marner. I'm not sure that would be a good thing."

"Seth could watch Amelia at my house—in fact, I've met Lucy and you could mention I'm the one volunteering to help out. I'll care for the little girl myself, but I'll need backup. See, Tom insists this wedding will happen regardless of what's going on with the murder case and Mike's death."

"I know. That man gets his mind set on something, he will make it happen. That's why I'm trying to recruit young people with enough energy to keep up with a four-year-old." She chuckled. "The child is wearing this grandma out. Lucy agreed to split her shift and come back this evening, so I'm kinda desperate."

"I'll ask for everyone's help—Finn, Seth, Lindsey, anyone—and you mention my name to Lucy."

"Thanks Jillian. You are such a sweetie." She disconnected.

Lindsey as a babysitter? Could she handle being around a child when she seemed so troubled by what had happened to her years ago?

All I could do was ask.

# Twenty-six

When I returned home, I found Lindsey sitting on my dock and staring out at the lake. Now that the wind had subsided, the water was still. A low orange sun peeked from behind charcoal gray clouds. I joined her, sat nearby and said nothing.

A sideways glance revealed the glisten of tears in her eyes and the face of a young woman who felt a pain I could not fathom. We sat in silence for a good five minutes. But that was fine with me. I knew sometimes the quiet can heal.

Finally she spoke. "Thank you."

"No need to thank me. After our first meeting, I told you I liked you."

She looked at me then. "Even though I was pretty darn rude. But I'm thanking you for giving me my power back. You're okay with who I am." She said this with surprise and understanding and warmth in her voice. She'd had an epiphany, it would seem.

I touched the fist resting on the wet wood of the dock and her fingers relaxed. I said, "It's what you deserve. To be yourself."

She nodded. "It was as bad as I thought it would be, seeing my mom. You know, I've never seen my mother cry before—but she was crying today. I believe she liked Mike a lot, but I don't think she ever got over what my dad did to her. I took his side, thought she pushed him into that affair with Zoe. Maybe I was wrong."

"You knew that's why they divorced?" I couldn't keep the surprise out of my voice.

"Oh, for sure. You understand, that's why my mom and Zoe act like such good friends."

"You mean they *aren't*?" I couldn't keep the surprise out of my voice.

"My mom always says 'keep your friends close and your enemies closer' when she talks about Zoe."

*It was all an act? Wow.* And then I wondered if *both* women were pretending—and pretending about more than their friendship, perhaps.

"Here's what I think," I said. "You should never have known why your parents split—at least not back then. It was an adult issue and you weren't an adult yet."

"But I asked her—asked my dad, too. I mean, I was upset."

I put an arm around her. "All kids ask. That doesn't mean the answers have to be the raw truth. 'We can't live together anymore' is sometimes enough."

Lindsey leaned into me, resting her head on my shoulder. "I wish you'd been my mom. Then none of this would have happened."

"That's one of the nicest things anyone's ever said to

me. But you're a great daughter and I hope that you and your mom can find your way back to each other—call a truce at least." But I sure hoped it wasn't in the visiting room at some women's prison.

Rebecca Marner was an enigma. Her public behavior toward Zoe was an outright lie. She manipulated her way into a friendship with a woman she didn't like—no, probably despised. What else was she hiding? Had whatever seethed beneath the surface all these years led her to murder her ex-husband and then kill Mike because he figured it all out? I wasn't sure I wanted to know the answers.

"Let's change the subject," I said. "Belle Lowry—you know Belle, right?"

Lindsey turned to face me and smiled. "Sure. She's pretty awesome."

"She hired this lady who's kind of down on her luck. And the lady has a little girl. To make a long story short, this person—her name is Lucy—needs a babysitter for a couple hours today and maybe on and off for the next couple weeks. I was thinking we could all pitch in to help her out. Belle is willing to pay."

"Who's *we*?"

"You, me, Seth, Finn—it takes a village, right?"

"I can help her out today, no classes for me, but I won't always be available. And I don't need any money. My mom handed over a hundred bucks' worth of guilt cash when I was over there today."

*"Guilt cash?"* I said.

"The money she gives me when she feels guilty—like for not even talking to me after my dad died. She gave me a car after the whole baby thing—even though I couldn't drive yet. So why not one word of sympathy after Daddy was murdered?"

*The whole baby thing?* Lindsey didn't sound like the shamed girl who'd cried the other night. "Why did your mother feel guilty? I mean, it sounds to me like she was more supportive during that time than she usually is. She went with you, stayed nearby, right?"

Lindsey sucked in her upper lip, looked down. "I'm sorry. It was just a tough time. Anyway, I'm sure Seth will be happy to help out with the babysitting job when I can't. It'll give him something to do other than play video games now that he has no job. What's the little girl's name?"

"Amelia." I stood, my jeans damp from sitting on the dock. "I don't know about you, but I could use some warm clothes."

We went to the house together and were greeted by four eager cats and one exuberant dog who'd been cooped up too long. Lindsey offered to take Yoshi out to play ball. I went to my bedroom, and the cats followed me.

They watched me change into jeans and a sweatshirt. I often wondered if what I wore offered them a clue as to what was next on the agenda. Would I stay home? Or would I be leaving again? They seemed satisfied with my choice, because Chablis jumped on the bed to resume the nap I'd probably interrupted. Cats sleep as much as eighteen hours in one day, after all. Silly Magpie attempted to pull my dirty jeans out of the hamper and when that seemed impossible, she jumped on my dresser, grabbed a comb and took off.

I had to laugh, but I knew I might not see that comb in the near future.

Before I called Belle to let her know Lindsey could take care of Amelia this evening, I reaffirmed Lindsey was fine with this arrangement, and she was. She asked if she could pick up Seth and the little girl and bring them here to watch a movie. It sounded like a great idea to me.

"I have nothing planned so—*wait a minute*." I thunked the heel of my hand against my forehead.

Lindsey was standing in the kitchen, a cup of yogurt in one hand. Her spoon stopped halfway to her mouth. "Is something wrong?"

"Is this Thursday?"

"Um, yeah."

I pulled the phone out of my pocket and glanced at the time. "I'm supposed to be at church for the wedding rehearsal in an hour. How could I have forgotten?"

"Duh. Because so much has happened this week. Who wouldn't forget?"

I glanced down at what I'd just changed into. "What should I wear?"

Lindsey smiled. "You wear whatever you want. It's *your* wedding."

A series of texts and phone calls confirmed that this was indeed the rehearsal night. But not everyone could come. Tom, Ed, Karen and Finn would be there. But Candace was running down several leads. She'd try to get to the church if she could, but she said she'd been a bridesmaid many times and wasn't worried at all.

I'd decided on the slacks and sweater I'd worn out to dinner. Meanwhile, I made sure Lindsey had the security and lock codes to the back door before she left to pick up Seth and Amelia. Once I changed, I took off to get Finn from the shelter so we could head to the mill town together. He was waiting outside Shawn's office and thank goodness I'd brought him a change of clothes. He smelled as though he'd been working in a kennel all afternoon, that's for sure.

"Thanks for picking me up, Jillian. I forgot all about this rehearsal thing until Kara texted me."

"Why didn't she text me? I nearly forgot myself."

As if she were telepathic, Kara phoned a few minutes later. "Are you on your way?"

"I am, Wedding Planner. Finn and I will be at the church in a few minutes."

When I mentioned how I'd nearly forgotten, she told me she was sorry she didn't remind me as she'd reminded everyone else. "I thought you'd remember—and yes, I got all caught up in the story for tomorrow's paper."

"What story?"

"Tom asked me to write a piece requesting help from the public. He gave me a couple pictures—one is of that old truck that was used to carry Rhett Marner's body at some point. He's hoping someone will recall seeing it being driven by people other than Bo or Wilbur Strickland."

"What's the other picture?"

"It's this nasty old sofa. He said the body came in contact with that sofa at some point. Maybe someone remembers seeing it being dumped by the donation box. Not many folks travel that road unless they're headed to Shawn's shelter, though. He thinks it's a long shot."

"No, it's a great idea," I said.

Before she disconnected, she said she had to lock up the office and not to start the rehearsal without her.

*I'd like to rehearse the kiss,* I thought. I could sure use a few kisses about now. Nearly forgetting my own wedding rehearsal seemed so unlike me. It made me nervous and by the time I walked into the church, my hands were trembling.

Elizabeth and Pastor Mitch were waiting, but no one else had arrived except Finn and me. Elizabeth offered to show Finn where the restroom was so he could change. When they left the sanctuary, Pastor Mitch came to where I stood in the center aisle and put an arm around my shoulder.

"I've never seen you look so panicky, Jillian. There's nothing to this. It's all quite simple."

His strong arm and kind voice were reassuring, but so many feelings swirled inside that tears threatened. A profound sadness that Mike wouldn't be here combined with the swell of pleasure I felt at finally being so close to marrying Tom made for a confusing mix of emotions.

But when I heard Tom's voice from the vestibule say, "Let's get this party started," I laughed and felt the tension drain away.

He'd picked up Ed and Karen and they all walked toward us down the aisle just as Elizabeth and a cleaned-up Finn came in from the side entrance.

Karen enjoyed her vintage clothing and tonight she wore a green wool suit with a jacket that flared beneath the matching belt. Her skirt was long and straight and she hadn't forgotten her gloves—black gloves with a spatter of rhinestones. I was surprised she wasn't wearing a hat, since she loved hats.

She hugged me tightly and I smelled her cherry-scented shampoo. Her hair had been dyed pitch-black—she'd told me she wanted a new look for autumn and it was definitely eye-catching. The color accented the blue eyes that matched her son's so perfectly.

Ed had even forgone his usual overalls for a pair of khakis and a white shirt buttoned up to his neck. He looked so uncomfortable I felt sorry for him.

He stroked his beard. "Karen says I need to trim this way back for the big day. What do you think, Jillian?"

I smiled. "You look wonderful, Ed. Whatever you want to do is fine."

Karen said, "Don't encourage the man, sweetheart. He needs to look his best walking you down the aisle. Wait until you see the suit I found him."

Ed did not look happy. "I guess if Karen can make me wear this getup, a suit is just one step further to me being the dreamboat she wants."

Finn seemed amused. "You two crack me up."

Kara came running in, out of breath. "I am so sorry to be late. But I think we have a quorum, even without Candace."

Pastor Mitch had Kara's notes and walked us through each step of the ceremony. He showed which scripture he planned to read, and the verse he chose brought new tears to my eyes. Tom put an arm around me and I hugged his waist.

"You will remember to wear waterproof mascara," Kara said. "That's not on your list, but—"

"Mascara? I never wear mascara."

Ed piped in with a grin, "If I have to wear a suit, well . . . you can finish that sentence."

We all laughed and everyone seemed to know their role. Finn was best man and I'd decided that both Karen and Ed would walk me down the aisle and then Karen would take a seat in the front pew. With Mike no longer with us, Ed would not only play father of the bride; he would stand up for Tom beside Finn.

"Candace and I will need escorts down the aisle at the end of the ceremony, after all," Kara told us.

I hugged Tom tighter. "And I will have the best escort of all. Forever."

"Is this where we rehearse the kiss?" Tom didn't wait for an answer—he just pressed his lips to mine. But we were interrupted when we heard Candace's voice echo through the near-empty sanctuary.

"Am I too late?"

I smiled, so happy she could make it despite probably being exhausted. "You are *never* too late."

Pastor Mitch and Kara went over the whole thing again while the rest of us sat in the first pew with Elizabeth. She told us how much she looked forward to Saturday.

She gestured at the cross centered on the wall behind the altar. "I am so sorry for the loss of your good friend Chief Baca. Just know he'll be standing next to God and offering his blessing."

We all nodded, each of us silent, thinking of the Mike we knew and loved. The pastor and Elizabeth left, saying they had a couple arriving for premarital counseling any minute but that we were welcome to stay as long as we wanted.

Though I was certain Candace would be too tired to even drag herself here, her eyes were bright and alert.

She was onto something.

"Can we get something to eat? I'm starving." She was looking at Tom. "Everyone? Anyone? What's a rehearsal without a dinner?"

But Ed and Karen said they were tired and Kara still had to put the paper to bed. She offered to drop Ed and Karen at their house. When the rehearsal day had been changed, we'd decided to skip the dinner part, but now it had been resurrected.

Finn, Tom, Candace and I decided the Main Street Diner was the perfect place to celebrate. But I knew this was about something else. What had she learned? Could she have a solid lead on the killer or killers even without those pictures running in the paper tomorrow?

Finn rode with Candace in the squad car, saying, "I have a need for speed."

He'd sure get it riding with her. I would follow Tom's Prius, but I told him I had to check the cat cam first, so he got in his car and waited for me to have a look. It could also be called a nanny cam tonight.

Sure enough, Lindsey, Amelia and Seth were sitting on my sofa with a bowl of popcorn. Well, Seth had the popcorn. Amelia was holding Chablis, and Lindsey was petting Magpie. I heard Disney-esque music from the TV playing in the background.

Merlot and Syrah weren't anywhere in sight, so I checked another camera and saw them in the foyer. Perhaps bugs had flown inside when the crew arrived; the cats liked to hunt them near the front door. I switched back to see Lindsey staring at Amelia fondly and then she took out her phone. I heard her say, "How about a selfie?"

Amelia's sweet face seemed awfully familiar as she posed with Lindsey. Of course I'd seen her before, but she'd been screaming her head off in a tantrum and the next minute she'd been sound asleep. I hadn't gotten a good look. *Those eyes.* What was it about those big brown eyes?

Tom gave a small honk to hurry me up. I closed the app and we took off, but I couldn't stop thinking about that child.

By the time we reached the diner, Finn and Candace were already seated in a back booth.

"Took you long enough," Candace said.

Tom nodded at me as I slid across from the two of them, saying, "Someone needed to check on her fur friends — and that takes priority."

"Not just on them. Lindsey and Seth are over at my place babysitting."

Candace appeared confused. "Babysitting your cats? Since when — "

"No, an actual real miniature human being," Finn explained.

"Pretty soon you'll need zoning reassignment as a group home, Jillian," Candace said with a laugh. "Is Seth staying with you, too?"

"No, but he's helping out with the little girl — a four-year-old. He'll be doing some of the babysitting until this lady gets on her feet. Maybe you've met her. She's working at Belle's."

Candace sat back and I recognized her wary *cop look* immediately. "Are you talking about Lucy Rucker?"

"Yes. She has a little girl named Amelia. But don't tell me she's some kind of con woman or — "

"No. Not that." Candace looked at Tom. "This ties in with what I wanted to tell you and why I decided to come to the church. It's a big deal." She glanced between

Finn and me and whispered, "And not for public consumption."

"Go on," Tom said. "You know these two can be trusted with anything and everything."

Just then the waitress arrived to take our order. Once we finished and she left to get our drinks, Candace went on.

"I got the financials for almost everyone, and turns out Rhett has been withdrawing fifteen hundred in cash every month for the last eight months."

"Extortion?" Tom asked.

"My first thought, too," she said. "I checked the post office to see if maybe he'd rented a PO box for a dead drop. You get the feds involved in extortion and it's serious business. But Sally—you know her, worked behind that counter at the post office for years?"

Tom and I both nodded.

"Anyway, she told me Rhett's been sending something certified mail to Charleston every month like clockwork. She said she'd need a subpoena to tell us who but thought I should know."

"How quick can we get one?" Tom said. "Tomorrow, I hope, because the weekend is coming up and I have certain plans that—"

"Hang on. I'm not finished, Chief."

All of us were completely focused on what she had to say and hardly noticed when our drinks arrived, but all of a sudden I was sipping sweet tea through a straw as I stared at her.

"Remember I told you Rhett bought a house? And we thought it was some kind of investment?"

My mind began to race, my concentration on Candace

diverted. Money going to Charleston and a house that someone *gave* to Lucy . . . her hesitancy when I asked Lucy if she had relatives in town. No wonder Candace was interested in the woman.

And then it dawned on me.

Candace was talking, but I interrupted her. "The eyes. I know where I've seen those eyes."

"Huh?" Candace said.

"What is it, Jilly?" Tom said.

Of course that was when the waitress arrived with our order. Soon plates of burgers, fries and chili dogs sat in front of us, but no one started eating.

As soon as the waitress left, Tom said, "What did you mean when you mentioned seeing those eyes? Whose eyes?"

"Amelia's. I think she's Lindsey's child. She has Seth's eyes and she resembles the baby picture in that locket and the wallet, the picture Lindsey kept with her. Those three are definitely related. Seth is an uncle and he doesn't even know it."

We all sat in stunned silence for a second.

Finally Candace spoke. "Rhett Marner brought his grandchild here to Mercy, to be close to him."

"Exactly." I explained how Lucy's husband had died suddenly, that she had no money. "She and her husband must have been the adoptive parents and Rhett knew who they were. Or maybe the woman reached out to him for help."

"Doesn't matter how she ended up here," Tom said. "What *does* matter is, who else knew about the little girl and the woman Rhett had set up here in town?"

I started thinking out loud. "Rebecca Marner was

with her daughter when the baby was born. Maybe she even arranged the adoption, met with the prospective parents or picked them out herself. She *is* that controlling. She could know Lucy."

Finn was still listening carefully but decided not to let his food get cold. Candace followed suit, dipping about six fries at once into the cup of ketchup on her plate. Even as she took a huge bite, she never took her eyes off me.

She chewed in silence, then said, "I didn't even know you'd met this woman."

"She was a stranger who needed help. I had no idea . . ." I let my words trail off.

Tom picked up his burger. "If Rhett brought his grandchild to town, he was probably about to let the cat out of the bag. Did Rebecca or Lindsey know? Did it set one of them off?"

My heart felt heavy as I considered what this all meant. How could Rhett do that to his daughter? I didn't care about Rebecca, but *Lindsey*? She'd feel so betrayed if Rhett intended to reveal she'd given birth when she was so young. I said, "How can you be sure he planned on telling anyone? Maybe he just needed to help this woman out and get his grandchild close so he could get to know her."

Tom set his burger down and rested a hand on my thigh. "I understand you want to see the best in everyone and I know you've become close to Lindsey—and maybe even begun to understand that . . . *snob* Rebecca Marner. But if Lindsey's mom was present when the baby was born, and even had a hand in finding good adoptive parents, she was bound to run into this woman in town at some point. Rhett knew Rebecca had no interest in protecting her daughter from the pain it would cause if he let the world know about his daughter having a child out of wedlock. Maybe he even told his ex and his daughter he was going to reveal this secret."

"Maybe I'm wrong, but Lindsey would surely have told us if she knew. I mean, she agreed to care for Amelia tonight without hesitation." I looked at Finn. "She would have at least told you, Finn. Right?"

He'd devoured his first chili dog and was about to start on a second one. "She didn't say a thing. I suggest we go home and simply ask her. Or is that a way-too-crazy idea?"

Okay, he was annoyed, probably because both Tom and Candace had insinuated that Lindsey might be involved in murder.

"Actually that's a good idea," Tom said evenly. "But I'd rather do it in a formal interview at the station. Offer her a Miranda warning and tape what she says."

"*Really*? You'd do that?" Finn set down his chili dog and glared at Tom. "She didn't *do* anything, Dad. You don't know her like I do."

"The girl's your friend. I get that. But two men are dead and one of them was my closest friend." Tom's voice cracked and he had to pause for a second. "She may not be guilty of murder, but my gut has been telling me since the minute I met her that Lindsey was holding back. My guess is, she's protecting her mother."

Tom's hand was still on my leg and I put mine over his and squeezed. I said, "Children like Lindsey and Seth, who were put in the middle of family troubles when they were young, can be more protective of their parents than the parents are of them—even when there's bitterness and anger in the mix."

"True. I was like that myself." Finn took a deep breath and looked at Tom. "I'm sorry, Dad. You're probably right. I was out of line."

"Why don't we forget about this for now and enjoy our rehearsal dinner?" He removed his hand and started in on his burger. But Tom wasn't fooling me. I wasn't the only emotional one tonight.

# Twenty-seven

Finn and I headed for home while Candace and Tom went back to the station. From what I overheard Candace whisper to Tom on the way out of the diner, the autopsy report on Rhett had finally offered an approximate time of death and it was days before he'd been reported missing. Tom didn't bother keeping it a secret that he wanted to look over the information Candace had just gathered. They needed to firm up the timeline of both crimes.

When Finn and I arrived home, Seth met us at the back door, finger to his lips for us to be quiet. Amelia was probably sleeping. We tiptoed into the kitchen where cats were certainly *not* sleeping. Syrah, Merlot and Magpie were ready for their evening food, and Merlot didn't care about human hand signals to be silent. He followed Finn into the pantry, chirping and trilling like a hungry bird all the way.

I stepped into the living room and what I saw nearly melted my heart. Amelia's head was in Lindsey's lap and

Chablis was sleeping with Amelia's arm around her. I took out my phone and snapped a picture.

"I hate to wake her," Lindsey said softly. "Since her mom's shift isn't over until ten, we still have a little time to let her sleep."

The TV, though muted, was still playing *Frozen* and I wondered if this was the second or third time they'd watched it.

I smiled down at the sleeping child. "Looks like the two of you hit it off."

Lindsey nodded knowingly. "This is a special little girl."

The look she gave Amelia said everything. I was guessing she knew the truth.

Finn touched me on the arm and gestured me into the kitchen. In a low voice he said, "Seth needs to get home. I could take him."

"Sure. You know where my keys are."

They left, Yoshi happy to be included in the car ride. I went back into the living room and sat opposite Lindsey and Amelia. Finn was right. The truth needed to come out, and even though Tom might not like it, I had to say something.

"You know this little girl, don't you, Lindsey? You met her once before."

She looked at me, her eyes filled with tears. "Yes. At least I think so. How did you know?"

"A number of things came together for me tonight. It all makes sense. I should share—"

The doorbell rang.

Confused, I said, "Did Belle offer to pick Amelia up?"

Lindsey shook her head. "I said I'd bring her back to the coffee shop when Mrs. Rucker's shift was finished."

Whoever was at the door rang again and as I stood and turned, I noticed three cats sitting at the foyer entrance, staring at the front door.

Chablis was oblivious. She remained asleep in Amelia's arms.

Through the peephole I was surprised to see both Zoe and Rebecca standing on the stoop. What were they doing here this late?

I opened the door, but the only greeting came from Zoe. Rebecca had this deer-in-the-headlights look. What was going on?

Zoe said, "May we join you, Jillian? When I visited Belle's Beans tonight, Belle rambled on about how benevolent Lindsey and Seth were being, and how generous you were to help care for an employee's child. So I hurried over to Rebecca's house and picked her up. You have a special someone staying here with you this evening, am I right?"

Before I could speak, Zoe shoved Rebecca into the foyer ahead of her and then shut my door.

That was when I saw the gun Zoe had pressed against Rebecca's spine.

"I love your home, Jillian." Zoe glanced at the ceiling and into the living room.

She seemed as if it were the most ordinary thing in the world to come calling while holding another person at gunpoint.

Meanwhile, Lindsey had carefully lifted the still sleeping child's head off her lap and stood. "What are you two doing here? Checking up on me?"

Lindsey obviously couldn't see that her mother had a gun pointed at her. But when she came closer, she squinted at her mother. "Mom? What's wrong?"

"Sh-she's got a gun," Rebecca said. "Get out, Lindsey. Take Amelia with you."

Lindsey's eyes grew wide, but she didn't move. "I'm not going anywhere." She looked at Zoe. "What's wrong with you? There's a little girl here. You could hurt someone."

But I knew then that Zoe already *had* hurt people. This woman was crazy. Absolutely crazy. And Lindsey didn't understand that yet.

I said, "Why don't we all sit down and talk this over? I'm sure—"

"Shut up," Zoe said through clenched teeth. She turned back to Lindsey and smiled again, her eyes almost glazed, staring far off, but her finger oh so steady on that trigger.

My mind raced as I tried to think of a way to distract Zoe without anyone getting hurt, especially that innocent little girl.

Before I could come up with anything—and what was there to do when an unstable person was holding a weapon?—Zoe spoke.

"I came here to take care of business and I suppose sitting would be more comfortable." She pushed the gun harder into Rebecca's back. "Move slowly into the living room. And if you make a false step, so much as a twitch, anyone could take a bullet. *Even her.*" She nodded in Amelia's direction, and thank God the child was still sound asleep and oblivious of what was happening.

My cats had retreated when the door first opened, but now began to creep back out from their various corners to see what was going on. Chablis was awake now, her blue eyes crystal bright, her gaze directly on Zoe. But she didn't move away from the little girl she'd apparently adopted. Instead her coat, puffed out in fear, seemed to almost obscure Amelia from Zoe's prying eyes.

I gestured us all into the living room, the swish of the tassels on Zoe's suede boots eerie, the click of Rebecca's heels on the wooden floor halting, echoing her fear.

Zoe glanced first at me and then at Lindsey. "You two sit where I can see you—and just so you know, I have a very twitchy finger. This gun could go off without warning if you so much as step toward me. Meanwhile, the two of us will just stand here, thank you very much. Isn't that a good idea, Rebecca?"

Rebecca nodded. Her face was drained of color. Her skin bore a thin layer of perspiration. She seemed terrified and I belonged to that awful club, too. We were all terrified—except for Zoe. She seemed as calm as the lake on a quiet morning.

I eased into the chair next to the sofa, and Lindsey sat by Amelia. Her leg jiggled and she clasped her hands in her lap. From the look she gave Zoe—fear and compassion seeming to merge—I felt confused. But Lindsey knew what this was about. Too bad my racing heart and I had no idea.

Zoe stared intently at Amelia. "So much trouble over someone so tiny. Isn't it strange how that can happen?"

Ah. Amelia *was* the focus of Zoe coming here with Rebecca in tow. Why?

I took a deep breath. The why wasn't important right now. Getting this woman to put down the gun was all that mattered.

Taking a page out of Finn's book, I decided on the direct approach. "Zoe, can you tell me what this is about?"

"Your new best friend, Lindsey, hasn't come clean?" Zoe cocked her head and smiled this odd smile. "Oh, she's still keeping Mommy dearest's secret, isn't she?" She glanced at her prisoner. "How do you manage to control everyone so well, Rebecca? I simply don't understand how you do it."

Syrah was sitting at the edge of the foyer, his eyes on Magpie. The little tortie was stealthily moving toward the shiny ornament and tassel on Zoe's boot. My heart skipped. If this woman had no problem killing a human being, she wouldn't blink at shooting a cat.

Then I saw Merlot slinking right behind Magpie.

*No, no, no. Please stop, kitties. This is no game.*

I heard the back door open. It had to be Finn returning. *Oh my gosh, no. Not him, too.*

But cats do love it when their prey is distracted. Magpie struck first, her mouth clamping on to the tassel in an attempt to tear it off Zoe's boot. She then got help from her brute of a boyfriend, Merlot, who leapt onto Zoe's leg and wrapped both paws around her calf.

As Zoe dropped her gaze to the cats, Rebecca's elbow came up and smashed into her chin. Between the blow and the cats wrestling with her, the woman went down.

Yoshi got to them first, just as Finn and I raced to prevent that gun from going off. The little dog grabbed the sleeve of her gun hand and began pulling. Finn called him off and we were on top of Zoe before she could make another move. Finn grabbed her wrist and pulled the gun away while Rebecca and I pinned Zoe down.

She started fighting to free herself, so Rebecca sat on her legs. "Finn, call 9-1-1 and get that gun as far away from here as possible."

I heard Lindsey say, "I already called 9-1-1."

Finn stepped back, but rather than leave us, he unloaded the weapon and put the magazine from the automatic in his pocket. Then he helped restrain Zoe. How did he know how to do that? But his dad had been a cop, after all. Was a cop again. I'm sure gun safety had been part of his parenting when Finn was younger.

Since I faced the still thrashing woman, I said in the calmest voice I could muster, "It's over, Zoe. Stop fighting."

She answered by spitting in my face.

# Twenty-eight

Tom and Candace arrived together, bursting in through the front door with panic in their eyes. But the steel and strength of two trained officers took control once they realized no one was hurt. They took over, cuffed Zoe and raised her to her feet.

That was when I realized that Magpie had her prize. She held the tassel with its little gold attachment in her mouth, and Merlot followed as she took off for the basement, probably to stash it away. As I witnessed this, the relief was immediate and welcome. That little sneak had saved us all from who knows what—and she had absolutely no clue she was a hero. She just wanted that tassel and didn't care how she got it.

Tom and Candace led Zoe to my dining room table, past the still sleeping Amelia. My days of slumber like that were long gone, but I was so glad the little girl hadn't seen or heard anything.

"Lindsey, why don't you take her into your room and put her to bed?"

"Shouldn't I call her mom? It's time for me to pick her up at Belle's Beans and I said I'd give them both a ride home. She'll worry."

I thought about this. The child was sleeping so soundly and I didn't want her to be exposed to what was about to become an interrogation of everyone here. "Just put her to bed. I'll call Belle and make an excuse."

Lindsey nodded and carefully picked up the sleeping child. Rebecca was still sitting on the floor, head down, shoulders shaking. She was crying and with good reason. I sat next to her and put an arm around her. "It's over. Just take a deep breath."

But as Lindsey walked past with Amelia, she looked up and in a shaky voice said, "Can I see her?"

Lindsey turned so Rebecca could catch a glimpse of closed eyes, curled lashes and pouty mouth—but only briefly. She then went down the hall with her daughter.

I helped Rebecca up and led her to a living room chair. Tom and Candace had planted Zoe in a chair so she faced the kitchen. The two Marner women couldn't look at each other right now. Maybe that would come later, but for now it was a good thing.

Finn brought Rebecca a glass of water and she took it with trembling hands. He smiled at me and said, "Should I make coffee?"

I nodded. "Sounds great."

While he was doing that with Yoshi's invaluable assistance, I called Belle. "Could you ask Lucy if it's okay if Amelia spends the night? The poor baby is sound asleep."

"Sure, sweetie," Belle said. "I'll take Lucy home. She's worked two shifts today and maybe she could use the time alone to get a good night's sleep."

"Sounds like a plan." I disconnected.

Lindsey came down the hall with Syrah balanced on her shoulder. That boy of mine knew when comfort was needed.

"Amelia will stay the night. Her mother knows nothing about what happened, and we'll keep it that way for tonight."

"Good." Lindsey walked to the sofa and sat across from her mother. Chablis immediately claimed her lap.

I sat next to Lindsey, and Syrah stretched out behind me on the sofa back.

I heard Candace reading Zoe her Miranda rights, but I doubted the woman was even listening. She was rocking and humming, her mental state apparently deteriorating now that her endgame was over without a success—if killing people could *ever* be called a success.

But I still had no idea what brought her here tonight holding Rebecca at gunpoint—a woman who had comforted her in her grief only a few days ago, however insincere that comfort probably was.

"Is what happened here enough to make you finally tell the truth, Mom?" Lindsey's voice was as cold as the chill outdoors. "Tell Jillian who you nearly got killed tonight."

Rebecca sighed heavily, her tearstained face still pallid. "My daughter. No—my *daughters*."

I blinked, stunned. "What are you talking about?"

Tom had been listening and came around the sofa to

stare down at Rebecca. "Yeah, what *are* you talking about?"

"Amelia is *my* daughter. Lindsey saved me from being disgraced in this town." She focused on her Lindsey. "I am so sorry for what I made you do—and so very grateful."

"Are you *kidding* me?" I felt anger boiling up inside and I was about ready to spew out my disgust. If I understood what Rebecca was saying, I couldn't believe what she had put Lindsey through for the last five years—but it sure made sense. The child had been protecting the parent.

"It was wrong," Rebecca said. "But we thought it was best. People would talk, we knew, but a teenage pregnancy seemed almost . . . *normal*, whereas a divorced woman, a woman with standing in the community, with an unexplained pregnancy? Well, that would have destroyed me."

"It's okay to destroy your daughter, though? That's okay?" I couldn't hold back as the horrible thing she'd done to Lindsey sank in even more.

Tom put a hand up. "Wait a minute. You said *we*. Who's the *we*?"

"Rhett and me. He was Amelia's father. And that was another reason why we needed Lindsey's help. Zoe would take him for every penny if she found out we'd still had feelings after the divorce and—"

"Oh, but I wasn't as stupid as the two of you thought, was I?" Zoe called over her shoulder.

Maybe she wasn't crazy after all. Maybe she was just mad as hell.

Tom walked back to face Zoe. "You want a lawyer or

not?" His tone was harsh, disgusted. This room held a world of hurt and sadness right now.

I was guessing despite the handcuffs, Zoe felt as if she were in control. But it was Rebecca who spoke. "I can tell you everything you need to know."

Tom's face was scarlet, his fists clenched. But he managed to say in a controlled voice, "Tell me about you and Mike. Why him? Why did *he* have to die?"

Finn, who'd been silent in the kitchen and who'd made the soothing smell of coffee surround us all, rushed to Tom's side with Yoshi on his heels. Finn pulled at Tom's arm. "Dad. Come on. It'll be okay."

I joined Finn, the shock at seeing Tom so angry almost paralyzing me for a second. I'd never seen him react so forcefully before, but I totally understood.

"She'll just lie to you." Zoe apparently wanted the spotlight back on her. "Don't you want to know how I found out? Don't you want to—"

"You haven't waived your Miranda rights, Mrs. Marner," Candace said. "We can't let you speak to us without a lawyer unless you waive those rights."

"Okay, consider them waived. I want the truth out there. My truth, not *hers*."

Tom broke away from Finn and me. He gripped Zoe's upper arms and shook her. "Then start talking."

Candace put a hand on his back and in a quiet voice said, "We have to do this the right way. The legal way."

Tom took a deep breath. His arms went limp at his sides as he backed off.

Finn locked his arm with Tom's, and his dad winced in pain. "What's wrong? Are you hurt?" Finn said.

"Just a little cut. It's nothing. I need to get on with this."

We all walked to the table where Zoe sat cuffed with her hands behind her.

I kissed Tom's cheek, squeezed his hand. "We're getting answers. That's what matters now."

Zoe said, "How touching. Such a sweet family moment."

Candace's attitude changed in a flash. She pointed at Zoe. "You shut up until I've got your signature on a waiver. I want my tape recorder ready to save every word you say."

I wondered if they should be talking about all this at the police station, but Tom wanted an answer to his most pressing question about Mike right away, of that much I was certain.

Candace spoke to me before she left to get her evidence kit where she kept all her forms, along with her tools of the trade. "Do *not* let Tom talk to her until I get back." She looked at Finn. "You fixed coffee. I think several of us could use a cup, especially Tom."

She ran out through the back door just as Morris and Lois were about to knock. She pushed past them saying, "Need to get a waiver from the car. Make sure Zoe Marner says nothing until I get back."

Of course Morris's first words were "Do I smell coffee?" I was grateful for someone who could cut through all the tension.

Lois glanced my way before focusing on Zoe. "I take it the one in cuffs has some explaining to do."

"Oh, she sure does," Tom replied.

Finn handed mugs of coffee to Tom and me. He said, "Why don't you sit with Lindsey and Rebecca? They probably shouldn't be alone together. I'll be fine." He sipped his coffee, never taking his eyes off Zoe.

I walked back into the living area while Finn stayed with Tom.

I glanced between Rebecca and Lindsey. "Either of you want coffee? It'll be a long night, I assure you."

They both shook their heads. The silence between these two seemed as toxic as their relationship. I sat on the sofa. "Why did you protect her, Lindsey?"

"Because she's my mother. I may not like her one bit, but I will always love her."

But she still never so much as glanced at Rebecca.

# Twenty-nine

Candace slipped the waiver in front of Zoe, and once she read it and said she was ready to sign, Candace unlocked her handcuffs. Once she'd signed the form, those cuffs were slapped back on faster than I could blink.

Tom sat directly across from Zoe, and Candace took the chair to her left. I'd turned around from my spot on the couch to look at them, and I now focused on Tom. I wanted to offer anything I could to help him get through this.

Though Zoe's back was to me, her voice was full of scorn when she spoke. "Guess you figured out it wasn't suicide. How?"

"We ask the questions," Candace said. "Why did you kill Police Chief Michael Baca?"

"It was an easy decision. He died because he mattered to Rebecca. She told me she loved him—not that she's actually capable of loving anyone. That was all I needed to hear. She had to hurt as much as she'd hurt me. Rhett's death meant nothing to her. She didn't even shed a tear when they found his body. But Mike's suicide? Oh, I could tell that hurt her."

"You're saying you took a man's life to get back at a woman you hated?" Tom sounded incredulous and I saw a flush creeping up his neck.

Candace saw this, too, and she reached over to put a hand on his arm and nodded at the recorder sitting on the table.

"The police chief knew Rebecca hated me and I didn't want that getting out. It might make him suspicious. Though I am a great actress, I wasn't sure how long I could keep up the charade if he started questioning my loyalties to my very dead husband."

Syrah seemed to come out of nowhere and jumped on Tom's shoulder, offered a gentle head butt before leaping over to the nearby window seat ready to watch what happened next. We were all listening, even the cats. But Rebecca seemed to have shrunken in size and for me, she was a contagion, a patient zero. If she hadn't slept with her ex and used her daughter selfishly, none of this might have happened.

"How did you get to Mike?" Tom asked Zoe.

"He apparently had a soft spot for a bereaved widow knocking on his door late at night. He offered me a drink. I said I'd only have one if he did, too. When we were both sitting down in his living room, I turned on the tears and when he left to get me a tissue, I doctored his wine with the Rohypnol I suppose you found in his system."

Tom said, "You screwed up murdering a man you didn't really know."

"How's that? What was my mistake? I know I put the

gun in the correct hand. His TV table was on the left side, he picked up his drink with his left hand and—"

"Didn't I say we ask and you answer?" Candace's arms were crossed, her young smooth features tight with controlled anger.

"I'll find out later from my lawyer, I suppose." Zoe sounded so callous it made me feel sick to my stomach.

"Okay. Let's stop. Are you saying you now do want a lawyer?" Tom stared at the recorder. He didn't want to risk this confession being tossed out of court.

"No. I'm not saying that. I signed your stupid paper. How many times do I have to tell you that everyone in this town needs to know all about Rebecca Marner and what she's truly like?"

But Tom shut off the recorder anyway. "Hang on while I try to make sense of just how evil you are." He closed his eyes and took several deep breaths.

He shouldn't be talking to this woman. It wasn't good for him. But someone had to get the facts so they could put her away forever.

Morris and Lois had been speaking quietly with Finn, I supposed getting his side of what had happened. Morris then beckoned to me. I started to get up, but Lindsey grabbed my hand. "Please don't leave."

Her eyes were swimming. When Rebecca saw this, she started to get up, I thought perhaps to comfort her daughter.

Lindsey held up a hand. "Don't you *dare* come near me."

As Rebecca sank back into the chair, Morris gestured for me to stay where I was.

Candace seemed well aware way too much emotion had come into play with everyone gathered here. "Maybe it's time we stopped this interview for now so we can all head over to the station. Morris and Lois can get everyone else's statement here."

Zoe shook her head. "No friggin' way. Anyone leaves, I'm revoking that waiver and I'll want an attorney immediately. See, *she* needs to hear what I have to say. Every damn word." She tossed her head back and to the side. She was talking about Rebecca, of course.

Candace whispered to Tom and he whispered back. She appeared stoic when she pressed the record button. "Go on, then, Mrs. Marner."

Zoe began to speak. "It all started after Lindsey brought something to our house that belonged to her father, some tool he'd left in the garage of the house where he used to live. After she left for home, I found the locket in the bathroom, the one she'd been wearing. There was a picture of a baby inside. So when Rhett came home that night, I asked him about it."

"Can you describe this locket?" Candace asked. She was taking notes while Tom sat back, quietly observing with narrowed eyes.

She went on to describe what had to be the necklace found with blood on it, the one wrapped around Magpie's paw.

"What did your husband say about this locket?" Candace asked.

"He lied. Said it was probably a stock photo like they put in picture frames when they're put on the shelf for sale. I called him on it, told him I wasn't stupid and that the baby looked exactly like him."

Candace looked up from her notepad. "What was his response?"

"He said he was sorry and asked if I remembered when Rebecca and Lindsey left town together and stayed away for a long time. The story at the time was that Lindsey had to go to some special school. But that was a lie, he said. His daughter got pregnant and Rebecca took her out of town, stayed with her at some home for pregnant teenagers. He said the baby looked like him because it was his grandchild."

"And what did you do then?" Candace asked.

"I pretended to accept yet another lie, but he wasn't fooling me."

Tom spoke up then. "How could you know it wasn't the truth?"

"Because I'd gotten to know Rebecca since all that happened. She would *never* take her daughter anywhere and stay with her for that long. Not in a million years. She's far too self-centered for that. She'd simply drop the girl off and leave as fast as she could. Pick her up when it was all over—or send someone to get her."

*She's right,* I thought. *That's exactly what Rebecca would have done.* Finn was leaning against the kitchen counter between Morris and Lois, Yoshi in his arms. I caught his almost imperceptible nod. He believed Zoe was correct in her assumption, too.

Candace said, "Is that all it took for you to decide to kill your husband?"

"Yes and no. A part of me wanted more proof. But it didn't take much snooping around to find out about the money he was sending to that woman in Charleston. Did you know I went to see her? I watched her house, watched her pick up the money Rhett was sending to her PO box. The For Sale sign was the perfect way to waltz in and talk to her. I pretended to be a Realtor. Silly woman never even asked for a business card. Didn't take long for her to start pouring out her sob story about losing her husband, about her adopted daughter and how they would have to pull up stakes and move to this little town upstate called Mercy because the biological father had given her a little house. He wanted to be close, to help out." She turned her head in Rebecca's direction again. "Isn't that the sweetest thing you ever heard, Rebecca?"

I looked at Lindsey and then at her mom. Neither of them showed any emotion, but Zoe's sarcasm cut like a razor. They both had to be hurting.

"See," she went on, "she'd confirmed that Rhett fathered that child and I was certain Lindsey wasn't the mother, that Rebecca used Lindsey as an excuse to hide her pregnancy from the gossip mongers in Mercy—and from me, of course." Zoe turned in our direction again and made eye contact with Lindsey. "Did you believe that if you went along with that charade, your mother might actually show appreciation, show you that she loved you?"

"Direct your answers to me, Mrs. Marner," Candace said.

I'd had about all I could stand. This confession had to be tearing Lindsey up inside. "This is *so* wrong. Does Lindsey have to listen to this, Tom?"

But Lindsey was quick to respond. "I want to hear everything. I *need* to understand. So it's okay, Jillian." The look on her face said it wasn't okay, not for a minute, but she needed the truth so she could close the chapter on Zoe's and her mother's twisted game of deceit.

Finn came from the kitchen and sat on the floor by

Lindsey's feet to offer support. Yoshi settled next to him. Magpie joined them, once again holding her prize tassel. She jumped into Lindsey's lap and curled up. Lindsey stroked her and I could see the muscles in her tight jaw relax a bit.

The questions turned to Rhett's murder. Zoe related how she found an opportunity to get Rhett away from the house on the pretext of picking up a sofa for the charity store after Floretta Strickland called and said she wanted furniture removed before her husband returned to town.

She shot him in the Strickland garage on Floretta's bingo night, knowing the woman wouldn't be there. She even put the locket in Rhett's pocket, not realizing it would fall out later. Her sons had made the trip with them, on the pretext of helping to move the sofa. When Zoe saw the keys to Wilbur Strickland's truck sitting in plain sight on the work bench, she drove home while her sons handled the rest—hiding Rhett's body and the stolen truck in the woods until they had an opportunity to put him in the parking lot. If not for Seth finding that shoelace, Rhett would have been buried in concrete and no one might have learned the truth. No one had paid any attention to their activities and I was certain Tom was beating himself up this very minute because he'd focused on Bo Strickland when he should have been looking closer to home for suspects. But he was doing what any cop would—eliminating suspects.

When Zoe was finally finished talking, Tom turned to Morris. "Go pick up those boys and book them on accessory to murder, obstruction of justice, stealing a car, destroying evidence and anything else you can think of."

"Wait a minute." Zoe stood. "They just wanted to help their mother."

Candace shoved her down in the chair. "Sit, lady."

She stared up at Candace. "Okay. I'm taking back my waiver. I want a lawyer."

Tom smiled. "Fine, but your sons will give you up in a heartbeat. See, in the police business we're used to making deals with little fish swimming as fast as they can away from the big one, the one that would eat them alive, given half the chance."

# Thirty

After a fitful, troubled sleep, I finally stumbled out of bed around eight. I showered and dressed while four cats watched my every move. I heard no cries for food—probably because they'd already been fed. They just wanted to make sure where I was; perhaps they needed to be reassured that life would return to normal. So much had happened last night that the stress still had them on high alert.

They followed me to the kitchen, where I found Lindsey, Finn and Amelia eating cereal at the breakfast bar. Yoshi was strategically placed under Amelia's barstool waiting for any morsel she might drop.

The coffee was made, and indeed the cats had been fed. I might have to keep Lindsey and Finn around—like *forever*. I poured a mug of a smoky brew and said, "This is new. Not my usual."

"I brought it from my house," Lindsey said. "The woman who lives there will never miss it."

But that woman was Amelia's mother. I could only hope she'd keep her distance from this precious child.

I leaned on the counter and smiled at Lindsey's sister. "Amelia, how are you this morning?"

"Fine. Where's my mommy?"

Chablis jumped on the counter and stared at Amelia's bowl. She was waiting for a taste.

Lindsey said, "As soon as you finish your cereal, Finn and I will take you home. I'll bet she missed you while she was working."

Her left hand on Chablis, Amelia picked up her spoon with the other hand. "Good. I missed her, too."

After I'd had two much-needed cups of fantastic coffee, Amelia hugged me good-bye and told me I had coffee breath. "But that's okay. You're nice." The little girl smiled not only with her lips but with those big brown eyes—the ones that looked exactly like her brother Seth's.

I imagined Tom, Candace and the rest of the small police force had been working all night "wrapping up," as Mike used to say. He would be sorely missed by everyone, but most of all by Tom and Candace.

I was just about to text Tom and see how things were going when Kara burst in through the back door. "What the heck happened last night? My scanner was absolutely dead and then Liam called me saying his office had a call about arrests and I realized I missed *everything*." Apparently Tom and Candace accomplished quite a bit after leaving here.

Kara eyed my third cup of coffee hungrily. "Is there more where that came from?"

"Absolutely."

We sat at the table that looked out on the lake, its peaceful ripples against the shore in stark contrast to the story I told—the one that took me almost an hour to explain.

Kara's remarks when I'd finished summed it up well: "What twisted people. No conscience, no empathy, no love for anyone but themselves."

"And yet they volunteered for a charity," I said. "I don't understand that part. It seems like a mockery, because mostly they both used anything and anyone to their advantage."

"*Narcissist* is an overused word these days, but it fits those two women." She stood. "I'm late to this party. The story I ran this morning will now be followed up by a special edition. You think Tom will have time to talk to me right away? I'll need an official statement from the police, and Mike always used to do that for me."

"He'll make time for you," I said quietly.

We hugged good-bye and I texted Tom to let him know Kara was on her way to the police station.

His response was to call and his first words when I answered were "You know how to love. I am so grateful for that."

"Hey, so do you. Now tell me, how is Zoe enjoying her jail cell? It's not quite the accommodations she's used to."

"I don't know and I don't care. This case is done. We finished the paperwork, got a judge on board to hurry up the process of getting into that safe-deposit box where Rhett kept his will. This case is wrapped up tighter than a caterpillar in a cocoon. As expected, the boys flipped on their mother. They know everything. Her confession isn't even needed now."

"I'm glad this is behind us, but what about Mike? His arrangements?"

"His sister can't get here until next week—she cares for her mother-in-law, who has Alzheimer's, and has to find a caregiver. We thought we'd have a candlelight service in the park tonight, since the funeral is days away. Kara can play town crier with that special edition you mentioned in your text."

"Sounds perfect. I'll set it up. I need something to do to take my mind off everything that happened here last night."

We disconnected and I felt the warmth of a cat pressing against my leg. I looked down to see Magpie, her prize in her mouth again. The tassel that probably saved a lot of lives.


The turnout that evening was unbelievable. The Mercy grapevine could spread the word—both good and bad—faster than any technology invented. Twitter had something to do with the whole town showing up, but I was still amazed.

I'd had to drive to a party supply warehouse out of town so we'd have enough candles, and we nearly did. Though we ran out, no one complained. People shared, joined hands, and raised their lit candles high.

Candace wasn't used to speaking in public, but that was about to change. She and Tom shared the gazebo in the center of the park and used the PA system the mayor offered us. He'd been a great help in directing this effort to bring the town together tonight. He introduced Tom and Candace after offering his own high praise for our fallen chief.

Tom cleared his throat and I stood by the gazebo stairs and offered a thumbs-up for encouragement.

"Mike Baca was my closest friend. The events that led to his death can be read about and talked about and we all need to do that. It's part of dealing with our loss. But in the end, when the talking is done, when the space he used to fill is so empty it hurts, we will pause in quiet moments and remember what a good man he was." Tom, head down, handed the mic to Candace.

"He was the chief to me, the boss," she began haltingly. "But he was so much more. My mentor, my friend, the guy who put up with my obsessing over stuff like cat hair at a crime scene."

A small current of laughter and nodding of heads followed. Raised candles bobbed in the stark, cold evening air.

"I loved my chief. He took care of all of us and he'll be missed."

Someone in the crowd began to sing "Let It Be," and soon voices quietly joined in the perfect song to say good-bye to a wonderful friend.

# Thirty-one

The next day, Saturday, came so quickly I felt harried and unprepared. As Candace, Kara and I stood in the church's basement dressing room, I said, "I never wear much makeup and if I get even a tiny bit of mascara on my grandmother's dress, it will break my heart."

In a few minutes, I would walk down the aisle. People called them butterflies—that feeling in your stomach when happiness and nerves meld—because that was exactly what they felt like. And I had a lot of butterflies acting up right now.

We were all facing a full-length mirror and Kara said, "You won't get anything on the dress. And I brought this waterproof mascara because I knew you would totally forget to buy any. Let me put just a little bit on. Please?"

"She made *me* put some on, so why not join the club?" Candace craned toward the mirror. "Looks okay, I guess."

"You both look beautiful," I said.

Candace's dress—a simple teal wrap—showed off her

curves and revealed legs that were well toned. I'd never seen her legs before today, and probably few people had. They were awesome.

Kara's magenta stretch-lace dress suited her slim figure perfectly. She was absolutely stunning.

"Jillian, you're the one people won't be able to take their eyes off," Kara said. "That dress is perfect. So simple and elegant."

Candace smiled and rubbed hair mousse into her hands and fussed with my hair a little more. "We all clean up pretty well."

Kara held my chin and applied a light coating of mascara. "That wasn't so bad, was it?"

I glanced down at the dress, its cowl neckline plunging just enough and draping perfectly. "Good. No spots."

Kara glanced at her thin diamond-studded wristwatch. "Time for the big reveal. This is definitely a fashion show and you're the top model today."

Kara lifted the train of my dress and hung the satin carefully over one arm. Candace gathered all our bouquets for the short trek up the stairs. The white roses with pale pink smaller roses interspersed looked so lovely when I'd held them earlier for a quick glance in the mirror.

Minutes later we took our places in the vestibule. Ed and Karen joined me, each taking me by one arm. Ed actually looked handsome in his charcoal suit and drastically trimmed beard. Karen was stunning as always, in a vintage lavender dress with beaded and embroidered leaves. She even had on elbow-length gloves one shade darker than her dress. A perfect accent. She wore a small satin hat and was the only one of us with any headpiece.

Kara, Candace and I had decided none of us wanted to deal with anything in our hair.

"Ode to Joy," one of my all-time-favorite classical pieces, swelled from the organ located in the small space above the sanctuary. Candace gave me my flowers and she and Kara started down the aisle side by side. Karen, Ed and I followed. I held the bouquet tightly with two hands as Ed and Karen each linked their arms with mine.

The butterflies disappeared the minute I locked eyes with Tom. His smile was all I could see, was all I needed. When I walked up the steps to the altar and gave my bouquet to Kara, he faced me. I caught a glimpse of Finn at his side, grinning from ear to ear. He was indeed Tom's best man in every way.

Our fingers intertwined and I was so lost in the moment that Pastor Mitch's words seemed to float above me like tiny, shimmering stars. The actual exchange of vows couldn't have taken more than ten minutes.

When Tom was told to "kiss the bride" and our lips met, I felt as if I'd truly found everything I would ever need. Tom and I were home.

We faced our friends to a burst of applause, but the people gathered here were still a blur through my misty eyes. I couldn't wait to get to Kara's house and spend time with each and every one of them.

But Kara took her job as photographer seriously. While the guests made their way to her house, she took so many pictures inside the church and out that I thought the smile on my face might freeze and become permanent.

Tom finally led me to his car and we took off for the party we'd been waiting for.

"Did that just happen?" I said.

"It's a thing now, as Finn would say. A forever thing. And by the way, I whispered to you at the altar that you looked gorgeous, but I got the feeling you weren't exactly taking in everything that happened. So I must repeat, you look amazing, wife of mine." He slowed and pulled over to the side of the road.

"What are you doing, Tom?"

"I'd like a moment with just you and me."

We spent more than a moment holding each other, telling each other how much love we shared and then quietly staring into each other's eyes. And then we were back on our way again to the party. Party rather than reception, I decided. This day so far had been formal enough.

Kara had outdone herself and I was finally able to properly greet all the people who'd made it to the wedding. Hugs and laughter and joyful chatter followed. So many people from my last few years in Mercy joined us today. They included Ritaestelle Longworth, whose cat, Isis, had stolen my heart. Dustin Gray, a structural engineer who had helped Candace with a case involving the old mill, made the trip from Greenville. I knew he was smitten with Candace back then and I could tell nothing had changed. He only had eyes for her today and they were engaged in conversation near the hallway to the bedrooms where all the cats and Yoshi had been sequestered until the guests left. All of our many cats and a dog would become too exuberant and ruin the celebration for others—but never for me. I couldn't wait to set them all free.

Belle gave me the biggest hug by far. She wore a lovely pink dress and was wearing her glasses, so her neon pink lipstick was perfectly applied today.

Tom and I talked with every single friend—B.J., Lois, Morris, as well as Shawn and Allison. I'd seen so little of Shawn's wife since she started vet school, but she told us she was almost finished. Billy Cranor and a few other Mercy firemen, as well as Marcy and Jake, the best paramedics in the world, congratulated us. Of course Pastor Mitch and Elizabeth joined us, too. Resting her bones on the sofa was a new and dear friend, Birdie Roberts, whose son was now owned by the last cat I'd fostered—a ginger tabby with loads of personality. Birdie wore her "church clothes," a pretty rose-colored dress and a hat with netting that covered her eyes. She reminded me of Queen Elizabeth—even down to her "sensible" shoes. Ed and Karen sat with her and when Tom and I drifted away toward the food, they continued the conversation we'd probably interrupted. One person who had complied with her noninvitation? Lydia Monk. But maybe she'd show up and surprise us—but I surely hoped not.

Kara and Liam played the perfect host and hostess, carrying hors d'oeuvres on silver platters and refilling champagne glasses. There were toasts galore, and kindness, respect and love filled the room with more warmth than Kara's fireplace provided for a cold but sunny day. I noticed at some point that Finn was nowhere to be seen and I assumed he'd gone to keep our fur friends company.

But when he showed up with Lindsey and Seth in tow, I had to smile. Lindsey had told me this morning she would feel awkward at the wedding, even though I asked her to join us. She said she needed time to talk to Seth about all that had transpired. He deserved to hear a more in-depth truth from her, not the version Rebecca would tell him.

We'd decided on cupcakes rather than a big fancy cake, and as people began to leave, I noticed they carried their wedding favor wineglass in one hand and a cupcake in the other. Soon only a few of us remained, but I was glad that group included Seth and Lindsey. Candace, Kara and I changed out of our wedding clothes and into jeans and sweaters. I was certain Tom was dying to get out of his suit pants and dress shirt and into something more comfortable, too. The tie and jacket had been discarded the minute the picture taking was over.

Once everyone was settled in the living room to relax, I said, "Anyone object to cats and a dog joining the party now?"

Of course no one did. Ed and Karen had dropped off Dashiell before the ceremony, so with my three, Magpie, Pulitzer and Prize, that meant seven cats. Yoshi knew he was outnumbered and stuck close to Finn, who took a spot on the floor with a can of Dr Pepper in hand.

Cat races commenced, but no one seemed to mind. Seth loved watching them, but a pensive Lindsey concerned me.

She was sitting on the floor next to Finn, and I settled next to her. "You look worried. Is everything okay?"

"I don't want to trouble you. This is a big day and you don't need to be thinking about me."

"It is a big day, but it's one about friends and family. You've become one of my friends, so tell me what's wrong."

"I don't think this is the time to burden you with any more of my problems. You've handled so much. You and Finn have been so kind and generous. Enjoy your day with your new husband. I'll be fine."

"I'd enjoy this day a lot more if all my guests were happy—and you're upset. You know you can tell me, right?"

She nodded but said nothing.

I took her hand. "Come on, Lindsey. Spill whatever is bothering you."

"You don't give up, do you?" she said with a laugh.

"Glad you finally understand that about me. Come on. The straight scoop. Right now."

She took a deep breath. "Okay. See, my dad left a lot of money to Amelia, and now my mother is trying to get all chummy with Lucy—even saying she can probably have the big house that Zoe, Toby and Owen lived in. I can't let my mother control and ruin another child. She's my sister and I want to protect her from that."

"You know, I spent a little time with Lucy. My guess is she'd like to return to Charleston. You might want to encourage her to take the money and run. Get as far away from Rebecca as possible."

Lindsey's relief was almost palpable. "Thank goodness you said that. It's a great idea. And I should be getting out of your hair, too. I've overstayed my welcome."

"No way. You stay as long as you want. Maybe you and your mother will never work things out, but time apart might be a good thing for a while. Besides, you can help with what's become a taxi service until Finn saves enough money for a car. We told him we'd foot the bill for the university, but he'd have to buy his own wheels."

She smiled. "Sorry. I may have stepped on your parental toes a little. I lent him money to buy a truck. Seems Daddy left me a bundle, too, and Finn's been such a friend to me when I felt as if I had no one—before you and Tom, that is."

"Don't forget Seth. He loves you a lot."

"I could never forget Seth. Thank goodness he'll be leaving for school soon. He needs distance, too."

Magpie, who'd been in a furious game of chase with Syrah, Pultizer and Prize, stopped dead in front of Lindsey. She crawled into her lap and put her paws on Lindsey's chest so she could see her up close. Apparently satisfied, she dropped one of Kara's earrings in her lap and sped off again.

*That little sneak,* I thought.

We arrived home late after spending hours talking and joking and watching cats and a confused dog as our entertainment. Finn, Lindsey and Seth left before we did and offered to bring the animals back to my house. That didn't mean the whole crew didn't beg for treats the minute Tom and I came in through the back door. Even Dashiell was eager, though his special diet didn't include anything with too many carbs because of his diabetes. Tom had treats for him that were pure protein, but we did have to separate him from the others so he wouldn't sneak a little kitty junk food on the side. Try explaining diabetes to a cat. It doesn't work.

Other than the pets, the house was quiet and as soon as Tom took Yoshi out for one last potty break, the dog raced down to the basement to be with Finn.

I'd left my dress with Kara and she said she'd box it

up carefully and bring it to me next week. I was grateful for how easy she'd made this wedding for me and told her so with big hugs and a kiss. Everything had been absolutely perfect.

Tom spread his arms. "Our home. I can't believe we finally made this happen. Come here, wife."

"Sure, husband."

We kissed and as we made our way down the hall toward our bedroom, the kitties trailing behind, I said, "Have you ever slept with five cats?"

"Nope."

"Good. Neither have I. But if I'm in your arms, I can handle anything."

Read on for a look at the first book
in Leann Sweeney's Cats in Trouble Series,

# The Cat, the Quilt
# and the Corpse

Available from Obsidian.

My cat is allergic to people—yes, odd, I know—so when I came in the back door and heard Chablis sneeze, I stopped dead. Why was she sneezing? This couldn't be a reaction to me. I use special shampoo, take precautions. Chablis and I are cool.

Besides, she hadn't been near any humans for more than twenty-four hours, since I was just arriving back from an overnight business trip to Spartanburg, a two-hour drive from my upstate South Carolina home. I'd left her and my two other cats, Merlot and Syrah, alone in the house, as I'd done many times before when I took short trips out of town. So how did human dander, better known as dandruff, find its way up her nose?

I released my grip on the rolling suitcase and started for the living room, thinking there could be a simple explanation for a sneezing cat other than allergies. Like an illness.

The thought of a sick Chablis pushed logic down to the hippocampus or wherever common sense goes when you have more important matters to attend to. I dropped my tote on the counter and hurried past the teak dining table. Since my kitchen, dining area and living room all blend together, the trip to where I'd heard Chablis sneeze wasn't more than twenty feet. But before I'd taken five steps, I stopped again. Something else besides a sneezing cat now had my attention.

Silence. No background noise. No Animal Planet playing on the television. I always leave the TV tuned to that station when I go away. If the cats were entertained by *The Jeff Corwin Experience* or *Heroes* or *E-Vet*, I'd convinced myself, my absences were more tolerable. Okay, I'm neurotic about my three friends. Not cat-lady neurotic. At forty-one I'm a little young for that. But cats have been my best friends for as long as I can remember, and the ones that live with me now have been amazing since my husband, John, died ten months ago. They take care of me. So I try my best to take care of them.

*Could the TV be off because of a power failure?*

Glancing back at the microwave, I saw that the clock showed the correct time — one p.m. Perhaps the high-def plasma TV blew up in a cloud of electronic smoke? Maybe. Didn't matter, though. Not now. I'd only heard from Chablis, and none of my cats had shown their faces. I was getting a bad vibe — and I can usually rely on my intuition.

"Chablis, I'm home," I called. I kept walking, slowly now — didn't want to panic them if I was overreacting — and went into the living area. "Syrah, where are you? Merlot, I missed you."

I breathed a sigh of relief when I found Chablis sitting on the olive chenille sofa, her blue eyes gazing up at me. Himalayans look like long-haired Siamese cats and Chablis was no different. Her gorgeous crystal blue eyes and her champagne fur were accented by deep brown feet, and she had a precious dark face and a fluffy wand of a tail.

Her nose was running and she seemed awfully puffed out—even for an already puffy cat. Was she totally swollen up by an allergen other than dandruff?

I knelt and stroked the side of her cheek with the back of my fingers, ran my hands over her body, looking for the mass of giant hives I was sure I'd find.

Nothing. She was simply all bloated fur and loud purrs.

"I am truly sorry for leaving you overnight. Are you telling me you have feline separation anxiety?"

Chablis blinked slowly, opened her mouth and squeaked. How pitiful. She'd lost her voice. She *had* to be sick. With a virus? Or leukemia? Cats do get leukemia.

*Quit it, Jillian. Call the vet.*

When I stood to pull my phone from my jeans pocket, I heard Merlot's deep, loud meow and saw him perched on the seat cushions that line the dining area's bay window—a spot that provides a spectacular view of Mercy Lake. He knows the entire lake belongs to him, despite never having been closer than the window. But he hadn't been sitting there when I first came in, and he wasn't gazing out on the water. No, Merlot was looking right at me and his fur was all wild and big, too.

Since he isn't allergic to anything, dumb me finally realized that they were both scared.

And then I saw why.

Broken glass glittered near Merlot's paws—paws that could each substitute for a Swiffer duster.

My heart skipped. Broken glass . . . a broken *window*. "Merlot! Be careful." Fear escaped with my words. I attempted to mask my distress by smiling as I walked over to him.

Yeah, like Mr. Brainiac Cat would buy this fakery.

I petted his broad orange-and-white tiger-striped head while making sure none of his paws was bleeding. He seemed fine other than that he reminded me more than ever of one of those huge, shaggy stuffed animals at a carnival.

I hefted him off the cushions—he's a Maine coon, a breed that weighs four times more than the smallest felines. Merlot stays lean, usually hovers around twenty pounds. I was hoping to keep him clear of the glass, but he was having none of that. He squirmed free and jumped right back on the window seat and proved himself amazingly nimble by staying away from any shards. While I examined the damaged window, he intently examined me as if to ask, "How will you rectify this now that you're finally home, Miss Gadabout?"

The jagged hole in the lowest pane was large enough for a hand to reach in and unlatch that window. And it *was* unlatched.

"Someone's broken in. Someone's been in our house." But stating the obvious couldn't help them explain what had happened. Figuring this out was human territory. For a millisecond, I wondered if this—this *intruder* might still be here. I shook my head no. My cats are not fools. They'd be in the basement or under a bed if any danger still remained.

And exactly where was Syrah? My Abyssinian hadn't made an appearance yet. I supposed he could have been frightened enough to stay in hiding, but no. He was the alpha cat of my little pack.

Okay, I decided. This break-in had upset him. That was why he wasn't making an appearance. Either that or he was so angry I'd left him and his friends to be threatened by a burglar that he was hiding to teach me a lesson.

The thought of a thief frightening my cats produced anger and fear and the sincere wish that I'd had a human friend who could watch out for things just like this while I was away. Since my husband's death, though, I'd been caught up in my own troubles and too proud to reach out to anyone. But making friends, getting to know my neighbors, might have prevented this whole episode.

I inhaled deeply, let the air out slowly. *You can change that, Jillian. But right now you need to find Syrah.*

That was what John would do if he were here. Hunt for the cat in a methodical, logical way. Solve this problem quickly. But I wasn't John and my calm began to crack like crusted snow before an avalanche. Between the silent TV, the scared animals and the absent Syrah, fear now claimed top billing.

"Where are you, baby?" I called, my voice tremulous. "Come here, Syrah."

I hurried toward the hallway leading to the bedrooms, Merlot on my heels. Poor Chablis would have been on his tail, but was stopped by a fit of sneezing. I began the search through all three thousand square feet of my house, the house that was supposed to be our dream home, the one John and I had designed ourselves.

But this was no longer a dream come true. John, at fifty-five, had been far too young to die of a sudden and unexpected heart attack. Though I was coming to terms with his death, letting go day by day, thoughts of him always seemed to flood my brain when I was stressed.

And a broken window and a missing cat were certainly enough to produce that state of mind.

I rushed from room to room, but didn't find Syrah hiding behind my armoires or beneath the dressers or under any beds. He wasn't in the closets or the basement, either. I went outside and checked the trees and the roof for a third scared cat. After all, the intruder might have let him out when he made his escape. But leaves had been falling for weeks, and spotting Syrah's rusty gold fur against the reds, browns and yellows of the oak, hickory and pecan trees in my yard would be difficult.

Syrah, however, is my most vocal cat, and when I didn't hear any meowing in response to my calls, I was sure he wasn't nearby. Cats have such good hearing that they can detect the sound of a bat stretching its wings, and I was nearly shrieking his name.

I finally gave up, and when I came inside I found Merlot sitting by the back door. I was trembling all over as I crouched next to him. He rubbed against my knees and purred while I took my cell phone from my pocket, ready to report the break-in.

"Are you trying to comfort yourself or me?" I asked as I dialed 911. The last time I'd had to do that—when John collapsed—had been the worst day of my life. This event certainly wasn't as horrible, but punching those three numbers again made it seem like John had died only yesterday.

My big cat circled me lovingly as I stood, nudging me, trying to comfort me as best he could. He knew how upset I was.

"What is your emergency?" said the woman who answered.